A TASTE OF SIN

PASSION AND POLITICS

BOOK 2

J.L. SEEGARS

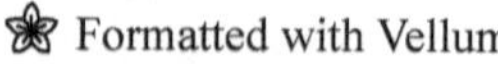 Formatted with Vellum

To all the Black girls biting their tongues and constantly fixing their faces. Crash out, queen. You earned it.

Revenge is a dish best served cold.

— PIERRE CHODERLOS DE LACLOS

CONTENTS

AUTHOR NOTE

Please be aware this story involves sensitive topics such as **gun violence, racism, misogynoir, loss of a child, school shootings, infidelity, domestic violence, suicide, murder, mentions of stalking, corruption and collusion.**

While I always endeavor to be thorough when compiling this list, I'm aware that there are things I might have missed. Please charge it to my head, and not my heart.

I strongly advise you to consider your own health and well-being before diving into the final installment of Selene, Cal and Beck's story.

THE PLAYLIST

01./ If I Die Young by The Band Perry
02./ Little Things by Ella Mai
03./ A Couple Minutes by Olivia Dean
04./ Hard Part by Teyana Taylor & Lucky Daye
05./ Don't Hurt Yourself (feat. Jack White) by Beyoncé
06./ Go Baby by Cleo Sol
07./ Is It a Crime by Mariah the Scientist & Kali Uchis
08./ TYG (feat. Spiritbox) by Megan Thee Stallion
09./ Sexy Soulaan by Monaleo
10./ II Hands II Heaven by Beyoncé

SELENE

Devastation has a scent.

A sound.

A taste.

A weight that presses down on your shoulders and curves your spine. That makes your knees weak, and forces you to the ground even when it's the last place you want to be.

It's happening to me now.

I'm sinking when I want to be standing. The heels I always reach for when I need to mix power with comfort disappearing into a ground softened by rain.

My ears are ringing when I need them clear, when I want to be listening to the officer on the other side of the caution tape. He just walked out of the building we haven't been allowed to get near. He has all the information I need but don't necessarily want.

Aubrey catches me by the elbows. His arms strong and sure. The reassurance he tries to offer me a song of broken and wrong words that barely register over the voices, sirens, and flashing lights. Bodies are pressing in on us from all sides. Family members of people who haven't been escorted outside of the building all clamoring to hear the update that's taken hours to come.

"Senator Taylor," Officer Langham begins, addressing Aubrey as if he's the only one who matters here. The officer swallows hard, throat working to produce words I fear will obliterate me. Aubrey's left hand slides down the length of my arm, and he closes his fingers around mine to stop me from flicking my thumb and forefinger together.

"Don't," he orders gently. "We don't know anything yet."

But don't we? Can't he, the man who always urges me to choose emotion over logic, feel it? The hollow ache that's begun to weave its way through the huddled masses toeing the line of grief with us. The echoing throb of anticipated loss. And if, for some reason I can't understand, he doesn't feel it, he has to know that reason can only dictate one outcome in this situation.

AJ didn't walk out of the doors of the high school he strolled into this morning. He wasn't carried out on a stretcher and rushed to the triage area before being placed in the back of an ambulance. So there's only one rational conclusion to draw: our son is still in there, and he won't walk out. He'll be carried. His lifeless form enclosed in a black bag that will be marched past us with a marked lack of urgency that rings with the hopelessness I'll shoulder for the rest of my life.

Bile rises in my throat.

"Please," I beg, forcing myself to meet the officer's eyes. "Just say it."

The faceless people on either side of us voice their agreement through sniffles and premature sobs while reporters and photographers shuffle around, trying to get the best angle. Several larger cameras pan the crowd, capturing the group in its entirety, but the others are trained on Aubrey and me.

He steps in closer, his chest pressed to my back, a rough exhale leaving him when Officer Langham starts to speak again.

"We've secured the scene," he says, gray-blue eyes focused on Aubrey's face. "All students, teachers, and staff have been accounted for. As you know, students who were not harmed were reunited with their families. Anyone who was hurt has been triaged on site and sent to the hospital for further treatment if necessary. There are thirty-two individuals left inside the building. Twenty-eight students, three teachers, and a janitor, but they were all….beyond help. We've been able to identify them all using their ID badges."

A woman to my right wails loudly, crumbling to the ground, nearly knocking down the two young girls who have been clinging to her all day. They can't be any older than nine years old, and yet, they have suppressed their own tears to wipe away their mothers. No one else moves to comfort her. We're all too focused on the clipboard in Officer Langham's hands now. His gaze flicks to the woman for just a second, a distant kind of sorrow on his face.

"Among those lost," he continues grimly, calling out names one by one. I tune him out, more focused on the way each of them sends horror ripping through the crowd like a bullet with no discernment. Aimless and somehow still hitting its mark every time.

It strikes me last, and I'm shocked at the power still left in it.

How it sears my flesh and shreds my muscle.

How it tears ligaments and tendons.

How it shatters my bones.

But most of all, I'm shocked that when Officer Langham speaks our son's name, confirming the greatest loss of our lives, I'm the only one who cries out for him.

1

SELENE

One hundred days.

Twenty-four hundred hours.

One hundred and forty-four thousand minutes.

Eight million, six hundred and forty thousand seconds and counting.

That's it. The amount of time that's passed since Aubrey Taylor began his first term as President of the United States. Everyone knows the first hundred days of a President's tenure set the stage for the rest of his time in the Oval, but no one thinks—or cares—about what those days feel like for the First Lady. They don't notice her slowly unraveling, morphing into the sort of person who breaks her existence down into milliseconds just so she doesn't get overwhelmed by the thought of her next breath. They don't see that her entire life has become numbers.

That *my* entire life has become numbers.

Twenty-three items on my agenda for the day.

Two days dedicated to my actual career.

Ninety-three full-time staffers who see everything and comment on nothing.

One hundred and thirty-two rooms to sit in and be ignored.

Twenty-eight fireplaces to stare into and contemplate my life choices.

Six floors, two basements, three elevators and eight staircases.

One mind quickly rotting.

One heart slowly dying, waiting for brief flashes of hope that are far too infrequent to sustain me.

"How is this my life?" I mutter, pacing the length of floor that exists outside of the security camera's field of vision.

There's only one in the stairway that takes staffers from the second floor to the third without being seen by the public, but that's all the space needs. It's tiny, secluded, and, despite its designation, rarely occupied. The camera is perched high in the far left corner, focused on the stairs but not the door designed to blend with the wall it's built into, which means there's no random Secret Service agent watching me wring my hands and talk to myself while I wait to see if I'll get to taste hope today.

My phone vibrates, and I pull it out of my pocket, heart pounding as I read the text.

> Agent Shaw: 5 and 1. ETA 30 seconds.

More numbers, but these make me smile. I shove my phone back into the pocket of my trousers and run a hand through my hair, enjoying the feel of the blunt ends as they pass through my fingers. I talked Diane into cutting it into a bob a few days ago, and despite the influx of articles and news segments questioning if the style is too severe for my features and wondering how I'm going to put it in an up-do for formal occasions like the upcoming State Dinner, I'm in love with the decision.

The door opens, and a mountain of muscle in a black suit joins me inside the space. My breath stalls in my lungs as I watch him maneuver around the door carefully, making sure not to let even an inch of his broad shoulders come into the camera's line of sight. He turns to face me, and I see it on his face: confirmation that he's in love with the change I've made too.

Onyx eyes run gentle lines over me, caressing the crown of my head and skating down until they reach the tips of my toes. The examination is equal parts lust and love, and although the intensity of his gaze starts a slow thrum of anticipation in my core, we both know we only have time for love.

Five minutes, to be exact, and we've already spent a solid forty-five seconds staring at each other.

He crosses over to me in two strides of his long legs, hands going to my ass and lifting me up. I wrap myself around him, squeezing tight. I'm not afraid of falling. I just need the closeness.

"Beck."

His name is a desperate, broken whimper that's accompanied by the gathering of tears in my eyes. I force them away, knowing I don't have time to fix my makeup before my next meeting.

"Gorgeous." His tone reassures me that I'm not alone in this longing. It's in his kiss too, an ache that causes a tightness in my chest when his lips glide against mine in two filthy, yet unsatisfactory, kisses.

One from him.

One from Cal, who couldn't be here because they can never get away from Aubrey at the same time. Part of me wonders why Agent Shaw even bothers to specify how many men I should expect during these clandestine meetings. Never once has she had cause to say two instead of one.

Beck presses me to the wall, his hands shifting to my waist. "I've missed you."

"I've missed you, too."

I miss him all the time. I miss *them* all the time. I miss us. Who we were to each other in the early days of this forbidden love. Who we could have become if it wasn't for Aubrey's malicious intervention.

He'd meant for it to break us.

For a moment, I thought that it had. My heart still clenches painfully every time I relive the day they committed to Aubrey's detail. Every second after that meeting was filled with the kind of grating hurt that I can only compare to what I felt after losing my son. And then came the letters. Handwritten letters delivered to me by Agent Shaw but penned by the two men who love me most, who couldn't go a single day letting me believe they'd chosen their careers over me.

The first were written on napkins from a cafe I know they frequent often. I always like to imagine them rushing out to whosever car they took that day to pen urgent explanations that started with promises of their continued love and went on to detail Aubrey's threats and warn me about the pictures he had.

Agent Shaw was stone-faced when she delivered the letters to me, and she bore the same expression when I sent her back with two notes of my own thanking them for explaining and agreeing with their suggestion that we take a large step back from each other to allow Aubrey to believe he won.

In a lot of ways, it feels like he has. The only thing he didn't succeed at was making me live in a false reality where my men chose anything over me. But knowing that hasn't actually changed anything. I'm still tied to him because I don't know what he'll do to us if I leave. I'm still living every day without them. I'm still in this fucked up place where it feels like my life is happening *to* me, and I'm angry as hell about it.

That anger manifests itself into nails digging into the skin of Beck's neck.

"Ouch," he says, wincing.

My fingers relax immediately. "I'm sorry."

Explaining where my mind is and why is unnecessary. The anger building inside of me has been simmering for months now, and it has been discussed ad nauseam. Going into it right now would be a massive waste of the few minutes we have left. I lean in, resting my forehead against his.

"How was the trip?"

"Mentally exhausting, as usual. He insisted on running with us every morning. Did you know it takes him twelve minutes to run a mile?"

I snort, the pettiest part of me lighting up at the thought of Aubrey slugging along the trails around Camp David trying to keep up with

Beck's long strides. "No, but it doesn't surprise me. He's never been a fan of cardio."

"You should have seen how red his face was by the end of each run. We'd laugh about it for the rest of the day," he recounts, lips quirking in fleeting amusement.

I move my hands around to cup his dear face, tracing my finger tips over the remnants of the foreign expression. "I miss your smile."

There's a weight to the words I didn't intend to place there. One that transcends the obvious pain of our lack of proximity and taps into the dark, shameful wall of guilt wrapped around his heart because of what he had to do to save me and Cal. I know from the brief moments I've shared with the man who captured both of our hearts that Beck is struggling with being responsible for the death of Agent Charlie Monroe.

It doesn't matter that she betrayed her badge and oath. That she led him and Cal to what would have been certain death. It doesn't matter that every report he wrote and statement he gave after the fact stated it was him or her. All that matters is she's gone, and he's responsible.

And that harsh truth has stolen his light.

Which isn't to say the man was ever a ray of sunshine. Because he wasn't. Not by any stretch of the imagination. He was carrying ghosts with him before. His wife. His son. But they were benevolent presences. The love he still holds for them a soft, aching glow that surrounds him, turning him into this mesmerizing and sometimes untouchable entity. They were there. They still are, but they weren't haunting him.

Charlie is, though.

She's a shadow over his features. A rain cloud above his head, stealing the small bits of sun we share in these stolen moments.

I just wish I fully understood why. I mean, of course I can't imagine it's easy being responsible for the end of someone's life, but I know for a fact she isn't the first person Beck has killed. And even if that was the case, his actions were justified because she intended to kill him. That reasoning would be enough to comfort me, but it's not enough for Beck. The most frustrating part of all of this is I can't ask him to explain it because I can't risk him looking at me the way Aubrey used to when I would ask for clarification on something that felt so obvious to him and every other neurotypical person around.

Beck sighs, and the heat of his breath skates over my lips. I lean in closer, chasing the warmth, needing the pressure of his mouth more than whatever response he was going to give. He caves easily, and I open for him the second his tongue emerges from his mouth. My fingers are in his skin again, but he doesn't wince this time. He groans, and I drink the sound down in greedy gulps, feeding him my own moans when he rocks up into me making me feel the erection I can't take advantage of.

That realization hits us both at the same time, and we snap out of the high of our collective madness, crash landing on Earth with desperate gasps that leave us with no choice but to let go of each other lest we risk blowing our cover. Beck lowers me to the ground slowly, and I back away from him, needing the distance.

"I saw your segment on Good Morning America," he says, reaching into his pants to adjust himself. "You were beautiful."

"Thank you," I murmur, breath growing ragged as he stretches out a hand to cup my cheek. He rubs at the corner of my mouth with the pad of his thumb, fixing what I can only guess is smudged lipstick.

"Not as beautiful as you are now, though," he whispers, dark eyes burning a hole into my very soul. "Doesn't matter what kind of lighting they have, how they do your makeup or what brand they put you in. Nothing compares to seeing you live and in color, gorgeous."

Heat floods my cheeks, and I'm hit with the sudden urge to kiss him again. I push it down. There's not enough time. There's never enough time. Despite the lovely compliment, I frown.

"Yeah, well, if I had my way, that's the only way anyone would ever see me. I think I could live the rest of my life without another camera pointed in my face."

He tilts his head to the side, examining me. "Developing a bit of camera fatigue?"

"Is that even a thing?"

"You're the First Lady of the United States. It's a thing if you say it is."

"Wouldn't that be something? Using my platform to lend meaning and credence to a feeling I only have because of it?"

Beck's hand moves from my cheek to the nape of my neck, using a light grip to urge me forward until my head his resting on his shoulder and my hands linked at his back. This will be the last hug we share for God knows how long, and we make the most of it. Our bodies melting into each other until his muscle is my muscle, his flesh is my flesh, his bone is my bone.

"Can't you take a break?" he asks. "Go home. See your parents and your sisters. Re-calibrate just for a little while?"

"No," I answer simply.

Months ago, the thought of going home would have sounded anything but relaxing to me. These days, I find myself longing for my mother's arms and the constant chatter of my sisters balanced among the quiet power of my father's presence. I wake up from dreams of falling asleep between Cal and Beck in my childhood bed and laugh at the ridiculousness of thinking my parents would allow that before crying over the small likelihood that I'll find myself needing to pitch the idea to them.

So much of life now is longing. Wanting things I will never get to have because Aubrey won't allow it. After all, he's the architect behind my schedule. Not literally. He isn't the hand holding the pen that writes everything into my overpacked calendar, but he gave Jordan the order to keep me busy. She disseminated it to everyone else on staff. On the outside looking in, Aubrey appears to be a supportive husband, helping his wife in her endeavor to be something more than ornamental. What no one seems to see is the malice it takes to give someone who thrives on having a purpose a schedule filled with nothing more than busywork.

Even the interview Beck referred to minutes ago fits that bill.

I'd gone to Good Morning America to discuss the successful place-ment of mental health professionals whose sole purpose is to create emotionally safe environments in hopes of preventing school shootings like the one that claimed AJ's life in twenty schools across the DMV area. It should have been a gratifying moment, a nationally televised celebration of a dream I'd worked towards for years now finally coming true, but I found no joy in it because the entire conversation was about Aubrey. How gracious he is, how supportive he is, how kind he is to make backing my First Lady initiative one of the top priorities for his first hundred days.

I know that's why he did it.

Why he honored the terms of the contract I could no longer hold him to because I'd been the one to break it.

And it wasn't about grace or altruism.

It was about control. About making sure every conversation regarding the promise I worked so hard to keep included him. About taking the joy out of getting the work done. About turning me into a villain if I leave him and a frivolous figurine if I stay.

How is this my life?

The internal question slithers through my mind, only drowned out by the sound of Agent Shaw's knuckles colliding with the door a few feet away.

"Time's up," Beck mutters, pulling back reluctantly. "Kiss me goodbye, gorgeous."

I rise up on the tips of my toes, dropping two chaste kisses on his lips. "I love you."

"I love you, too."

He doesn't linger, but his words do, staying with me long after he's begun his ascent up the stairs I came down minutes ago. It's an extra precaution. If any one ever bothers to check the camera, which Agent Shaw assures me no one ever does, all they'll find is footage with altered time stamps that shows us entering the stairwell on one floor and exiting on the other moments later.

Logically, I know it's not the smartest plan, but it's all we have until we can find a way to truly have each other.

2

CAL

A gun to his temple.

Or maybe in his mouth. The cold glide of the metal harsh and bitter on his tongue. His blue eyes wide and desperate. Muffled pleas for his life landing on deaf ears, processed by a brain that holds no sympathy for him, only hatred. Only the desire to see his life end with no thought or concern for what it will mean to be the one to end it.

With a subtle shake of my head, I put an end to my silent exploration. Fantasizing about killing the President is usually one of my favorite pastimes, but I'm feeling particularly disappointed in the lack of creativity I'm displaying today. There's nothing groundbreaking about a spent bullet and splattered brain matter in a country where a hundred or so people die by firearm every day. Outside of being commonplace, it's also far too quick and kind of a death to give to a man like Aubrey Taylor.

No, what he deserves is a slow, painful death. Something tailored to fit his specific brand of depravity. Something that will ensure his final moments are filled with the same agony Selene, Beck and I have endured since he made us pawns in the game of chess he calls his life. Shooting him just doesn't meet those requirements.

Unless of course, it's a bullet in the stomach, I muse. *Gut shots are incredibly painful.*

"Something funny, Agent Drake?"

The unwelcome question comes from the other side of the expansive, oval-shaped room, behind the large, wooden desk with ornate designs where Aubrey is sitting. Cordelia Barnes, who's across from him, glances over her shoulder, waiting for me to answer. I force my features to relax and shake my head.

"Nothing at all."

"Sir," the former Senator and current Secretary of State adds. "You're addressing the President of the United States, agent. You should call him sir."

Her Southern drawl adds a sprinkling of racism to her attempt to correct me. I haven't called Aubrey 'sir' since he strong-armed me into taking this job, and I won't start today. You'd think her previous failures on this front would make her give up, but she's as incorrigible as she is annoying.

Aubrey waves a dismissive hand. "It's fine, Cordelia."

The smile he aims in my direction before returning his attention to his colleague is relaxed yet condescending. It's a true reflection of the air of arrogance that floats around him every day. One I'm constantly subjected to because he insists on having me do dumb shit like stand inside the Oval and watch him and Cordelia pat themselves on the back for doing everything but keep the promises he made to earn his place behind the desk.

During the campaign, I never had much reason to interact with the woman. She was, like so many other people, a background actor in a play starring Selene. Nothing more than a figure moving around in the blurred edges of a scene with the only woman I've ever loved in the foreground. Sometimes I regret not paying more attention to her then because I might have been better prepared to deal with her constant presence.

She and Aubrey are joined at the hip, closer now than they were during the campaign. It's clear to anyone paying attention that she has Aubrey's ear. What's evident to me, especially in private meetings like this or the multiple weekends at Camp David, is that she isn't above gripping that appendage and using it to turn his head in whatever direction she wants it to go.

Remnants of frustration from my insubordination color her tone as she crosses her legs and glares at Aubrey. "What exactly are your concerns here?"

He doesn't look at her. His focus is back on the papers in front of him detailing a military operation in Sudan that went sideways last night. "You know what my concerns are, Cordelia. Your bill has passed. An Executive Order demanding the Department of Education to require the implementation of security cameras enhanced with facial recognition software would be overkill."

"Or it would be exactly the push needed to actually make schools safer. Feelings wheels and therapy sessions aren't going to cut it, Aubrey," she says, tacking on a dig at Selene's First Lady Initiative before continuing. "Our children need real solutions for the threats they face in school *today*. Not tomorrow, next week or next year."

"I've heard you make this same pitch a hundred times, Cordelia. There's no need to do it again," Aubrey gripes, a flare of authority in his tone that rarely comes out when he speaks to her. He closes the folder in front of him and sighs. "The answer is no."

Her head rears back. "No?"

I don't think she's ever heard him say the word before, or rather, never been on the receiving end of it. Her posture sharpens, shoulders rising to meet her ears, spine straight as a needle, head tilted to the side. I can't see her face, but I imagine she's shooting daggers out of her eyes. Everything in her protesting the rejection he's emphasizing with a nod of his head.

"You heard me correctly." He crosses his arms over his chest and leans back in his chair, withering under the weight of her gaze even as he attempts to appear unmoved. "I understand how important this is to you, Madame Secretary. The bill was the last one you introduced in the Senate before you rose to this post."

"Yes, it—"

"*However,*" he continues. "As the Secretary of State, this bill and its implementation no longer fall under your purview. You have sworn an oath to protect the interests of the American people by turning a keen eye to the rest of the world, which means you cannot allow yourself to be distracted by domestic issues that are already being resolved."

Cordelia pulls in a breath through her nostrils and forces the air out between her clenched teeth. "I *implore* you to reconsider, Mr. President."

Word choice aside, the command is clear, and it catapults the two of them into a silent standoff where I am the sole spectator. Since this is the most interesting thing that's happened to me all day, I watch closely, trying to make sense of the battle of wills that shouldn't be happening. Cordelia has always operated outside of the carefully drawn lines around her position, taking more liberties than what have been afforded to any other member of the Cabinet, but push back in the face of Aubrey's meager and infrequent attempt to pull rank is egregious even for her.

It's almost like she believes herself to be entitled to his agreement.

The silence only lasts for about twenty seconds before Jordan St. James—Aubrey's campaign manager turned press secretary—interrupts by barging into the room. All eyes fall to her. Aubrey and Cordelia both frown in her direction, and the bubble of tension around them pops, allowing their displeasure with each other to morph into the joint annoyance with her that always seems to be present lately.

I'm not sure what Jordan has done to earn their disdain, and when the three of them are in a room together, I'm never allowed to stick around long enough to find out.

"Agent Drake, give us the room."

The order comes from Aubrey, and despite my curiosity about the working dynamics of the trio who conspired to ruin the best thing that's ever happened to me, I'm happy to take my leave, exiting the office and immediately seeking out to Beck to hear how his visit with Selene went. Not being able to see her, to hold her precious face in my hands and kiss her long and slow before pulling her into one of those bone-crushing hugs she loves so much had killed me. The only solace I found in being denied that luxury is knowing that Beck got to have it, and when I find him in the small office we share as lead agents, I find new relief in her scent on his skin when we embrace.

Clinging to him is a risk since any one of the agents under our charge could walk in at any moment, but I do it anyway. My palm pressing into the nape of his neck. My fingers applying gentle but firm pressure to keep him in place. He exhales roughly as I pull in lungfuls of them, imagining what they might have packed into the five minutes they shared. Beck holds still, indulging this act of desperation the way I do for him when I'm the one lucky enough to steal a few moments with our love.

"How is she?" I ask, finally releasing him.

"Tired. Frustrated. Sad." He runs a hand over his freshly shaven head and gives me a half smile. "Beautiful."

"As always."

Daily sweeps of this room to ensure there are no listening devices make this one of the few places we are safe to discuss Selene. Still, we never use her name. Never speak about her for too long. Never go into full details until we're outside of these walls, which means I won't know the full story behind Beck's observations until our shift is over.

"Who sprung you from the penalty box early?" he asks, referring to the Oval as the punishment device it is for both of us. Agents don't typically stand guard inside the office, but Aubrey insists on having one, or both, of us do exactly that, sacrificing what little privacy he has to make sure we see him being a Master of Universe.

I'm sure he believes it's a power play, but true power doesn't require total control or constant monitoring. It's quiet confidence. It's skill and certainty. It's indulging your enemy as they strategize against you, allowing them to imagine defeating you, and knowing that no matter how well prepared they are, you'll crush them anyway.

Aubrey doesn't know power. He doesn't have it, but he's familiar with the illusion of it.

I lower myself onto the corner of the desk. "Jordan. She interrupted a spat between Aubrey and Cordelia."

Beck follows suit, returning to the office chair he was occupying when I arrived. He leans back, resting linked fingers over his stomach. "Aubrey and Cordelia, arguing? That's odd."

"Very," I confirm, giving him a quick rundown of the tense discussion. He lets out a low whistle when I finish.

"Sounds like trouble in paradise." He rubs his chin. "Could be good for us."

Whenever we're not working, we're doing this.

Discussing Aubrey and the people around him, looking for weaknesses to exploit, searching for something, anything, we can use to keep him from making good on his promise to have Selene hurt if she steps out of line. With all the time we spend immersed in his world, you would think it'd be easy, but it's not. He's always careful to expose us to only the most mundane parts of his life, ordering us out of rooms at the White House or banning us from entering whole structures at Camp David whenever things get interesting.

He obviously wasn't anticipating the conversation with Cordelia to go left or else he would have dismissed me before it even began.

"Possibly," I agree. "There's also something weird happening between them and Jordan. I haven't quite put my finger on it yet, but I know it's there."

"Do you want to do some digging?"

"No, let's give it time to play out. If we start pushing for information, they'll close ranks. The last thing we want is to be an enemy they can unite against."

"I hate this shit, Drake," he mutters, dark eyes narrowing into slits that indicate he's preparing to go into a rant I've heard a million times. Hell, I've even participated in it a time or two, matched his anger with my rage, paired it with the burn of hard liquor and the bliss of a blackout knowing that it won't change a thing.

"I know, Beckham."

The enraged speech I'm expecting doesn't come. I watch Beck choke it down—swallowing his disappointment in the people who betrayed us as well as the frustration at having the assignment we worked so hard to earn be weaponized against us—and when I open my mouth to ask him why he's gone quiet, he tips his head towards the door.

I turn to find Sam Granger staring at us through the sliver of glass meant to provide light in the windowless room. With a quick dip of my chin, I invite the agent into our space.

"Drake. Beckham," he says, closing the door behind him. Granger isn't a big man. He's average height with a solid build and an unimposing presence, but the room still feels overcrowded now that he's in it. His entire existence is an affront to my nervous system, putting me on high alert and setting my teeth on edge.

The discomfort is a familiar sensation, something I experience every time I'm around the men on our team. Men Beck and I hand-selected. Men we vetted independently. Men we should trust with our lives but keep at arm's length because experience has taught us that we can only trust each other.

That distrust, that anticipation of betrayal, keeps me silent in moments like this, leaving Beck to navigate conversations while I watch for the signs I missed with Charlie and Harris.

"You're early," Beck says, glancing at his watch. "We still have another half hour left on shift."

"Yes, sir. I figured you and Agent Drake would want to head out early given you've been on all weekend."

"Nice," Beck muses.

"Calculated," I add. Granger's gaze snaps to my face. Blonde brows folded in confusion.

"Excuse me?"

"This isn't the first time you've made this offer, so tell me, what's your angle, Sam? Hoping to parlay your acting lead title into the real deal by proving persistent negligence on our parts?"

A red tint creeps up into his cheeks as he looks to Beck for help. I suppress the urge to laugh, remembering the days when people used to look to me for assistance with calming Beck down. To no one's surprise but Sam's, Beck doesn't come to his defense. Instead, he leans back in his chair and waits for an answer.

"I was just trying to be nice," Sam insists. "You've given me the opportunity to gain supervisory agent experience without actually having to lead a detail, and I thought I'd find a way to show my appreciation."

His expression is earnest, but I'm still wary. Maybe because I know our reasons for placing him in charge when we're off duty weren't exactly above board. Out of everyone on our team, Sam has the least experience. He's got no situational awareness and slow reflexes, so he's less likely to spot and neutralize a threat. None of these are traits you want in a Secret Service agent if you want the person you're protecting to live, but they're perfect qualities if you spend every day hoping their charge will die.

Beck lets out an amused huff, rising to his feet and clapping me on the shoulder. "That's very thoughtful of you, Granger. Agent Drake and I will happily take you up on that offer."

Left with no choice but to vacate the office, I stand as well. Granger moves to the side as we head for the door, genuine pride in his eyes as he watches us go.

"The brief is on the desk," I tell him, nodding toward the folder that contains our report on the shift we're closing out and lists important information for the one he's about to begin. "Call if you need anything."

"*Don't* need anything," Beck calls over his shoulder, urging me down the hallway. Within minutes, we're in the car, the White House in our rear view, and some much-needed sleep ahead of us. Beck is already getting a jump start on that. His head leaning against the headrest and his eyes closed.

"You could at least wait until we get home to fall asleep," I tell him, easing to a stop at a busy intersection.

"I'm not asleep. I'm just picturing it happening."

I don't have to ask what it is. Our brains are so eerily similar that I can dive right into his silent musings with no further clarification.

"Plane crash," I offer.

"Too many innocent bystanders. A well-placed bomb?"

"Same issue. Poison, maybe. Something engineered to attack his DNA specifically."

"Is that even a thing?"

I shrug. "Probably."

"Can't exactly Google it though, can we?"

"We're already risking a lot just talking about it."

Beck sighs, turning sleepy onyx eyes on me. "Two bullets to the back of the head."

"Execution style. I like it."

"We could do it together," he says.

There isn't a single thing in this world I'm not willing to do with Lance Beckham including assassinating a President, but there's a whole other person to consider in this scenario and every other one we play out where we're responsible for ending Aubrey's life.

"We'd go to prison for the rest of our lives. She'd be alone."

"Yeah," Beck agrees. "But at least she'd be free."

3

BECK

No one ever talks about how peaceful cemeteries are.

The quiet calm that finds you when you're sitting among the headstones of people you hope were loved well and are missed terribly. I can't speak for anyone else here, but I know for certain that both things are true for the two souls who were laid to rest in the spots in front of me.

I wasn't planning on visiting Diana and Cameron's graves today, but after receiving a call from my realtor confirming the sale of what was supposed to be our forever home, there was only one place I really wanted to be. Cal let me leave the circle of his arms without much protest, knowing I needed the space to process this final loss of my old life.

Blades of freshly mowed grass brush against my legs as I kneel before my wife, replacing the bouquet I brought last week with a fresh one. This is the first time in a while I've been able to visit before the flowers wither and die, and I find myself smiling at that as I reach over and put the old arrangement next to the set of blocks I got Cameron.

He would have been inching up into the teenage years if he'd lived to see today, but I can only ever picture him as a baby. Small and fragile and in need of protection I wish every day I would have been able to provide.

A sharp lancing pain rips through me, forcing my eyes shut for a second.

"I'm sorry," I whisper, letting the useless words find a home in the timid warmth of the early May afternoon. As I open my eyes, I imagine them floating up to the leaves of the cherry blossom trees looming above, acquainting themselves with every other apology and grief-riddled sentence that's escaped my lips and been captured by the branches.

The image brings me no peace.

Few things do these days.

Instead of dwelling, I settle myself into the spot between Diana and Cameron and give the trees more things to hold. I spend an hour unburdening myself only to stand and find I'm carrying the same heaviness I was when I sat down. It came in the days after we rescued Selene from Jacob Marsh when the air of relief that she was safe dissipated and the weight of what I'd done to make that a reality set in.

First, it was the what-ifs.

What if I hadn't stumbled out onto that landing? What if I had thrown Charlie to the side instead of over the railing? What if it had been Cal? Would he have been able to talk her down? What if she didn't have to die?

What if, what if, what if.

Then came the nightmares I refused to talk about with Cal because I didn't know how to explain that it wasn't always Charlie's broken body on that factory floor. Sometimes it was Selene's. Sometimes it was his. Sometimes it was Diana's, and she'd have Cameron in her arms. And no matter who the victim was, the perpetrator was always me. Me, doing damage, inflicting pain, ruining everything.

Eventually, Cal got me to share. As soon as he heard what was going on in my head, he went into superhero mode, long speeches validating the choices I made to protect myself, him and Selene. Even longer ones about how I'd never hurt any of the people I loved. Passing remarks about returning to the therapist I was mandated to see after the incident to make sense of the fucked up connections my brain decided to make. Worried looks when none of those things worked.

He tries to hide them, but I read concern in his every expression, hear it in his voice, see it in everything he does like the carefully spaced out texts and phone calls I get whenever I'm out of his sight for too long.

I'm climbing back into my truck when my phone rings, announcing his arrival at the end of his rope. Deciding to let him sweat for a bit more, I crank the engine and wait for my phone to connect to the vehicle before answering the call.

"I'm heading home now, Cal."

A hum of approval that's more about me calling his house 'home' than anything else fills the space around me. We made the decision to move in together not too long after Aubrey forced us into taking the job because something about knowing our access to Selene was going to be damn near non-existent for the foreseeable future made waking up next to each other every morning and falling asleep together every night feel necessary to our survival. Like our closeness is the only thing making living without her bearable.

"Glad to hear it," Cal says. "That's not why I'm calling though."

"Oh. What's up, then?"

"You didn't see my text?"

"Uh, no. What'd it say?" I ask, plucking my phone from the cup holder and opening our text thread before he can even answer. There's only one new message, and it's a link to an article from a fledgling blog that appears to specialize in doling out right-wing propaganda. Above the link, there's a photo of a ruddy-faced white man with beady blue eyes and a bald head in a prison jumpsuit.

Leland Marsh.

Underneath his ugly mug is a headline that leaves my vision red.

A Father's Love: Leland Marsh speaks about the tragic death of his son, Jacob.

"What the fuck is this?"

"Some twisted sympathy piece that makes Jacob out to be some kind of victim and paints Leland as the grieving father instead of a hateful motherfucker who raised another hateful motherfucker," Cal growls.

I click the link, scrolling through the page to find that his description is pretty much spot-on. Aside from a few paragraphs at the beginning to provide context, the article is kind of sparse. The questions Leland was asked are in bold, and his corresponding answers are underneath. I guess the so-called journalist didn't want anything getting in the way of Leland telling his side of a story he still claims to have nothing to do with.

Thanks to the lackluster formatting, I'm able to make note of every subject they touched on, paying close attention to when they discuss Jacob's rebuilding of the Brothers of Confederate Pride—which Leland frames as a place where true Americans can embrace their heritage and be among like-minded individuals who want to see our country return to her former glory. When asked about Selene's kidnapping and attempted murder, Leland stated that all change comes with a cost. The only semi-respectable question asked throughout the entire interview was the one that followed that statement.

Apparently it was so good, the reporter decided to include a video clip of the moment.

Cal is silent as I start the video, pin pricks of irritation dancing down my spine when I see the walls of the same room we visited the bastard in months ago on my screen. The interviewer is out of frame because the camera is focused on their subject, but their voice is crystal clear as it filters through my speakers.

"Is that what Jacob's death is? The cost of change?"

Leland's expression turns harsh, his top lip curling into a snarl as the vein in the center of his forehead bulges. "My boy was a victim. Do you hear me? He was murdered in cold blood by two Black bastards who collected their medals with his blood on their filthy hands. Can you believe that?" He growls, banging a fist into the table. "MY BOY IS DEAD, and they're just living their lives, thinking they've won." He lifts his hand, pointing a finger at the camera as he stares directly into it like he's speaking just to me. "But you haven't won anything. Jacob might be dead, but his vision for this country is alive and well. *You have no idea what you've awakened.*"

"When you say 'you'," the interviewer chimes in. "Who exactly are you speaking to?"

"Everyone who walked out of that clothing factory alive when my boy didn't."

"Does that include the current First Lady, Selene Taylor?"

"Did she make it out of that factory alive?" he retorts.

"Um, yes, she did."

"Then, yeah, that includes her too."

The clip ends with Leland's dead stare fixed on the camera. I swipe the article away with an angry flick of my thumb and throw the phone down in disgust. "Do we know who the interviewer is?"

"Ian Conlon. 41. Lives in his mom's basement in some shitty town in Ohio. He owns the site."

Of course, Cal has already done his due diligence. He probably memorized Ian's entire life story while I was sitting in the cemetery trying to find peace among the dead. The thought sets me into motion immediately. I throw the truck in reverse and strap on my seat belt as I pull into oncoming traffic, gunning the engine because moving fast makes me feel less shitty about being so many steps behind.

"What's his connection to Marsh?"

"That, I don't know. The warden wasn't exactly forthcoming when I called and asked to see his visitor logs."

I wish I could say I was surprised, but I'm not. The last time we had the pleasure of making Warden Ethan Bennet's acquaintance, he had us escorted out of his prison for using excessive force against Leland. Clearly he's still pissy about me slamming Marsh's head into a table and Cal threatening to do the same to one of his guards.

"Asshole," I mutter. "We can go around him. Find Conlon and see if this is all for clicks and views or if he's trying to be Jacob 2.0."

"*We* can't do anything."

My brows furrow. "What are you talking about? Conlon could be a danger to Selene, we have to..." The burn of urgency and purpose leave me in a quiet whoosh as the realization sets in. Cal and I are no longer in charge of Selene's safety. We're not even supposed to acknowledge her existence because that might set Aubrey off, so investigating the possibility of a threat to her is not an option. "We could give compile the information and give it to Shaw," I offer lamely, hating the idea of ceding control to anyone, even someone I trust and respect as much as the head of Selene's detail.

Since coming on the scene, she's proven herself to be extremely capable. Every member of her team I've had the chance to interact with speaks highly of her, calling her a dynamic leader with a vision for protecting that requires flexibility and accounts for the humanity of those under her care. I've seen her work firsthand, benefited from her unusual philosophy, and yet, it still burns down to my core to know we'll have to hand over this lead and hope she sees the value in pursuing it.

"That's probably for the best." I listen to the faint clicking of his fingers flying across the keys of his laptop and know instantly that he's drafting an email to the woman in question. Seconds later, he sighs. "Done."

"Shaw can handle this, right?" I ask, leg bouncing impatiently as I wait for the car in front of me to find a break in traffic to execute a left turn.

"Yes," Cal answers confidently.

That same certainty is in his voice hours later when we're on a FaceTime call with Selene's parents, Justine and Albert, or as they like for us to call them, Mama J and Al. Somewhere between saving Selene and putting the entire Grant crew on flights back to Georgia, Cal and I ended up exchanging numbers with Mama J. At that time, I don't think either of us realized we'd be talking to her more than we even see Selene.

She calls all the time. Sometimes to ask questions about her daughter that we can't answer, but other times, it's to check on us. To make sure we're eating and sleeping and not giving in to the prevalent urge to kill Aubrey's dumb ass. Today's call is a surprising balance of both concern for us and for Selene. A result of Conlon's video of Marsh going viral on social media.

"I just can't stand the sight of that hateful man." Mama J shakes her head, shoulders up around her ears as she shivers with disgust. "Why would anyone give him a platform to say such terrible things?"

She poses the question directly to us, staring into our souls with the brown eyes she passed down to her oldest daughter. The phone is propped up on the kitchen counter, so we have a plain view of her slicing vegetables while Al stirs something in the pot on the stove behind her. He glances over his shoulder, mouth set in a disapproving line.

"Hate will always find a home in this country, Jus, you know that."

"Of course I know that, Albert. It doesn't mean I have to accept it, especially when it's aimed at *my baby*."

"Selene has a great team around her," I remind them, stealing Cal's line of reassurance because I'm sure he's tired of saying it by now. We've been on the phone with the Grants for almost thirty minutes, listening to Mama J rant and trying to convince her it will all be fine. Nothing seems to truly soothe her, though, and I understand that. I won't be soothed until Marsh and every other threat to Selene has been obliterated.

"I don't doubt that at all," she says, softening a little. "I just wish you two were a part of that team as well."

Cal reaches for me, wrapping his fingers around the clenched fist resting on my thigh. It loosens immediately, shifting to an open palm for him to press his against.

"We wish that too," he tells her.

"More than you know," I add.

4

SELENE

I used to love coming to work.

The thrill of walking into a building that doesn't have my name on the door but bears my mark anyway.

The satisfaction of being around people who hate small talk as much as I do and don't look at me weird when I order the same dish from the same restaurant for lunch every day for three months.

The buzz of excitement that would roll through my body and shoot out of my fingertips when inspiration for a new program struck. I'm waiting to feel it now, fingers poised over the keyboard, teeth digging into my bottom lip, brain frustratingly quiet. I've passed hours like this. Not today, but over the course of the nearly four months Aubrey has been in office. As First Lady, my duty is to this country and not my business, so I only get to come to Culture Code twice a week, and every minute of my limited time is spent suspended in the agony of *trying* to create.

Anyone who's ever taken something fluid and given it shape, blessed it with form, imbued it with purpose, knows creation isn't something that can be forced. You have to be willing to surrender control, if only for a second, so it can flow through you. That part has always been hard for me, but decades of coding have taught me that it's possible under the right conditions. The most important of which is the one thing I have less and less of whenever I'm here: time.

Back in January, I made it clear to Allegra—my social secretary—that my days at Culture Code were to be blocked off. No appearances. No interviews. No stupid meetings about rehearsals for State Dinners. Just me, my work, my office, my people. She promised to honor the request, and for a while there she did. I would get to spend two full days at the office, even managing to work late sometimes Then, slowly, but surely, that changed. A quick meeting before you go to the office here. An appearance that will require you to leave the office there. Suddenly, my designated days were mere hours I was lucky to have, and my ability to curate an environment conducive to creating was gone.

I slam my laptop shut and push back from my desk, blowing out a harsh breath.

"No luck?" Monique asks, glancing up from her makeshift work station at the conference table in the far corner of the office. We were supposed to be having a work date of sorts, using the other's presence as motivation to get things done. Usually body doubling works great for me, but today it seems to only be benefiting her.

"None. I should have let you sit at the desk."

A frown forms between her brows as she scribbles a note on one of the papers in front of her. "It's your desk, Sel. I'm fine right here."

"You work at it more than I do, Mo. At this point, it's yours. The office too."

While this is the first time I've lent my voice to the thought, it's not the first time it's run across my mind. I feel like an imposter in this space. A child playing pretend while all the grown ups look on indulgently, waiting for me to finish so they can get back to work. No one has ever said that to me, of course, but the energy is there. Present in Monique's coffee mug on the coaster to my right. Obvious in the way employees direct their inquiries to her even when I'm in the room. Demonstrated by my repeated failure to have a single moment of productivity.

"Why are you talking like that?" she asks, tossing her pen down and pinning me with a hard stare. "You planning on killing yourself or something?"

Her ridiculous question pulls a snort of laughter out of me. "No, Monique, I'm not planning on killing myself."

"Then why are you trying to give me your office and that ugly ass desk?"

My mouth drops open. "My desk isn't ugly!"

"Wrong. It's hideous, but it's yours, and it's going to stay that way."

"We can get you a new one."

"Selene," she groans, throwing her head back on her shoulders. "I don't want a new one. I like the one I have in my office."

"But it's too small for this space. It'll look ridiculous." I push to my feet and round the desk, standing a few feet away from it to really try to envision Monique's dainty furniture here. "You need something grand. Something commanding. Something that says Monique Walker, CEO."

The next time she speaks, she's right beside me. Her voice is soft, but firm, with a hint of worry underneath the sass and severity.

"What's going on with you?"

I twist my lips to the side and shrug. "I'm just being realistic, Mo. I'm not the leader Culture Code needs right now. I'm never here."

"You're here twice a week. That's more than most people in your position would give a job."

"It's not enough for me, and it's not just a job. It's my business."

She throws her hands up, eyes stretching wide. "Exactly! It's *your* business, which means you will always belong at the helm of it. You don't just give that shit away to anyone, not even your best friend."

I want to accept her words as the validation they're so clearly meant to be, but it's hard to believe when I can't do my favorite part of my job. "I can't even write a line of code, Mo," I whisper.

"Bitch, neither can I," she exclaims, and despite my sour mood, I find myself diving into a pit of laughter behind her. Somehow, we end up holding each other upright. When we've recovered, Monique grabs my hand and leads me back around to the chair I abandoned, placing her hands on my shoulders to force me down into it. Once I'm settled, she takes a seat in one of the arm chairs opposite me and stretches her legs out, propping her red-bottomed heels up on the edge of the desk.

"Level with me, Sel. Are you really thinking of leaving Culture Code?"

Just the thought of it makes my stomach twist into knots. The last thing I want is to leave this company, to abandon the work that was once the only reason I got out of bed in the morning, but the reality is I might.

"I just feel like I don't have anything to offer," I confess, my voice low, weighed down by shame. "Coming here is starting to feel like an exercise in futility. You have things well in hand. You don't need me barging in and interrupting your stride twice a week."

She rolls her eyes. "One, you're not interrupting anything so cut that shit out. Two, if you don't come down here that means I'll have to come bang on the doors of the White House to see you, and they'll probably arrest me. Is that what you want?"

Reminding her that she'd have to get past the gates and multiple security points before she could even get to the doors seems unnecessary, so I don't bother.

"No, Monique, that's not what I want."

"Okay, so in order to keep you sane, me free and the company functioning, let's end this conversation. There is no Culture Code without you, Selene. Whether you're here for a second or here for eighteen hours a day, you're still the heart and soul of this place."

"If you say so."

"I do say so," she insists, eyes running anxious lines over my face. "Can you really not be here more often? I thought you said he was supportive of you continuing to work."

"He is."

The lie burns like acid on my tongue, and it comes too quickly. Monique's brows pull together. She is constantly suspicious of my marriage, picking apart everything I say and do as it relates to Aubrey because she can't believe I could still love a man who apparently didn't shed a tear for me while I was being held hostage by a man determined to kill me on national television. I don't blame her for being skeptical. I don't blame my parents or my sisters either. Everyone has questions, and all I have are the lies I tell to perpetuate the narrative Aubrey promised to kill me for contradicting.

"Okayyyyy," Monique says slowly after a few tense seconds, where I force myself to hold perfectly still and maintain eye contact. "Then it shouldn't be a problem for you to come into the office more. Just tell Allegory to keep it cute with the scheduling."

Once again, I find myself laughing. "Her name is Allegra, and it's not that simple, Mo."

"Of course it is. You're the First Lady. She works for you."

"Right," I drawl sarcastically. "How could I forget that?"

"That's what I'm trying to figure out," she says, tilting her head to the side. "Did you get any sleep last night?"

"What?"

"Sleep, Selene. Rest, recuperation, you know, when you lay down and close your eyes and your brain shuts off?"

I pick the pad of sticky notes next to the mouse and launch it at her head. "I know what sleep is, girl. I was just wondering where the question came from."

She swats away the projectile just before it collides with her face. "Jesus! I was just curious!"

"Your curiosity wasn't the problem. Your tone was."

"Just answer the question, heffa."

"No, Monique." I let out a heavy sigh, knowing exactly where this conversation is going. "I didn't get much sleep last night because I had a nightmare. What about you? Did you get your suggested eight hours?"

We both know the answer is no. Neither of us does a good job of taking care of ourselves, but Monique is usually worse than me about going to bed at a decent hour. After the kidnapping, that changed.

"This isn't about me," she says.

"Well, I don't want it to be about me."

"You're the one having nightmares about the very real trauma you experienced that resulted in the death of three people. One of whom has a crazy ass racist daddy who told the world he was gunning for you."

Monique's recounting of Leland's viral video is just as dramatic as Mama's was when she called me about it yesterday after she got done talking to Cal and Beck. I roll my eyes, and I'm not sure if the annoyance trickling down my spine is for my best friend or my mother and her ability to talk to my men whenever she wants.

"He did not say he was gunning for me."

Her nostrils flare. "I'm not about to argue about word choice with you, Selene."

"We're not arguing. We're not just discussing a series of facts you think are connected."

"So you just think it's a coincidence that you had your first nightmare in weeks after that video came out?"

Anyone with an ounce of common sense would know seeing Jacob's face reflected in his father's sneer was the cause of that awful dream returning, but I still resent Monique for making me admit it.

"No."

It's a low, defeated confession that my best friend takes no pleasure in extracting. She's been riding the wave of my subconscious' betrayal with me for months now, and I know I should do us both a favor and be a little less combative when it comes to addressing her concerns.

"Are you still against speaking to someone about all of this?"

"Thanks for talking me down earlier," I say, switching subjects much to Monique's frustration.

"You are getting on my last nerve today, you know that?" she growls, checking her watch and pushing to her feet. "You're lucky I have a meeting with the coding academy coordinators, or else I'd beat your ass for all the shit you put me through."

"No, you won't. You love me too much," I remind her, moving over to the door to give her a hug before we part ways. Even with her hands full, she manages to wrap me up in a tight hug. I'm so glad to have the physical contact, I don't even complain about her laptop digging into my back.

"I do love you," she confirms, pulling back to set a serious gaze on my face. "That's why I want you to seriously think about going to therapy, okay?"

"Okay, Mo."

She smiles and hurries off to her meeting, genuinely soothed by yet another lie. The truth, I haven't just thought about therapy, I've longed for it. Yearned for a safe place to put all the emotions zipping around underneath my skin.

The problem is there is nothing and no one who meets that criteria because of who I am, or rather, who my husband is. There are no sacred spaces for me anymore, and as long as I'm attached to Aubrey, that will always be the case. It's infuriating really. He has bunkers, situations rooms, offices with armed guards and bullet proofed vehicles. Every space he exists in is fortified while I remain vulnerable to him and the rest of the world.

A visible target with nowhere to privately lick my wounds and safely plot a way to get my life, career and men back.

The door clicks shut seconds after Monique's departure, bathing the room in blessed silence that stops me in my tracks.

I look around the space—*my* space, the place I've built my dreams and forged my legacy in the tech space—and wonder why the hell it never occurred to me that everything I want in the way of privacy and security exists right here in this building I was prepared to give up just moments ago. Unsteady feet carry me back to my desk, and I sink into the chair with hope swelling in my chest. Culture Code isn't a break from from my life as the First Lady of the United States of America.

It's the key to being free of the title and the man attached to it forever.

5

SELENE

"Monique says you've been in the office a lot more."

Pride colors my mother's voice, the warmth of it washing over me through my headphones. She'd called in the middle of me conducting my post-nightmare routine, which consists of listening to guided meditation recordings while I lie in bed staring at the ceiling. Initially, I was a little dismayed by the interruption, but I'm glad that I answered because her constant chattering is actually exactly what I need.

I close my eyes and will the lingering tension in my muscles to fade while the sounds of Mama moving around the kitchen transport me back to my childhood. A pot of Folgers coffee brewing on the counter. Sausage patties sizzling on the stove. Slices of bread toasted in the oven with pools of salted butter in the center.

"Selene? You still there, baby?"

"Yes, ma'am."

"Well say something then, girl. You had me thinking I pressed the mute button by mistake again."

She's right to be concerned since muting herself by accident is a regular occurrence.

"Sorry." I wince at her light admonishment as I sit up and rest my back against the headboard. "What did you say a second ago? I missed it."

She repeats herself, adding more context this time, so I have a full understanding of how she and Monique ended up discussing my attendance record at work.

"Don't you two have anything better to talk about?"

The clang of a pan hitting the stove rings in my ear, prompting me to open my eyes. I blink into the darkness of the room, grateful for the black out curtains that are currently hiding the sun from me. It's a little after seven, and I need to be getting up to start my day.

"We don't spend all day talking about you," Mama says. "She just happened to mention that you were spending more time at work, and I wanted to let you know how proud I am of you for not letting anything keep you from your dreams."

"Thank you."

It feels wrong to accept her praise when I haven't accomplished anything significant professionally or personally in months. I decided to use Culture Code as my base of operations to get out from under Aubrey's thumb two weeks ago, but I haven't made any real progress on that front. Mostly, I've just been compiling data, studying Aubrey's voting record from his senatorial career, comparing his campaign promises to his accomplishments in office thus far.

There hasn't been anything of interest outside of the complaints about his actions sometimes contradicting his words. Entire forums are dedicated to what President Sanders once called Aubrey's 'fair weather politics', filled with posts that put clips of him on the campaign trail promising a foreign country would never have an independent military base on US soil next to an article published in February about him being in talks with the Emir of Qatar to build one in the Midwest.

None of it means anything yet. I mean, politicians lie to get elected all the time. Still, I bookmarked every forum and news article, adding them to my growing database of things I hope will amount to something but most likely won't because it's hard to blackmail someone with things that are already public knowledge. I need something bigger, something darker, something undeniable and ruinous, something no one knows but the people closest to him.

Unfortunately, I'm no longer a part of his inner circle, and I wouldn't be able to stomach the things I'd have to do to change that fact, so I'm just stuck. No access. No leads. Nothing but the desire to not just be free of Aubrey but to burn his entire world down on my way out.

"You don't have to thank me," Mama says, pulling me out of my head and back into the present. "I'm always proud of you, baby girl. I'm sorry I never said it enough when you were growing up."

I hear the wobbly notes of regret in her tone and push out a soft breath. Lots of positive changes have happened in our relationship between her impromptu trip to Vegas during the campaign and now. We had long conversations about what I needed as a child and what I got from her. She's owned her mistakes and promised to do the work to show up how I need her to now. I've trusted her to make those changes and forgiven her, but she can't seem to forgive herself.

"*Mama.*"

"I know. I won't cry." She laughs, the sound wispy and sad, sending the image of her wiping away tears floating through my mind. We're both quiet for a beat, and then she perks back up, steering the conversation in a new direction. "What's on your agenda for the day?"

"We have the first forum for Aubrey's Promise at AJ's old school."

"I thought you were going to be doing these on your own. Who's we?"

"Me and Aubrey." I grimace as I speak his name, hating the thought of doing this appearance with him almost as much as I hate the name he insisted on attaching to my labor of love. Initially, he wasn't supposed to attend any of the forums, but Allegra informed me last night that he had changed his mind about missing this one in particular.

"Mmm." She hums disapprovingly.

"Cal and Beck will be there too."

That perks her right up.

"Oh, good! I always feel better when they've got their eyes on you."

"Me too."

Their eyes. Their lips. Their hands….

I bite my lip, vanquishing my wayward thoughts and vowing to spend some time with my vibrator and plethora of memories tonight because if I'm thinking about threesomes on the phone with my mother then I've gone far too long without an orgasm.

"How are you feeling about going back to the school?"

"Fine. It's just a building, Mama."

One that's undergone a full remodel since the shooting. The changes mean it won't be familiar to me at all. It won't feel like anywhere AJ has ever existed even though I'm told his name is engraved on a plaque in the main hall along with the other people who died that day.

"It's not just a building, Selene. It's the site of one of a major trauma, which means it could be extremely….what's the word?"

"Triggering?"

"Yes." She snaps her fingers. "Triggering. That's exactly why you need to be going to therapy, ain't that right, Al?"

Up until this point, she hadn't so much as hinted at my father's presence in the kitchen, but now I hear the deep rumble of his voice from far off, which means he's probably at the table eating his breakfast and hoping to be left out of his wife's early morning meddling.

"Good morning, Daddy!"

"Good morning, baby girl," he shouts.

My brows pull together. "Have I been on speaker this whole time?"

"Of course. I need both hands to cook breakfast, Selene," she says, sass all up and through her tone. "Now, back to this therapy thing…"

"*Mamaaa,*" I groan at the same time Daddy says, "Justine. Leave it alone."

She sucks her teeth. "Can't tell the two of your stubborn fools nothing."

A knock on my door presents the excuse I was looking for to end the call, and I waste no time saying my goodbyes, promising to call later and let them know how the forum went. The knock sounds again, and I sigh, throwing the covers back and stretching before getting up to finally start my day.

Agent Shaw's signature frown greets me when I open the door.

"Good morning, ma'am."

"Good morning, Agent Shaw."

With everything the woman knows about me, you'd think we'd have abandoned the formality by now, but she seems to prefer to keep those boundaries in place. As someone who thrives inside the space between crisp and clear lines, I understand the desire. I even get how that need for order led her to accept my relationship with Cal and Beck. She'd hinted at it on the night she found out about us, explaining that her job was to keep me safe and doing that meant knowing every aspect of my life so she could sort them into the corresponding boxes.

Often, I imagine that my men and I reside in one she's marked messy, inconvenient, and potentially career ruining. Of course, that's just me projecting. I don't really know how she feels about us or anything at all, actually, because her professional facade doesn't ever have a crack in it. Even now, when I'm sure I look a mess with ruffled pajamas and my bonnet halfway off my head, her expression remains neutral.

"The motorcade will be departing for Beaumont High School at nine sharp," she announces. "I've been asked to inform you that the President will be arriving separately."

"Perfect. Anything else?"

"No, ma'am."

"Do you know if Diane and Ayanna have arrived?" I ask, hoping my firecracker of a hair stylist and the ethereal makeup artist I poached from Ursula Upshaw's morning show are already on site and prepared for the challenge of making me look something other than stressed.

She nods. "Agent Morgan has just escorted them to the salon."

"Okay, please let them know I'll be with them shortly."

"Yes, ma'am."

With the conversation done, Agent Shaw resumes her post to the right of my door, and I return to the solitude of my room, moving through my shower and the rest of my morning routine slowly because

I know it'll be the last time I'm alone for the next twelve to fourteen hours.

* * *

Just the thought of being 'on' for so long has me stressed. The buzz of preemptive overstimulation starts in the shower and lasts long after the forum at Beaumont High is over. Waves of anxious energy twist their way through me, emanating from the spot on my back where Aubrey's hand has been for the last minute or so. He's holding me in place, forcing me to pose for photos on the stage they erected in the gym for us while the students look on with distant interest.

The thrill of having the President and First Lady at their school wore off around the time we started talking about the link between bullying and school shootings, and now they're all ready to return to their regular schedules. I don't blame them. I'm ready to go too. Desperate to get away from Aubrey, and the blown up photos of AJ's face I didn't know were going to be displayed around the gym, and the stage he would have walked across at graduation if he had finished high school instead of dying in it. Most of all, I'm ready to get away from the copper and brass stare that's caressing my face from afar.

Cal hasn't stopped looking at me. Well, technically, his eyes have left me several times over the last few hours, but they always, *always*, come back. Even when they shouldn't. Even when I don't want them to because Mama was right about me being triggered and now all I want is to run into his arms and cry for my baby, but I can't.

One second, I think to myself. *You can have one second of eye contact.*

My heart pounds as I slide my gaze in his direction without moving my head an inch. Aubrey is too busy making love to the camera and chatting up the pretty, blonde principal to notice the shift in my attention, and thank God for that because the moment our eyes lock, I'm swept up in Cal's love, lost in the sorrow and understanding emanating from every line of his still expression.

A sudden sob swells in my chest as I look away, and I grab my throat to stop it from making its way up. Aubrey turns a gaze made of quiet fury on me.

"What's wrong?" he asks, features melting into a mask of concern for the cameras pointing at us.

I step out of his hold, shaking my head. "I need to—"

The stalled wail tries to escape again, but I slam my lips shut. Several people start to move toward me, but I'm only cognizant of Cal breaking formation and Beck using a single hand to pull him back, even though he looks ready to step out of line too. Agent Shaw is the one who makes the approach. She swoops in, placing a hand on my elbow.

"I've got her, sir," she says to Aubrey. Determined to play up the role of loving husband, he reaches out, brushing a few strands of hair behind my ear as he ducks down to meet my eyes.

"I'll come and check on you in a few minutes, darling."

His act requires no response from me, so I don't give him one, opting instead to allow Agent Shaw to guide me out of the gym and into the hallway where everything is quiet except my brain.

"Take a seat right here, ma'am. I'll get you some water."

I sink onto the bench she's directed me to and rest my head against the white brick of the wall, relishing the cool feel of it against my skin. Agent Shaw's footsteps grow quieter the further away she gets on her quest for water, and I relax into the silence that only lasts a minute before it's interrupted by the appearance of two teenage girls who share the same face.

"Are you okay, Mrs. Taylor?" The one on the left asks, lines of genuine worry between her brows. They're set deep into her mahogany skin like she spends most of her time fretting over one thing or another. She tucks her hands into the back pockets of her worn jeans, stopping just a few feet away from the bench while her sister lingers behind her. "I can call you that right? Or do you prefer First Lady?"

Adjusting myself so I don't look like I'm on the verge of falling apart, I offer her a smile. "Mrs. Taylor is fine. Selene is better."

"Our foster mom doesn't let us call adults by their first name," the other girl says. She's inching closer now, hugging the wall.

"Then Mrs. Taylor is fine," I assure her. "What are your names?"

"Isis," the twin closest to me says, pointing to herself. "And that's Imani."

"I'm the oldest," Imani tells me crossing her arms over her chest. I stare at them both, running a mental compare and contrast. Imani is taller and more solid than her sister. Her features are hard where Isis' are soft, which makes for a stunning juxtaposition since they have the same round eyes, button nose and thick dark brows that remind me of someone I can't place at the moment.

"The oldest *twin*," Isis reminds her with a glare. Her gaze softens when she turns it back to me. "We had an older brother, but he….died during the shooting."

My heart drops as grief echoes between the three of us. All these years, I've thought of the parents who lost their children and the children who lost their parents, but I'm ashamed to admit that I've never thought past that. Never considered what it would be like for the Isis and Imanis of the world to attend the same school where their siblings are memorialized forever.

"I'm sorry," I whisper fiercely, knowing the two words from a stranger won't mean a thing to them. "Is that why you two weren't at the assembly?"

We were told several children had been excused. I could certainly see their loss being a valid reason to sit it out. Isis drops onto the bench beside me. "No, we decided to skip so we could spend some extra time in the computer lab."

Imani's nostrils flare in annoyance. She's clearly the more closed off of the two. "Isis! You're not supposed to tell her that."

"Why not?" I ask, genuinely curious. "I don't have any authority here. I can't give you detention or any other punishment even if I wanted to, which I don't."

Imani tilts her head to the side, her long black braids spilling over one shoulder. "Why don't you?"

"Because I also prefer time on the computer to pretty much anything else."

Both girls seem impressed by my answer, and the slow trickle of validation moves through me, reminding me of what it was like to hear AJ's friends call me cool when they thought I wasn't listening. The key to maintaining cool status as an adult is knowing when to stop asking questions. I know this. And still, I find myself posing a question to them.

"What were you working on?"

Isis slides a careful, questioning look to her big sister who graciously gives a shrug of encouragement. She squeals softly and then spins to face me, eyes wide with excitement.

"We're building a video game!"

From there, the words spill out of her at rapid speed. Details of character development and world building flying at me faster than I can process them. Imani has joined in by the time Agent Shaw returns with water, a granola bar and the school nurse who orders the girls into the gym to find their homeroom teachers before I can say goodbye or remember who exactly they remind me of.

6

CAL

The most interesting thing happens when you meet the makers of a monster.

All the pieces of the horrific puzzle that is them fall into place, and you can finally make sense of them. Finally see that their selfishness and entitlement isn't a mistake, it's a learned behavior. A weapon they were taught to wield and were rewarded for using successfully.

Aubrey's list of rewards is long and vast, ranging from things as grand as the presidency to something as small as one of his arms around the back of Selene's chair while she picks at the lunch he insisted she share with him and his parents after their joint appearance at Beaumont High.

Chip and Arlene Taylor are everything you'd expect the parents of a man like Aubrey to be. Chip is quiet vulgarity dressed in an expensive suit, and Arlene is poised submission wrapped in an understated dress and string of pearls. When you put them next to their son, they're the picture-perfect American family.

The only thing that doesn't fit is the melanated goddess among them.

Everything from the glow of her skin to the sadness behind her eyes sets her apart. While they laugh boisterously and talk about how handsome AJ looked in the photo the school had displayed in the gym, she mourns him silently. It's infuriating. How they look right past her. Talk around her. Pretend her pain isn't palpable. Real enough, raw enough, big enough to fill up the entire private dining room at the back of Dahlia's—an upscale Asian fusion restaurant Aubrey eats at often.

Maybe it isn't to them.

Maybe I'm the only one here who cares enough to see it. If Beck were in here instead of with the cars, he'd see it too. We'd share looks from across the room and vow right then and there to add this moment to the long list of things we have to atone for when we finally have her back in our arms. It's longer than I'd like, and I hate not knowing when we'll be able to start checking things off it.

If we'll ever be able to start checking things off of it.

I shake my head, banishing the thought as soon as it's fully formed. The key to surviving this is staying positive. It's looking ahead to the future and keeping an eye out for glimmers of hope in the present. My glimmer comes seconds later, appearing in the form of Selene excusing herself from the table to go to the restroom. Agent Morgan—Shaw's right hand—steps in immediately to escort her, and I hold my breath as they approach the open doorway I've made my post, willing Selene to look at me even as I force my eyes away from her.

She doesn't, and I know that's probably for the best because Aubrey is watching. He's paused his entire conversation with his father just to witness the pain it causes us to be this close to each other and act like we don't know what it feels like to be closer. What he doesn't see, though, is Selene drop her hands to her sides as she passes between me and the wall. He doesn't notice my pinky stretching out, the single digit straining for the faintest bit of contact, and he damn sure doesn't catch how hers does the same.

The fleeting touch sends shock waves through me, but I remain expressionless even as Selene gasps quietly, leaving me with the small, private sound as she disappears down the hall.

Aubrey's smile is a dark curve of satisfaction as he turns back to his parents. He picks up the glass goblet filled with sparkling water and takes a long sip, continuing the conversation they were having before Selene left the table.

"Don't get me wrong, the plaque is nice, but I think I'd like to see my son's memory represented in a much more significant way."

Chip cuts another slice of his ribeye and pops it into his mouth. "I agree. Having the President's son sharing a memorial plaque with everyone else seems distasteful."

"Exactly!" Aubrey agrees. "They're building a new sports complex. I think the Aubrey Taylor Jr. Stadium has a nice ring to it."

"Well, I'm sure Principal Mathers would be more than happy to discuss different options," Arlene chirps, taking a dainty bite of her salad. She chews slowly and swallows with a napkin covering her mouth, wiping the corners when she's done. "She seemed quite fond of you, Aubrey. You could have Jordan invite her to the State Dinner. It'd be the perfect way to endear yourself to her even more."

Aubrey appears to be intrigued by the idea until his father shakes his head. "Why on Earth would he do all of that when he can just write a check and have her do whatever he wants, Arlene?"

The woman's response is lost on me, drowned out by Agent Thorpe's voice flowing out of my comms. "Secretary Barnes is on site with four men who refuse to show identification. Dower and I attempted to block entry, but the Secretary insisted to be let through. They are heading your way now."

Turning toward the door, I lift my wrist to my mouth, pressing down to activate my microphone. "Are you fucking kidding me, Thorpe?"

Dower is the one who responds. "She insisted, sir."

"And I might insist on putting my foot up your ass, Dower, does that mean you're just going to bend over and take it?" Beck growls. "Drake, hold tight, Shaw and I are coming inside."

"Negative. Hold your position while I assess the situation."

Moments later, the situation walks through the door. Cordelia is first, waltzing through the door and past Agent Morgan who has just emerged from the short hall to my right that leads to the bathrooms where, as far as I can tell, Selene still is. Morgan catches my eye, silently asking if she needs to engage. I shake my head, stepping into the center of the hall and stopping Cordelia and her cronies in their tracks.

"Madame Secretary, I've been informed by my agents that your guests have refused to show identification."

She glances over her shoulder at the four men who pretty much all the look the same to me. They're all white with short cropped hair with non-descript, but expensive, suits draped over their muscular frames and bored expressions. You would think they crash the private lunches of world leaders every day.

"They prefer their privacy," she drawls, turning back to me with a smug smile.

"Privacy is their right. Holding court with the President without proper vetting is not. If your guests refuse to comply with security protocol, I'll be forced to have them removed from the premises."

There are so many things I hate about the job Beck and I worked our asses off for, but more than anything I hate instances like this when honor and competence override my desire to see Aubrey dead. I don't know who these men are or what they're here for, but it's a very slight, but real, possibility they're here to kill him, and here I am, standing in the way because I swore a fucking oath.

One of the men sniffs, drawing my attention. He's standing closest to Cordelia, and now that I'm really looking at him, I notice he's older than the men behind him, who are in their mid to late thirties. There are streaks of gray starting at his temples, running throughout his dark brown strands, and harsh lines at the outer corners of his green eyes. Impatience radiates off of him, but he doesn't say a word, allowing Cordelia to do the talking.

Her chin rises defiantly. "*I* vetted them. Now, if you'll excuse us—"

She tries to side-step me, but I anticipate the move, blocking her with ease. "Your guests need to identify themselves."

"That won't be necessary, Agent Drake," Aubrey says, his voice carrying from the end of the hall. I turn to find him standing there in the same spot I occupied just seconds ago, his expression stricken.

My jaw turns rigid. "These men have not been properly screened. I cannot guarantee your safety."

My warning holds no weight. He barely acknowledges it as he waves Cordelia and the men through. They file past me as if their entry was a foregone conclusion and I was nothing more than an unnecessary obstacle. Aubrey greets them all with a strained smile, instructing them to get comfortable at the table before shifting his focus back to me.

"Give us the room," he barks, disappearing into the dining area.

Frustrated, and more than a little confused, I'm left with no choice but to follow the order. I head down the hall, meeting Morgan at the opening she hasn't moved from.

"Who the hell are they?" she asks, voice pitched low.

"I have no idea." And truthfully, I don't care. Aubrey can entertain as many unidentified subjects as he wants. It doesn't matter to me. All that matters now is their sudden appearance has created an opening for me and Selene that I am going to take. Agent Morgan follows my intense gaze down the short corridor and sighs.

"I'll keep watch."

"He wanted total privacy so stay out of sight and update Shaw and Beckham so they don't come rushing in," I tell her, already heading toward the bathroom. My steps are quiet but hurried, and I make it to the door just as Selene is coming out of it.

Her eyes go wide with surprise when she sees me, and I place my hand over her mouth to stop her from saying anything.

"Everything is fine, but we don't have long, okay?" I whisper, backing her into the bathroom.

She nods, heels clicking softly against the jade green tiles that cover the floors and walls. I kick the door closed with my foot and remove my hand from her mouth.

"Are you crazy?!" she whisper-shouts as I lock the door. "You can't be here, Cal. He'll know."

"He's occupied."

"Occupied? With what?"

It's been so long since I've been alone with her, since I've found myself wrapped in the scent of sugared wild berries and cherry blossoms. Desperate for more than a passing whiff, I step into her space, taking her into my arms and lifting her up until I can plant my nose in the hollow of her neck. She shivers against me, cradling the back of my head in her hands to hold me in place.

"Occupied with what, Cal?" she asks, her voice part fear and part desire.

"Cordelia," I sigh the witch's name into Selene's skin. "And some random men. Aubrey told us to give him the room."

"But you came in here instead."

"I needed to see you." I pull back, wanting an up close view of her stunning features even though they're laced with sadness. "How are you doing?"

Tears gloss over her eyes, making the puddles of toffee in her irises shimmer. "I wasn't prepared for how hard it would be to be there. I didn't know they were going to have his face…" She swallows, twisting her lips to the side to stop the sob trying to claw its way out of her. "Can you just—"

She doesn't even need to finish the request. I lower us to the floor, tucking the hem of her dress in so it doesn't get dirty then pull her into the tightest hug possible. She hugs me back, returning a fraction of the pressure I'm giving as her breaths slow and then stop altogether.

"Is it too much?"

"No," Selene gasps, lungs expanding as they fill with air. "It's perfect."

I'm always afraid that I'll hurt her, but I've learned to trust her knowledge of her limits. We sit in perfect silence for a long while, until she finally taps my shoulder, signaling for me to let her go.

"Thank you," she murmurs. "It's all I've wanted all day."

"I know."

The desire was so clear on her face. The need to retreat to the safety of my arms evident to me from across the room. I didn't know then that I'd get to give her that today, but I'm so grateful I got the chance.

With her palms resting on the tops of my shoulders, Selene pushes back, allowing me to see a different desire taking over the lovely lines of her face. Heat dances in her eyes as she lowers her lips to mine. "Now, I want something else."

"Selene, I don't—"

"*Please*, Cal."

Her hands are already at my waist, deft fingers working to undo my belt. I want to say no, to tell her we don't have enough time, but she's kissing me again. They're slow, languid kisses accompanied by strokes of her tongue that stoke the fire burning in the pit of my stomach.

"Fuck it," I groan, hands fisting the fabric of her dress until it's up around her hips. My fingers rush over the smooth, taut skin of her thighs, loving the way her muscles tense and relax under my touch.

"I've missed you so much," she moans softly, fumbling with my zipper. "I love you so much."

"I love you too." I tap her hip with my left hand. "Lift up for a second."

She does as I ask, and I make short work of freeing my dick as my heart tries to pound its way out of my chest. It's been so long since I've been inside of her, and I almost lose my shit when she lines the wet heat of her pussy up with my tip.

"*Fuck.*" My head falls back when she slides down onto me, walls already rippling with the promise of an impending orgasm as she takes my full length in a single motion.

Selene whimpers, biting her lip to hold in what I'm sure would be an earth shattering moan as she swirls her hips, dragging her clit across the exposed skin of my lower abs. I grab her waist, digging the tips of my fingers into her sides to get her attention. She fixes a wild, lust-filled gaze on my face, and I'm sure I'm nothing more than a mirror, reflecting that need and desperation back at her.

"Look at me when you ride me, pet. I want you to see exactly what this pussy does to me."

Her walls clench around me, and I buck up into her, laughing darkly when she curses.

"I'm on top," she growls, swooping down to give me a kiss that ends with her biting my bottom lip. "That means I'm in charge, Drake."

If I had a response, which I don't, I wouldn't be able to vocalize it because as soon as Selene is done putting me in my place, she starts bouncing on my dick with an urgency that's as familiar to me as the curve of her exquisite lips.

Everything about us has always been rushed. Condensed. Big feelings packed into small interactions, overwhelming desire stuffed into forbidden circumstances. This moment is no different—I mean, it's a quickie on a bathroom floor of a restaurant with her husband and in-laws around the corner and one of my colleagues keeping watch—and yet, we treat it like it is.

Every kiss is a discovery.

Every wet glide of her pussy over my shaft a revelation.

Every moan a sacrifice to the gods in charge of happily ever afters for desperate fools who risk life and limb for love.

7

SELENE

My hair still smells like Cal's cologne.

I can't tell if it's my imagination or not, but every time I turn my head or run my fingers through my hair, I catch a whiff of him. The notes of smoke and spice combined with my aching knees and the faint bruise on my knee from the jade tiles of the bathroom floor are the only reminders I have of the stolen moment we shared two days ago, and I'm clinging to them desperately today, knowing they're the only thing that will get me through the tedium of the final planning meeting for the State Dinner.

Playing hostess has never been an interest of mine, and my apathy toward planning this event has been treated as a direct affront to everything the First Lady position stands for by Allegra, my social secretary, and Spencer, the White House Chief Usher. Every time I sit down with them, there's a new layer to my indifference and a new degree to their joint indignation.

"Ma'am," Spencer chides gently, rubbing at his temple while I stare blankly at the flower arrangements covering the small coffee table in the center of the sitting area in my office. "All you have to do is choose one."

"But I don't like any of them," I state plainly.

Spencer scoffs, fingers moving faster as his leg starts to bounce. He's a short, impeccably dressed Black man with a round belly, harsh features and a deep disdain for indecisive people. He cuts his eye at Allegra, and she hops in immediately, scooting to the edge of the armchair across from me and picking up one of the glass vases from the line up.

"What about this one?" she asks, hope clinging to the edges of her voice. She always grows a bit antsy when Spencer gets wound up. All of the staff members do. It's actually kind of comical, the way everyone assumes the White House is ruled by the President, when really a stubby man in a tweed jacket with elbow patches is actually keeping everything and everyone in line.

I eye the fragrant bouquet of roses, chrysanthemums and hydrangeas with the same disinterest I gave them from afar. "They're lovely, Allegra. All of the flowers are lovely, which is why I couldn't care less what we go with."

"But you have to care," she insists. "Every place setting will include a note from you giving context for the decor choices you've made. It's a personal touch that will—"

"You explained this when we chose the flowers the first time," I remind her, leaning back in my seat and folding my arms over my chest. "The notes were finalized yesterday, so I don't understand why we're even having this discussion right now."

Too often I find myself revisiting conversations with no context as to why the solutions we came up with previously are no longer viable. No one seems to think that kind of information matters, but when it's my time and mental energy being taxed it matters to me.

Allegra relaxes into her seat, smoothing a hand over the lines of her pleated skirt. It's sage green and matches perfectly with the blazer she's wearing but does nothing for her complexion, clashing with the pink undertones of her pale skin and making her look sallow.

"We, um, realized that the First Lady of Singapore is allergic to cherry blossoms," she admits, sliding a helpless look in Spencer's direction.

"It was an oversight," he adds. "Now our florist is scrambling to redo the arrangements and the calligrapher has to stay late penning another set of cards, but no one can *do* anything until *you* decide which arrangements to go with."

"Your tone suggests you believe the issue here is me when it sounds like the real problem is a lack of attention to detail and a refusal to hear me when I say I don't care what flowers end up on the table at this dinner." I stand, splitting a look between him and Allegra. "Please select the arrangement that will be easiest for Paige to put together and nix the note cards. It doesn't make sense for the calligrapher to stay late working on something no one will bother to read anyway. I'll be at the office for the rest of the day. Please don't disturb me with anymore last-minute emergencies you can sort out yourselves."

I take my leave before either of them can respond, stepping out into the halls of the East Wing that are never quiet but don't come anywhere close to the hustle and bustle of the West. Agent Shaw is waiting for me outside of my office, falling into easy step behind me as I make my way toward the exit where I know Agent Morgan is already waiting with the car. I'm eager to get to Culture Code and dig into the situation that unfolded at Dahlia's. Before we went our separate ways, Cal gave me as much information as he could about the encounter with Cordelia and the men who refused to make themselves known to him, emphasizing how distressed Aubrey looked when he waved them through.

Fear isn't an expression I normally see on that man's face—especially now when he feels like he's untouchable—so I would have given anything to witness it, to lay eyes on the people who inspired it. The result of missing a moment that could be the key to finally being free of Aubrey is sparks of anxious excitement dancing underneath my skin and a level of hyper vigilance that makes no sense for someone who spends the majority of her day being monitored by people who specialize in neutralizing threats before they ever become a problem.

As we move through the East Colonnade, I find myself paying close attention to everything. The way my heels sound against the lacquered brick of the herringbone floor. The number of people soaking in the sunshine through the large windows overlooking the garden. And even the tinkle of feminine laughter coming from the Family Theater we never use. *That* gives me pause. I stop abruptly just outside the door, straining my ears to see if I hear it again. Agent Shaw slows too.

"What is it, ma'am?"

"I thought I heard something."

Everything is quiet now, but I still push the door open and step inside, taking in the plush red carpet and reclining chairs that match. There are no windows in this room, so it's dark save for the light spilling in from the hall, which makes it easy for me to identify the woman nestled in one of the chairs in the third row.

"Jordan?" I scan the room. "What are you doing in here?"

Her presence in this wing, but especially this room, make no sense to me. From the day Aubrey took office, she's existed solely in the West Wing. I don't think I've ever seen her outside of it, but here she is, looking completely at home in a recliner in the middle of the work day, laughing at nothing and with no one.

"Are you okay?"

The question pops out of my mouth before I can stop it, before I can remember that this is the woman who went out of her way to make my life hell for years. Based on the bags under her eyes she's failed to hide with concealer, karma is catching up to her, which is exactly what she deserves, not my concern.

"I'm fine," she says, approaching me with her phone in hand, waving it around like it's proof of something. "Just taking a little social media break."

Not once in my years of knowing her, have I seen the woman open a social media app without an explicit goal in mind. Aimless scrolling seems like the last thing she'd indulge in, especially this far from the center of the action.

"In the theater? Why wouldn't you use your office for that?"

"Do I need your permission to exist outside of my office, Selene?"

"No, giving you marching orders is more of Aubrey's domain." I tilt my head to the side, slipping easily into our adversarial banter. "Or has he handed your reins over to Cordelia?"

My question strikes a chord somewhere deep inside Jordan. Her nostrils flare, and tension cuts jagged lines into her features. "Do you know what I do every day, Selene? I stand in front of reporters and cameras from the most prestigious publications in our nation, and I field question after question about you and Aubrey and Cordelia *fucking* Barnes. I answer for everything your husband has done in his life including the shit he took this morning and the amount of time he spent wiping his ass. When I stand behind that podium, narratives shift and legacies are formed all through the power of *my* tongue, so trust me when I say the *only* person holding any reins here is me."

I know what confidence looks like on Jordan. I've seen it turn her spine into a steel rod and the tongue she's bragging about into a poison-tipped dagger. *This* is not confidence. This is the incessant bark of a small dog that wants you to believe it's big, that needs you to buy into its act because scaring you means it doesn't have to be ruled by its fear anymore.

She storms out of the room, and I watch her go, wondering what exactly she's afraid of.

8

BECK

It's been years since I've lived with a partner, so I'd forgotten what it was like to go from sipping coffee and watching the morning news as you get ready for work to being balls deep in a person you're incapable of saying no to in the span of a second.

Cal so rarely lets me have this.

The honor of control. The gift of sacred invasion. The sight of his back muscles straining to maintain the position I've put him in. The soft, crushing weight of his walls contracting around my dick as a reward for every inch I feed into him only to take it back and start the process all over again.

"Don't fucking tease me," he grunts, rocking his hips.

"Always trying to top from the bottom," I mutter, holding his ass cheeks apart to enjoy the view of my length disappearing inside him. "Trust me to take care of you, Drake. It's all I want to do."

He softens then, surrendering to the pace I've set. It's a slow, demanding rhythm filled with restraint and tenderness that suggests we have all the time in the world to indulge in each other when we're really flirting with being late.

Still, I can't find it in me to rush.

My hands move to Cal's hips. One set of fingers finding purchase in the hard flesh while the other continues up his body, coming to a rest at his throat. Cal pulls in a harsh breath when they wrap around it, my palm barely grazing his Adam's Apple as I bury my fingertips in his skin, using my grip to pull him into my chest.

We're both kneeling now, and the new position turns us both feral. All thoughts of careful control turned to ash in the wake of a flame that knows nothing but the impatience of desire, the demand of need that erupts like a volcano between his body and mine, leaving us both panting and filthy on the closet floor.

Cal recovers first, because of course he does, and goes to the bathroom to wash up. I'm still trying to find the strength to do the same when he returns with a warm, soapy wash cloth and an adoring smile on his face. He makes quick work of cleaning me up and drops a kiss on my forehead when he's done.

"You know I'll always trust you to take care of me, right?"

I curse myself silently for the inadvertent exposure of my insecurity. "Of course," I answer, finally making my way to my feet. It's not a lie. I know Cal trusts me. The problem is I don't always feel worthy of that trust. Mostly, I just feel destructive, like I can break anything or anyone.

Like I broke Charlie.

Before the thought can take root and cast a shadow over my day, I push it away, maneuvering around Cal's large form to get back to my side of the closet to finish selecting an outfit. It's not a hard choice since the only thing either one of us ever wears to work is a black suit, and yet, we always find ourselves standing back-to-back considering the options on our overfilled shelves.

"We need a bigger closet," I announce, pulling a crisp white shirt from the folded stack in front of me and shrugging it on.

"No, we just need less clothes."

"Yeah, that's true too, but even if we get rid of half of our stuff this closet still wouldn't be big enough for the three of us."

Thinking about the future we will hopefully get to share with Selene is the only thing that seems to help me forget how fucked up I am. I don't get the logic behind it, can't see how daydreaming about a future I don't think I deserve soothes any part of me, but somehow it does.

Cal's eyes are bright with hope and the taste of future joy when I turn to face him.

"You're right," he says, gazing around the space. Before I moved in, it would have been considered generous, but now it can only be described as cozy. There's no word for what it would be if we tried to fit even a fourth of Selene's shoe collection in here. "I guess we'll just have to get a bigger house," he concludes as he makes his way into the bedroom with me on his heels. The news is still on, and the anchors are, yet again, discussing Aubrey pulling out of talks with Qatar about a military base here in the states. I grab the remote and shut the TV off.

"Just like that?"

He nods, stepping into his pants while I do the same. "Just like that. I never planned to stay in this house forever anyway. It was always supposed to become a rental property."

"Yes, I know, but you said that was a few years down the line, not anytime soon."

"That was when I only pictured sharing this house with you. I knew we could make this space work with no problem, but I didn't see her coming."

A soft smile curves his lips as he tucks the hem of his shirt into his pants, and I fasten my belt, shaking my head. "Neither did I."

"Of course you didn't, Beckham. You didn't see me coming either."

Although I agree with his statement, I find myself flipping him off as I sit on the edge of the bed to put on my shoes. "Go to hell, Drake."

"We should probably look for something with more square footage," he says, ignoring me. "Four or five bedrooms so we'll have space for guests. An office so Selene can work from home. A big kitchen for holidays."

I straighten, studying the happiness that's written itself into his features. "You want to host holidays?"

His brows furrow. "Well, yeah, I thought it'd be nice to have everyone together. Hunter, Rae, Riley and—" He hesitates over my mother-in-law's name. "—and Erin. Unless, you were planning on keeping things separate."

Any significant holiday is months away, and yet, I can see the wheels in Cal's mind churning, trying to sort out what a holiday apart will look like when we've made so many strides towards building a real life together. Strides that included having a conversation with his younger brother, Hunter, who laughed and told us he already knew we were more than best friends, and Diana's mom, Erin, who tore me a new one for thinking my love for Cal somehow canceled out my love for her daughter. With everything out in the open, there's no reason for us to be considering anything but shared holidays and a house full of our favorite people, so I don't let him sit with the thought a second longer.

"No, of course not."

Relief settles over him immediately and then he narrows his eyes at me. "Then why would you ask me that dumb ass question, Beckham?!"

"I was just curious! Plus, we're talking about holidays in a home that would belong to someone besides us. We don't know what Selene would be comfortable with."

"She might get a bit overwhelmed, but I think she'd mostly enjoy it. Can't you just see her with Riley? Nerding out over some science shit while we all try to keep up?"

The image leaves me with no choice but to smile. I have no doubt Selene and Riley would adore each other, that she'd fit perfectly into our families the way she fits seamlessly with us.

"We'd have to tell them who she is to us," I say, heart beating a little faster at the thought of claiming her publicly even as the fear of being judged for our non-traditional dynamic trickles down my spine.

Cal huffs his amusement at my worry. "They'll know exactly who she is to us the moment they see how you look at her."

* * *

THE ENTIRE DRIVE into work is spent arguing about who has the worst case of heart eyes when it comes to Selene. I get the last word, whispering 'you' to Cal just before we walk through the doors of the situation room we reserved for the multi-team meeting we always have before large events like the State Dinner happening tonight.

Most of the people in the room are from our team and Agent Shaw's team, but we also have Lee, the head of Singapore's Presidential Guard, and representatives from the security details of a few key Cabinet members. Lee is a quiet, observant man who has enough respect for the authority Cal and I hold to let us run through our plan for the night without so much as a grunt. Agent Shaw and her team are just as respectful, but the same can't be said for the other assholes in the room who don't understand what it means to be seen and not heard.

Chief among the poorly behaved mongrels is none other than Daniel fucking Hicks. Our former team lead who managed to turn his numerous failures on the campaign trail into a promotion, though not the one he wanted. Instead of guarding Aubrey, he's stuck leading Cordelia's detail, and by leading I mean staying in the cushy office they gave him at Headquarters while his subordinates do all the work and only coming into the field when it suits him.

Unfortunately for us, today is one of those days.

"Your intervals are all wrong," Hicks mutters, interrupting Cal who went over the page he's currently staring at five minutes ago.

"We'll have uniformed agents at the gate," Cal continues, cutting an eye at Hicks but still addressing the rest of the room. "Any questions?"

Of course, Hicks raises his hand, speaking before anyone has called his name. "Yeah, I want to know why you've got the uniformed officers doing perimeter sweeps at fifteen minute intervals. That seems excessive. I would suggest once every hour."

He looks around the room for support, but I'm the only one who meets his eye. "No one asked for your suggestion, Dan."

"But I've got decades of experience—"

"Remind me, how much of that experience was gained guarding Presidents?"

Red creeps up his neck and into his cheeks. Satisfaction sweeps through me just as fast. Having the power to not only dismiss Hicks but to make him feel as small as he tried to make us feel when we worked under him, makes this one of the few times I've felt grateful for this position.

I tilt my head to the side. "Well, Dan, we're all waiting. Please share with the class how many years you've spent coordinating security for State Dinners at the White House."

"None," he grits through clenched teeth.

"Exactly." I nod. "So please do us all a favor and save your comments for discussions where the topics are within your limited realm of expertise."

If we weren't in mixed company, I'd get a little more specific, directing him to update his charge on proper security protocol so she never makes the mistake of bringing perfect strangers into what was supposed to be a secure space. I swallow that urge though, turning the meeting back over to Cal with a smirk. We wrap up minutes later, and Hicks storms out of the room before anyone else can leave their seats.

"That looked like it felt good," Agent Shaw muses, approaching me and Cal once the room has cleared out. "I take it there's history there?"

Cal lets out a low whistle. "That's an understatement."

"Former boss," I explain. "He's the asshole who was in charge of Selene's detail during the campaign."

"I thought he looked familiar," she says, shaking her head. "It must have been so frustrating to have to take orders from someone like him. Is it true he didn't take any of your assessments about the online threats and Marsh's connection to them seriously?"

"Unfortunately," I confirm with a grimace. My blood always starts to boil every time I think about how differently things could have gone if Hicks had listened to me and Cal all those months ago. We could have gotten to Jacob sooner. We could have avoided bringing Charlie in for intel. We could have had backup when we went into that factory. Cal wouldn't have walked away with a head injury, and I wouldn't have come out of there with blood on my hands.

Shaw's eyes harden, her gaze turning serious but sincere. "I want you to know I'm not like that. I investigate every piece of information I get regarding Mrs. Taylor's safety no matter where it comes from or what it might lead to."

"So we can assume you looked into Conlon?" Cal asks, taking advantage of the opening she's just given us to follow up on the intel we shared with her about the reporter who interviewed Leland.

"Absolutely," Shaw says. "Morgan and I paid him a visit."

My interest is immediately piqued. "And?"

"And we determined he doesn't pose a threat to the First Lady. He doesn't even seem to believe in all that right wing propaganda he's platforming on his site. I think he's in it for the views."

Cal and I share a look, the question of whether to trust Agent Shaw's judgment passing between us in an invisible wave of tension and fear. I want to push for more information, to ask Shaw for her notes and have her walk us through the entire meeting with Conlon so I can analyze it thoroughly. Cal looks ready to seek the man out and question him himself. Neither of us are in a position to do any of those things, so we do the only thing we can: thank Agent Shaw for pursuing the lead and rest easy in the knowledge that no one will protect a Black woman more than another Black woman.

9

SELENE

Tedious.

That's the only word that can be used to describe the evening thus far. Though I'm sure I'm the only person who would refer to it that way because everyone else seems to be having a lovely time. Laughter is constant interruption in the flow of conversation and tinkling of silverware as the hundreds of people—politicians, celebrities and titans of industry—in the tent erected on the South Lawn enjoy course after course of lavish dishes inspired by our guests' home country.

The food has been the highlight of my night, and I've found myself mentally deconstructing every dish placed in front of me while Aubrey and President Tao bounce from subject to subject with little to no input from anyone at the table besides Aubrey's VP, Torrance Belford, and Cordelia. Currently, they're discussing how the war in Iraq impacted Singapore's economy while I try to determine what exactly Chef Bloom used in the sticky glaze coating the succulent meat of the mud crab I've just devoured.

"Kecap manis," a soft voice says from across the table.

I look up to find First Lady Hana Tao watching me. Heat sweeps across my cheeks, and I wonder if it's bad form for me to have left the responsibility of starting a conversation in the hands of a guest. "I'm sorry?"

"Kecap manis," she repeats, gesturing to her plate. "It's a soy sauce sweetened with palm sugar. That's what makes the glaze so good."

"Oh!" I force a smile, searching for more to say. "I'm sure the chef will be happy to hear you've enjoyed his version of the dish."

"It was a little spicy for my taste," Anne Belford adds, sliding her plate over to her husband. Torrance spares her a sidelong glance but doesn't engage, continuing to give his attention to the world leaders who are giving him a rare bit of space to voice his thoughts on President Tao's reluctance to commit to a formal alliance with the U.S. Anne's unwelcome contribution to the conversation kills the First Lady's desire to continue engaging, which is just as well because I had nothing more to say.

The rest of dinner passes in a silence that's not exactly comfortable but is definitely preferable to the alternative, and I'm glad when we all have to move to the less formal portion of the evening even though the shift means having to dance with Aubrey. Every eye in the building is on us as he moves me around the parquet wood that makes up the dance floor in front of the stage where moments ago he gave a welcome speech. Flashes of lights from numerous cameras throughout the room blind me, but I know better than to blink, than to do anything but smile.

"You look beautiful tonight," Aubrey whispers, his lips too close to my ear and his breath too warm. "I've always loved you in red."

"Don't talk to me."

His hands travel down my back, stopping just above my ass. "It's a simple compliment, Selene. I know you're not well versed in the art of social interactions, but when someone pays you a compliment, you're supposed to say thank you."

My spine stiffens. "Your first mistake is assuming I want to hear you speak at all let alone desire a compliment from you."

He laughs, playing it up for the cameras and the crowd by tossing his head back and squeezing his eyes shut. When he's done, he presses his temple back to mine.

"Would you rather hear it from *them*?" he purrs, condescension coating the words.

"Absolutely because unlike you they never say anything they don't mean."

Feeling the weight of that truth, I force myself to focus on something other than the way my gut is churning because of Aubrey's proximity, finding Cordelia in the crowd with a phone to her ear and her face screwed up into a mask of frustration.

Aubrey scoffs. "Didn't mean it when they said they loved you, though, did they?"

This is his favorite thread to pull. The insult he always goes to. The one that doesn't sting nearly as much as he wants it to because it offers the reassurance I can't find in his brooding stares or fake smiles. Relief is a victorious trickle down my throat and into the pit of my stomach where the constant worry that the truth of my reconciliation with Cal and Beck has been revealed lives.

"Did you?" I toss back just as the song ends. The opening chords of the Marine Band's next selection start almost immediately, leaving little time for me to spin out of Aubrey's arms and into those of President Tao who, unlike my husband, seems reluctant to let his wife go. He watches her and Aubrey closely, barely sparing me a glance even as he maneuvers us around the dance floor with ease.

"You must think me terribly rude," he muses after a full minute of silence. Since he's a few inches shorter than me, I have to look down to meet his eyes.

"Not at all, Mr. President."

"Hana always gets nervous when she's left alone to deal with unfamiliar men," he explains, splitting his attention between his wife and me. Since he doesn't seem to need an actual response from me, I hum an acknowledgment and turn my attention back to the room, hoping to find Cordelia somewhere in the crowd. Just as I find her—in a corner arguing with a distressed-looking Jordan—President Tao whirls me around.

"You don't seem to share my beloved's fear."

"Are you someone I need to be afraid of?" I ask with an arched brow.

"Certainly not, Mrs. Taylor." Eyes the color of coal dance with humor and a hint of something close to cruelty. "I simply thought you'd be more wary of strange men after your unfortunate experience during the election."

It's probably the clumsiest segue I've encountered yet, but I know an attempt to transition into questions about my kidnapping when I see one. Since I'm not feeling particularly chatty tonight, I play dumb.

"I'm not sure what experience you're referring to."

People have this funny way of painting you as the asshole when they're trying to fish for information they aren't entitled to and you make them do all the heavy lifting. President Tao, who I'm sure is used to getting exactly what he wants before he even asks for it, is unfortunately no different.

"Your experience with Jacob Marsh, of course."

"Oh, you mean when I was abducted, beaten, berated and almost executed on national television? *That experience?*"

His jaw unhinges, opening and closing as he flounders for a response. I don't wait for him to find it, choosing instead to halt my steps and leave him with no choice but to do the same. I'm aware of the cameras on us, capturing a moment that will surely be on the nightly news and in the morning paper with God only knows what kind of headlines, but I don't care.

"Jacob Marsh didn't make me afraid of men, Mr. President. Like your beloved, I learned to be afraid of them as a young girl. I was warned about the kind man, the honorable man, the man who believes himself good even when his actions say otherwise. The man who would drag someone else's trauma out into the light for his own dark entertainment and play victim when confronted with the ugliness of what he's asked for. That is the kind of man I'm wary of, and as I'm sure Hana can tell you, those men aren't always strangers. Oftentimes, they're familiar. Husbands. Fathers. Elected officials who depend on their power to give them a pass."

I step back, forcing him to relinquish his hold as a million flashes erupt around us. "Unfortunately for you, I'm not in the mood to hand out any of those tonight."

Knowing I've ruined something that can't be fixed or smoothed over if I'm around, I make a beeline for the exit, ignoring the appalled looks and murmurs rippling through the crowd as I pass by. My first full breath doesn't come until I'm at the end of the long entryway that leads into the tent. The sweet, fragrant smell of grass from the perfectly manicured South Lawn tickles my nostrils, and I gulp down greedy lung fulls as I step into the warm night. I should stop here, should wait for Agent Shaw or Morgan or someone else from my detail to catch up with me, but I keep moving, wandering aimlessly until I'm standing in front of the entrance to the Oval that's being guarded by the only faces I actually want to see tonight.

Beck spots me first, brows wrinkled in confusion as he steps away from his post.

"What are you doing here?"

Cal is next, moving out of the shadows and into the light to give me the gift of his adoring, yet worried, gaze. "What happened? Where's Shaw?"

"I don't know, and nothing happened. I just—"

It's been so long since I've found myself alone with both of them, I can't seem to string a coherent sentence together. Everything in me is screaming for their touch, pleading for their kiss, demanding I close the space between us immediately.

And that's what I do.

I grab Beck's hand, squeezing his fingers tight as I walk towards Cal and bring him with me. Cal's arms open instantly, and I can't tell if I've collided with him or if he's used the vice grip he has on my waist to yank me into him. It doesn't matter. All that matters is that the hard lines of his body are pressed against my front while Beck's heat melts me from behind.

"You can't be here," Cal murmurs, his lips grazing mine in a ghost of a kiss.

I rise up on my tiptoes, chasing his mouth. "But I am."

Beck's hands are layered over Cal's at my waist. He's linked their fingers together, so I'm locked in an impossible strong hold I never want to be free from. My heart slams against my ribcage, joy singing through my blood at the layered contact. This is all I ever want. They are all I ever want.

Impatient with Cal's teasing, I cup the back of his head in my hand and bring him down to me for a searing kiss that he takes over immediately. Ceding control has always been hard for me, but it never is with them. I give myself over to Cal, parting my lips to clear a path for his tongue while my body sags into Beck. He's moved to the other side of my neck now, running his nose over my racing pulse. A low growl escapes his throat when I roll my ass into the hardened length of his erection.

"Fuck."

He bites down on my neck, and the moan it elicits pours out of my mouth and into Cal's, navigating the twisted path of tangled tongues to complete its journey. Distant voices carried by a light breeze meet our ears, and everything stops. Cal breaks the kiss. Beck's lips leave my neck. We all turn frantic eyes to the world around us, scanning the area but staying close to each other. When no one appears, a collective sigh of relief fills the air.

Beck sighs. "We should get you back to the party. There's no way they're not looking for you."

"He's right, pet," Cal says, trying to move back.

"No. I'm not going back in there."

Tension writes itself into Beck's limbs. "What happened? Who upset you?"

There's a lethal, accusatory note to his voice that leaves me with no choice but to soothe him face-to-face. I spin around in their hold and take his face in my hands. "Nothing and no one that matters now that I'm here with you two."

"But you can't stay here, Selene. Aubrey will be expecting you to—"

"Aubrey is too busy kissing up to the President of Singapore to give a damn about me."

I inject confidence I don't feel into my voice and pray its enough to manifest my words into reality. Aubrey has to be distracted. He has to be thinking about smoothing things over with President Tao more than he wants to ream me out. Otherwise, they're right and he'll be looking for me. I don't want them to be right. I don't want this moment to end. I don't want to schlep back to that tent and play nice or hide from Aubrey's wrath for the rest of the night.

I want this. I want them. I want us.

My touch turns tender, fingers slipping over the smooth skin of Beck's head. His eyes fall shut, resolve fading with every second that passes. "Please don't make me go back in there," I beg. "Let me stay with you. Let me have you." He's already caving, both of them are, but to seal the deal, I pull him into a slow, drugging kiss that builds and builds until I'm climbing him like a tree and Cal is cursing as he guides us backwards through the doors we're all supposed to be standing outside of.

I've been inside the Oval once since moving into the White House, posing for photos that ended up in a design magazine that claimed Aubrey and I chose the new slate blue window dressings and embroidered rugs together. Of course, I'd never seen any of the decor items before, and I don't look at them closely as we stumble into the room. Beck presses me against the nearest wall, the tips of his fingers digging into my ass through the silky chiffon of my Oscar De La Renta gown. Aubrey had complimented the color, but I'd chosen the gown because I adored the rosette detail at the bust and liked the amount of cleavage the sweetheart neckline put on display.

Beck buries his face between the exposed mounds and inhales deeply. "God, I've missed you," he moans, mouth wandering to my right breast where his tongue traces the curve of the fabric before his teeth pull it away from my skin, exposing the hard peak of my nipple.

"Bite her."

The order comes from behind us, and my eyes fly open, gaze locking on Cal's at the exact moment Beck follows his command. He's not as close as I thought he'd be. Instead of standing somewhere near the doors we just passed through or sitting on any one of the plush chairs in the space, he's behind *the* desk. The desk every President since Jimmy Carter has used during their tenure. The one Aubrey treats with the same reverence one might give a throne.

Wet, heated lashes of Beck's tongue steal my words, my thoughts, my questions about cameras and blind spots. All of it, including the knowledge that Aubrey requested the cameras in his office be turned off in the evenings—falls away as Cal settles into the buttery leather of the desk chair, his expression almost bored as he watches Beck ravage me. My sex clenches, liquid desire pooling in the fabric of my thong at the sight of his indifference.

"Do you want more?"

I bite my bottom lip and nod, hips churning. "Yes, please."

"Give her more, Beckham."

Whatever it is Cal and I have decided on is of no consequence to Beck because he ignores Cal, continuing to work me into a frenzy with nothing more than nipple play. Cal's lips curl into a smirk.

"I think he wants you to beg, pet."

Confirmation lives in the pools of onyx focused on my face, and the pleas spill from my mouth in an incoherent whimper. "Please, Beck, I need more."

"More what, gorgeous?" he rasps, fingers already drawing up the fabric of my dress to bare my legs. I start to tremble as they ghost over the inside of my thighs and nearly convulse when he uses the pad of his thumb to work my clit in hard circles through lace coated in my essence.

"She's so fucking wet, Drake."

"Bring her here, so I can see."

Beck's touch is precise, every rotation of his thumb applying the perfect pressure at the perfect spot. And it stays that way even as he carries me across the room and lays me out on the most important desk in this country. The oak is cold against my skin, but I can't bring myself to care because I'm with my men and on the brink of an orgasm so strong it's likely to destroy me.

I plant my feet on the edge of the desk, spreading my legs wide so

Beck has more room to work and Cal has an unobstructed view. He slides the chair in closer, dipping down to take my mouth into a filthy kiss while Beck pushes my thong to the side and kneels before me. As soon as he pulls my clit into his mouth, I come apart, back arching off the desk, thighs threatening to separate his head from the rest of his body, throat raw and aching from a howl of pleasure muted by Cal's mouth latched to mine.

His kisses guide me out of the haze of my orgasm and back into the present reality where Beck is adjusting his dick in his pants and staring at my pussy like he's never seen one before. Despite having just come, desire starts to swirl in the pit of belly again, louder and more demanding than before.

"Beck?"

His eyes snap to my face. "Yes, gorgeous?"

"More, please."

"Are you—"

"Positive. I want you inside me right now."

Cal sits back, eyes smoldering. "Give her what she wants, Beckham."

Without so much as another word, Beck unzips his pants, setting his dick free. I obsess over the bead of pre-cum leaking from his tip while he grips my thighs, pushing them up and back until my knees are at my chest. And then he's inside me, one perfect glide of his length through the slickness from my orgasm that takes him to the end of me.

"*Jesus,*" I hiss.

"He's not here, baby. It's just me," Beck growls, eyes rolling into the back of his head as he pulls out and drives back in, meeting no resistance. "And I've missed you so fucking much."

Between the way his voice breaks over the confession and the slow, thorough strokes he's giving me, my heart is ready to burst. Even in our most rushed moments, he handles me with care, with reverence, with love. The words spill from my lips, hitting the air in a rushed jumble of syllables that suggest it's my first time saying them.

"I love you."

His expression turns rabid, rapture writing itself into the lines of his face as he drops my legs and covers my body with his. "Say it again," he begs, strokes growing jerky but still hitting that perfect place inside of me that turns my brain to mush. "Tell me again, Selene."

"I…love…you," I moan, the tears gathering in the corners of my vision turning Cal and the rest of the room blurry. I wrap Beck up in my arms as my legs open further to give him space and whisper the words to him again and again until they become the soundtrack to a joint orgasm that leaves me filled with his cum.

"I love you too," he says once he's recovered, treating me to gentle kisses as he untangles his body from mine.

"Watching you two together will never get old," Cal says.

Forgetting that I'm sharing space with Callan Drake is an unlikely possibility, but I still jolt when I hear his voice. He's smiling when I turn my attention away from Beck, who's tucking himself back into his pants, and focus it all on him. And while his smile is incredible, it's not nearly as captivating as the erection tenting his pants.

I lick my lips. "Seeing what watching us together does to you will never get old."

Beck hums his agreement but doesn't say more. Still, I feel the weight of his gaze on me as I sit up and arrange myself on the desk so I'm facing our man. I lift my right foot, bringing it to his lap to trace his dick with my big toe. Cal shivers, pushing the chair back to slip out of my reach.

"We've pushed our luck enough, pet. We should be going now."

A pout tugs the corners of my mouth down. "But you didn't cum."

Cal taps his temple. "I've got plenty of images to work with when I jerk off in the shower later."

"Orrrr." I lift my dress and draw my legs up, dragging my fingers through folds glistening with Beck's release and mine. Cal curses under his breath. "You could come now."

Beck chuckles. "You should definitely come now, Drake."

"Yeah, Drake," I tease as Cal scoots closer. "You should come n—"

The rest of the word dissolves into a puddle of nothingness when Cal's fingers find my opening. Actually, they're just below it, scooping up the drops of Beck's cum that escaped me and guiding them back inside while he studies my face.

"You want me to come, pet?"

Two fingers move in and out of me with slow, shallow thrusts that fill the room with obscene sounds. My whines layer over top of them, and Cal lets a dark, dangerous smile curve his lips. He leans forward and plants a kiss on my knee then pulls away suddenly. I start to protest then fall quiet when I see his hands go to his belt.

"Then get over here and make me come."

My core clenches at the demand, and impatience becomes a riotous ball bouncing around my chest, only stopping when his dick is buried deep inside me. It should be impossible to feel anymore gratification than I already have tonight, but that's all I feel right now. That's all I *am* right now. A pleasure-driven being who couldn't stop chasing the high of an orgasm if she tried.

I don't intend to try.

In fact, I hunt down my orgasm and Cal's too, taking control of the rhythm the way I did in the bathroom at Dahlia's. It's a frantic fuck that lacks finesse but not passion, and I take great pleasure in dismantling the institution that is the man underneath me in a matter of minutes. He comes seconds after I do with his teeth in my shoulder and sweat beading his forehead, and finally, I'm done. The seemingly endless pit of lust inside of me satiated, at least for tonight.

The office we've just defiled is soaked in silence and the scent of forbidden sex as we put ourselves back together, preparing to return to a world where we pretend not to love each other. I escaped to the private bathroom to clean myself up, focusing mostly on hiding the tears that come every time I have to say goodbye to them, and when I emerge from it, Cal and Beck are huddled up near the doorway. Their heads are close together, eyes on the phone in Beck's hand.

"What is it?" I ask, hoping some overzealous news outlet hasn't already posted photos of my spat with President Tao online and put me in a position where I have to explain what happened and why I minimized it.

Neither of them appears upset or murderous as they look at me, but

I still approach with caution, taking the phone from Beck when he holds it out for me. The screen is open to an article in the New York Times, and the headline reads as follows:

BREAKING NEWS: PRESIDENT'S MISTRESS FOUND DEAD, MORE DETAILS TO COME

10

SELENE

"Was he still fucking her?"

Monique slams her hands on my desk, open palms landing with a slap that makes me jump. I close my laptop with a heavy sigh that's meant to relieve some of the tightness in my muscles but somehow only adds to the tension that's been building in my shoulders and neck since she entered my office five minutes ago. In that small amount of time, my best friend has subjected me to an interrogation that has left me with the distinct feeling that I'm sitting in front of a congressional committee.

There have been a lot of questions aimed in my direction in the two weeks since the news of Sutton Ellsworth's death broke. I should probably be grateful to the former speechwriter for succumbing to her severe peanut allergy when she did. Her going into anaphylactic shock in the middle of her parents' anniversary dinner on the night of the State Dinner ensured that the abrupt end of my dance with President Tao barely registered on the press' radar. They were much more interested in dredging up the affair and analyzing every photo taken of Aubrey since to try and answer the question Monique just asked me.

"I don't know."

She squints like there's a problem with her vision when really the issue is with my answer. It doesn't mesh with the lies I've been telling her for months about the state of my marriage.

"You. Don't. *Know*?" She drops into the chair opposite me. "How can you not know, Selene?"

"Because I don't spend my days monitoring Aubrey's dick, Mo. He could be fucking someone right now, and I wouldn't have any idea."

"Oh, no, don't do that technicality bullshit with me, Selene!" The excess fabric of her lavender wide-leg trousers swishes through the air as she crosses her legs and then her arms. "I know you've asked him. I know that after the first affair you can smell his bullshit a mile away, so tell me the truth even if you won't tell anyone else."

"There's no truth to tell. I don't know if the affair was still happening, and to be frank, I don't care."

"You don't care?" She twists her lips to the side. "You don't care if your husband, who you are supposedly happily married to, was fucking someone else? Did you open up your marriage without telling me because you know making that decision just because your partner has cheated isn't always the smartest thing."

"Are you done?"

I trace the lines of the nondescript black computer in front of me, anxious to get back to the many, many articles and photos I've compiled related to Sutton's death. Monique follows my fingers, watching absently at first and then more intently. With her brows knitted together, she leans forward.

"What's that?"

On instinct, my hands spread over the laptop protectively, but it's too late. I've already drawn her attention to it, and just like everything else today, she's not letting it go.

"A computer."

"No shit, Sel." She reaches for it, and I pull it back, which of course makes her more suspicious. "When did you get a new laptop?"

"I didn't."

The computer is almost as old as AJ would be today, and it doesn't take long for Monique's eyes to go wide with recognition. "You're working on a project?"

"Yes, I guess you could say that."

"And you're far enough along on it to need that?" She nods her head in the direction of the computer. Air-gapped and as immune to hacking as anything in this world can be, it's the device I use when I'm working on a project that needs to be protected from any and all outside influences. When the initial framework for Smart Sight was done, I put everything on an encrypted USB and moved it to this old beater, writing and workshopping everything on the worn out keys, only allowing it back onto networked computers once the patents and copyrights were in place.

Precautions like this aren't uncommon in my line of work, and knowing how to take them is coming in especially handy now that I need to find out if my husband killed his mistress. While everyone else in the world, including Monique, is preoccupied with questions like whether Aubrey was still fucking Sutton, I've been wondering if she's the key to my freedom. At first I wasn't convinced her untimely demise was an unfortunate accident.

A sous chef who mistook peanut butter for tahini.

An Epi-Pen missing from Sutton's purse.

A delayed ambulance response because of traffic caused by construction.

So many small things that when looked at separately seem like lethal coincidence. But when you put them together, and combine them with Cordelia's stressful phone call and the tension between her and Jordan minutes later, it feels like it could be something more.

"Don't you think that's something I should know, Selene?" Monique asks, her voice pulling me out of my wandering thoughts.

"What?"

"The project. You don't think you should have told me that you're working on something?"

"Oh." I bite my lip. "You're right. I just didn't think it was ready for anyone else's eyes yet."

Skepticism dances on the lines of her curved brows. "Bullshit."

She lunges for the computer again. This time I'm too slow to stop her, so I have no choice but to watch her pull it to her side of the desk and study the screen, imagining what exactly she's seeing. The screen is divided into two sections. On the left-hand side is a window with a notes app that holds all of my thoughts about Sutton's death. On the right, there's a gallery of photos from the day in question. I scoured the internet for hours on end for those, trying to get every possible angle inside of the restaurant and on the street outside of it

If I recall correctly, the last picture I was looking at was taken by Sutton herself. It was posted on Instagram moments before her throat began to close up. There are others of course, some I acquired in less-than-legal-ways. I know the exact moment when Monique comes across one of those because she covers her mouth and gasps, pushing the computer away.

"How the fuck did you get pictures of her body?"

Ashamed.

That's how I should feel. That's what I should have felt when I asked for the crime scene photos from AJ's school. And maybe I do feel it a little. Maybe it's a thin thread running through me, stitching my organs together. But it's not enough to silence my need for information. Monique doesn't understand that. Most people wouldn't, which is why my answer feels like it's not good enough even though it's the truth.

"I needed to see for myself."

"That she's dead?!"

Monique is standing now, pacing in front of my desk with trembling hands. She's trying really hard not to look at me with disgust. I admire her effort, but it's not necessary.

"That she died the way they said she did. I needed the pictures to make sure the coroner didn't miss anything."

"Anything like what, Selene?!" she shrieks, her voice loud enough to drown out the sound of the TV playing behind her.

"Like a puncture wound of some sort."

Monique pauses, turning her head in my direction slowly. "You think someone did this to her on purpose?"

It feels like forever since I've given my best friend a truth. So long that I can't seem to say the words. I nod, relief and regret hitting me at the same time. It feels so good to be honest with Monique, but I know this one truth will pour into others and then it all unravels. The lies, the secrets, everything. She'll be angry with me for keeping so much from her, and it won't matter that I only did so to keep her safe.

Pressing my lips together, I choose my words carefully. "I think it's highly unlikely that Sutton left home without her Epi-Pen. I think it's even less likely that a trained chef would mistake peanut butter for tahini."

"I think that part is bullshit too," Monique says, a bit calmer now. "I just thought the restaurant was throwing him under the bus to avoid being sued for his unauthorized substitution. But you think it's...you think someone did that to her on purpose?"

"No, I think *Aubrey* had that done to her on purpose. He sent someone to kill her. I just can't prove it yet."

I'm not sure if Monique's knees have given out or if she's grown tired of pacing, but she sinks into the chair across from me with her mouth agape. "But why? And how? How would he even pull something like that off?"

"He's the President of the United States, Monique. Do you really think it'd be hard for him to get rid of someone if he wanted them dead?"

A shiver runs through her. "Don't say that."

"Why not?"

"Because he's your husband! The man you love. You can't be in love with someone who would do something like that."

And there it is. The unraveling. The tugging of a thread that undoes the entire web of lies I've strung together since signing that contract and agreeing to sell a lie to everyone including the people closest to me. I have a choice in this moment. I can either grab my scissors and cut the thread, minimizing the damage, or I can place my hands over each of hers and *pull*.

I choose the latter.

"I'm not," I tell her, shaking my head for emphasis. "I'm not in love with Aubrey, and I haven't been for a very long time."

Monique is quiet, listening intently as the truths pour out of me.

One after another, after another until I've told her everything including how Cal, Beck and I had a threesome in the Oval Office. When I'm done, she doesn't say anything for a long time. I sit in the silence with her. The only sounds besides our breathing and the anxious flicking of my fingers is the evening news.

"Say something," I plead when a full five minutes has gone by.

She taps her index finger on her protruding lips. "I don't know *what* to say. For the first time in my life, I think I might be speechless."

All of my senses are attuned to her, trying to make sense of her tone and expression. There's not much for me to go on as far as her face is concerned, but she doesn't sound mad. She lifts her hand, scratching her head.

"Both of them? At the same time?"

I roll my eyes, letting all my worry subside for the moment. "Of course that's where you want to start."

"Well can you blame me?! I've spent our entire adult lives praying you'd be free of cock one day and here you are bouncing on two dicks and hiding it from me?"

My jaw drops. "Aubrey doesn't call it a cock."

"Not with you. He damn sure called it one with his little dead girlfriend."

"You're insane."

"You're the one with pictures of her body on your computer," she tosses back. "But we can talk about that later. Right now, I need to know how you managed to find two men who are obsessed with you AND each other."

Knowing that Cal and Beck are living their love more publicly these days made me feel comfortable with sharing the full extent of their relationship with Monique. Since she's one of the most open-minded people I know, I'm not at all surprised that she's so accepting of the complexities of our dynamic.

"I don't know," I whisper, cheeks growing hot as I think of my loves. "But I'm so glad I did."

Monique's eyes glisten with the soft sheen of tears. "I'm glad you did too. You deserve that kind of goodness, and fuck Aubrey for trying to stand in the way of it."

"Fuck Aubrey in general."

Her brows shoot up, all the soft emotion disappearing to make way for humor. "Oh hell yes! I love this version of you! You should have been taking two dicks at once YEARS AGO!"

I throw my head back, hardy laughter pouring from my throat. "It's not always two dicks at once."

"But sometimes it is?!" she squeals, mischief lining her features.

"It was only once," I admit. "We don't usually have the time we need to prep for that."

"Makes sense. I've never been DP'd myself, but I've heard it takes a lot of work to get your pussy ready for that kind of stretch."

My entire face is hot. "Okayyyy, time to change to the subject."

Monique cackles. "Don't get shy on me now, girl. I've been in the dark for months, and I need you to show me the light!"

She throws her hands in the air, waving them like she's in the pews of a church and the sermon being delivered to the crowd is speaking directly to her soul. When she's done with her shenanigans, she laughs at my exasperation.

"Okay, okay. I'll stop. Just tell me one thing, though."

"Yes, I've hated every minute of lying to you, and I promise to never do it again even though I'm terrified that you knowing the truth about everything has put you in danger."

The words tumble out of my mouth, and Monique rears back, hand on her chest as she digests them. "Girl, relax. I know you hate lying to me, and I understand your reasons. I'm a little worried about what me knowing everything means too, but I'm riding with you until the bitter end."

I breathe a sigh of relief. "Okay."

"That wasn't what I wanted to know, though."

"It wasn't?"

"Nope." She pops her lips on the 'p'. "I want to know when you had the time."

I bite my lip, thinking back to the first time I got to fall asleep between my men. "When we were in Vegas."

Her fist comes down hard on the desk. "I KNEW IT!"

"No, you didn't."

"Okay, well maybe I didn't know they were turning you into a fucking shish kabob, but I knew your story about needing to clear your head was some bullshit." She leans back in her seat, grinning like a Cheshire cat. "I'm so proud of you right now."

"Umm, thank you?"

"I'm serious, Selene. You managed to find and hold on to something real and amazing in the midst of a storm that was meant to destroy you. Not many people would have been able to hold their hearts open for a love like that after what Aubrey did to you."

"I guess you're right." I sigh. "I don't feel like I am holding on to them, though. I feel like we lose our grip on each other every day that passes with us living under Aubrey's thumb."

The lightness of the moment has faded, and now we're back in the somber space we started in. Monique makes the shift effortlessly.

"That's why you're investigating Sutton's death. To get away from Aubrey."

"Yes, but I don't know enough about anything, including whether he and Sutton were still together at the time of her death."

"You could always ask them," Monique suggests, hooking a thumb over her shoulder at the TV which is now teasing a special featuring Sutton's parents, Peter and Janice Ellsworth, that will be airing later tonight. Janice is crying, and her husband's arm is wrapped around her shoulder. She's not looking at the camera, but he is. His face red as he stares into the camera.

"I just hate that my baby girl will only be remembered as his mistress," he says.

The clip ends a few seconds after that, returning back to the news anchor who instructs viewers to tune in at nine tonight for the full story. I think it's interesting that Peter Ellsworth is concerned about the world remembering his daughter as Aubrey's mistress when I'm much more interested in making sure they know she was also his victim.

11

CAL

It doesn't happen often.

Beck waking up screaming.

The nightmares are frequent, I know that, but the broken, sorrowful cries that come from deep within his soul and rip apart the air are so rare they snatch me from the depths of unconsciousness and immediately send me reaching for my gun.

Tonight is no different.

The cold metal of my piece greets my warm palm before I've even really opened my eyes, and I'm on my feet in an instant, back to the wall, bleary eyes scanning the dark room only to find there is no threat. Not a physical one at least. My chest is heaving with unspent adrenaline as I catch sight of Beck's writhing form on the bed. His face is a twisted ball of pain, a clear indication of the internal war he's fighting. I return my weapon back to its rightful place, knowing neither it nor I will be of any assistance.

All I can do is wait.

For the dream to end. For the pain to stop.

With a sigh, I wipe the sleep from my eye and turn on the lamp by my bedside, hoping the soft light will start the process of waking Beck up. I know from experience that trying to wake him up on my own won't do either of us any good, so I sit on the edge of the bed and slowly peel the covers away from his body. He shivers, turning toward me and the light even though he's still asleep.

A whimper passes through his trembling lips as he claws at the sheets.

"Cameron."

My heart clenches. Dreams about his son are the most painful to witness. He always cries for him the longest, tears for a tarnished past and a stolen future streaming down his cheeks and making me wish for Selene because she's more familiar with this strand of grief than I could ever be. I've never fathered a child, never brought a life into this world only to have to go through it without the light of the young soul I was supposed to nurture and protect, so everything I say in hopes of comforting Beck feels empty when it comes to Cameron.

Selene's wouldn't though.

There would be a weight to her reassurances, a depth to her promises of brighter days, a sad but genuine understanding conveyed in every touch, kiss and hug.

Tears born of inadequacy and longing blur my vision as impatience rises in my chest. I want Selene. I need her. We both do. Everything about who Beck and I are and how we work is made better by her presence, and I'm tired of living without her. Tired of not being able to hold her or love her and get those things back in return.

Beck jolts awake, his lips parted on a scream that doesn't meet the air as he sits up. I watch him scan the room for threats and wait for him to realize there's no one here but us.

"You're safe," I whisper, keeping my voice soft to avoid startling him.

His head jerks in my direction, eyes wild for a moment as he processes my features. It only takes a second for him to adjust, and he swallows hard, falling back against the pillows with a frown pulling down the corners of his lips.

"Was I screaming again?"

He won't meet my eyes. That familiar cloak of shame slipping around his shoulders and squeezing until his breaths turn uneven. I crawl over the twisted sheets and comforter to get to him, grabbing him by the nape and pulling his face into my chest.

"Breathe, Beck."

Desperate hands claw at my back as gasps turn into sobs that shatter us both. I don't know how to help him. I don't know how to fix it, but God do I want to. I would do anything to take this pain from him.

"I keep failing," he says, voice breaking over the words. "I keep failing him. Every time I see him falling, I leap to catch him but it's too late. I'm always too late, Cal."

My hands are everywhere. Passing over his bare scalp and over his shoulders, down his back where the fabric of his tank top is clinging to his sweat-slicked skin. It's not enough. I'm not enough. No amount of love and comfort can heal what's been broken inside of Beck since his birth parents gave him up. This is an inherent pain, something he's carried for his entire life that's only been exacerbated by the long list of losses he's experienced. He's spent a long time ignoring it, pushing it down, hiding inside happiness he doesn't thinks he deserves in order to escape, but it keeps finding him and I don't know how to protect him from it.

I kiss the top of his head, my own tears falling onto his skin. "I know, love. I know."

He doesn't say more after that. He doesn't need to. We've shared this exact moment so many times before. There's a rhythm to it. A routine. A script we follow that dictates how this scene and the ones after will go. Beck knows it as well as I do. That's why he doesn't protest when I pull away once his tears have subsided. It's why he takes my hand and allows me to lead him to the shower. Why he stands there silently while steam fills the room and I strip off his sweaty clothes, tossing them in the hamper along with my own before moving us both under the spray of hot water.

Beck's breathing is a mix of shudders and hiccuping gasps that only ease when I begin to work shampoo into his scalp, turning the cleansing act into one of restoration with gentle kneading motions that go on for longer than necessary.

"Cal?"

"Yes, love?"

"You know I don't have hair, right?"

A soft laugh leaves me as I begin the rinsing process. "Yeah, I know. Your scalp still needs love though."

He grunts when I start to rub in conditioner. "Feels like you're coddling me."

"I definitely am," I confirm. "Sometimes you need to be coddled."

His lips twitch with incredulity, gaze sliding away from mine to concentrate on the tile on a spot somewhere over my head. "I don't deserve it."

"I don't think you're qualified to speak on what you do or don't deserve, Beck."

"What?"

"You're not being kind to yourself," I tell him, studying his face as water washes away all traces of the conditioner. "Ever since Charlie died, you've been giving in to the voice in your head that only exists to feed you lies about yourself."

"Charlie didn't just die, Cal. I killed her."

"You did what you had to do to save your life. To save my life. To save Selene's life."

As partners in the Bureau, we've seen each other through multiple uses of lethal force. Never once has he struggled this badly. I don't understand how this time is any different, and if Beck is aware of what sets it apart, he hasn't let me know yet.

A muscle in his jaw twitches, and I half expect him to pull away but he doesn't. He stays close, letting me run the washcloth I've just covered in body wash over his shoulders and chest.

"I brought Valinsky in," he says when I've made my way to his stomach. "Even after I saw what he did to..." He swallows hard, struggling to say his wife's name. "He fucking tore her apart, Drake. There was blood everywhere, and Cameron….he was…" Beck shakes his head, trapping the gruesome details I already know between his lips. Then he rolls his head around on his shoulders and starts again. "I could have killed him. No one in the world would have batted an eye. I wouldn't have even seen the inside of an interrogation room, but I brought him in."

A soft hum of acknowledgment is all I give him as I crouch to wash his lower half. Thick, muscled thighs, toned calves and feet Selene once said were too beautiful to belong to a man keep me distracted as he lays out his flawed reasoning.

"That bastard murdered my family," he growls, staring down at me. "He took everything I loved, and I still put the cuffs on him. He's alive and breathing because even at the lowest moment of my life I was able to exercise enough self-control to keep him that way. And he wanted me to kill him, Cal. He told me he could see the desire in my eyes, that he could smell the blood lust on me. What kind of shit is that?" he asks a dark, rueful laugh rumbling his chest. "Blood lust. Like I'm some kind of rabid animal. Like I was some monster. Like I was…"

"Him," I offer when he refuses to finish the sentence.

Beck eyes glow with anger and self-loathing. "I thought I was better than him, Drake. Really, I did. I'd never felt blood lust or any real desire to kill anyone before. It's always just been an outcome I couldn't avoid, but with Charlie it was all I wanted."

He pauses like he's expecting me to fill the silence with shock or outrage or disgust, but I remain quiet, placing my hands on his hips and urging him to turn around. I set about washing the backs of his legs and thighs and the confession hangs in the air. Beck doesn't speak again until I'm standing and scrubbing his back. He glances over his shoulder, brows furrowed.

"Did you hear what I said, Cal? I wanted her dead. I wanted to kill her."

"I heard you."

"And you don't have anything to say to that? She was your friend. You mentored her for years, watched her find her footing in the Bureau—"

"Missed every possible sign that she was a traitor," I add.

"Who cares if she was a traitor?! That doesn't make what I did right. It doesn't change the fact that I wanted her dead, and I acted on that desire. I did everything in my power to make it a reality."

With my hands on his shoulders, I turn him again, putting his sudsy back in the water's reach. Onyx eyes rush over my face, searching for something he'll never find.

"That makes me like him, Cal. It makes me like the monster who took Diana and Cameron from me. It makes me like the bastard who kidnapped Selene and beat her, who put her bruised face on national television and pressed a gun to her temple. And if I'm like them, how can I deserve you? How can I deserve her? How can I deserve the shared holidays and the house big enough for the three of us and the family we might want to build one day? How can I deserve any of it?"

My brows lift in surprise as I grasp on to the only shocking thing he's said. "You want a family?"

Little drops of water bounce off of his broad shoulders and into my face, but I stare at him unblinking. With all that he and Selene have loss on the kid front, I'd resigned myself to a reality where I got to have them and only them. I never allowed myself to picture kids, to envision bedtime routines and hectic schedules due to extracurricular activities. It would be enough for me, life with just Selene and Beck, but the thought of more than that makes my chest warm with hope I force myself to get a hold of because even if Beck and I agree we want children, we don't know if Selene does.

A huff made of frustration and amusement sends Beck's breath skating over my cheeks. His shoulders sag as he shakes his head like he can't believe I'm asking him that question in a moment like this.

"I want everything with you and Selene, Cal. You know this."

I take his face in my hands, transferring remnants of soap bubbles from my hands to the thick hairs of his beard. "I do know that. I just didn't think kids were on the table."

"That's part of everything, is it not?"

"Someone's feeling better," I muse and then say, "Yes, I suppose kids is a part of everything."

He brings his hand up, fingers tracing the smile on my lips. "Don't get too excited. We'd have to talk about it with Selene first, and that can only happen after we get her away from Aubrey."

"I know."

And I do. There are so many obstacles ahead of us, but there's goodness too. All of it waiting on the other side of the nightmares and guilty consciences and husbands who refuse to let go even when they don't want or appreciate what's trapped in their grasp. At the moment, I can't do anything about Aubrey. I haven't found a solution that allows us to have Selene and keeps him from making good on his threat to have her killed. The speculation surrounding Sutton's sudden death has left me feeling even more helpless on that front.

As usual, everything about Selene seems to be operating outside my circle of control, but tonight I've found a way to soothe our partner. Thanks to Beck's candidness, I finally feel confident in my ability to comfort him, to soothe the part of him that's slowly being smothered by a weight that only becomes bearable if someone else steps in and lifts it off your chest.

Beck reaches around me, grabbing the body wash and the same washcloth I used on him to start washing me. I always allow him to return the favor even though the showers are never for me, so he looks confused when my fingers wrap around his wrist, stilling him.

Our eyes lock, and I drop the mask, laying my heart and my hate bare for him.

"I wanted her dead too," I tell him. "And if it had been me instead of you, she would still be rotting away in a hole in the ground." His eyes stretch wide, but his gaze is soft with relief. "If you're a monster, Beckham, then I am too."

12

BECK

Dr. Penelope Pike has perfected the art of silence.

I've sat across from her for an hour now, and the only sound that's come from her side of the room is the scratching glide of her pen across the notepad she has pressed against her thigh. None of our previous sessions have gone this way—me, filling all the time with words I'd rather not say; her, writing down observations I'll never know the true extent of—so, it's awkward, leaving me impatient and desperate for the volley of dialogue instead of the loneliness of a monologue.

"Can you say something, please?"

She raises her head, tapping the end of her pen on her chin. "Does my silence bother you, Agent Beckham?"

I shift in my seat, running my palms over my pants. "Yes."

"And why do you think that is?"

"Because I'm tired of hearing my own voice."

There's only fifteen minutes left in our hour-long session, and my mouth is dry. I don't know how anyone talks for this long without taking a moment to breathe and hydrate.

"Or maybe you're uncomfortable with being left alone with your thoughts," she offers, uncrossing her legs. She's wearing wide legged jeans and an oversized sweater that's too warm for the sweltering heat of DC in the middle of June.

"Isn't everyone?"

"Would it make you feel better if I said yes?"

Frustration claws at my chest with long nails that turn my response sharp. "It would make me feel better if you could tell me what the purpose of giving me the silent treatment is."

"You have a background in psychology, Agent Beckham, years of experience with interrogating subjects and taking confessions, do you really not understand the value of silence in settings such as these?"

As she poses her question, she rearranges herself in the seat, folding her feet underneath her. Watching her get more comfortable in the face of my growing agitation makes me want to get up and walk out of here and never come back. I can't do that though. After my shower confession a week ago, I promised Cal I would go back to therapy and gain the tools I needed to heal the ache inside of me he'd already began to sooth with his own dark admissions.

Pulling a breath in through my nose and expelling it out of my mouth, I think back to her question. "I've only ever used silence during interrogations when they weren't really interrogations."

"How do you mean?"

"Well, some suspects just can't wait to talk. That's not usually the case, but it does happen sometimes. They can't wait to tell you what they've done, so there's no work for you to do. The words just flow out of them, and you have no choice but to just…let them."

The end of my explanation comes with the dawning of realization. Dr. Pike watches it wash over me, hiding a knowing smile behind the rim of the teacup she keeps on the table beside her chair.

"Exactly." She takes a slow sip of the hot liquid before saying more. "In our previous sessions, you were reluctant to share, which isn't uncommon when clients are mandated to come to me, but today, you came in and just let the words flow. It would have been a shame to interrupt that for the sake of hearing my own voice."

"Oh."

I deflate a little, feeling like an asshole. Dr. Pike reads me easily, shaking her head. "Don't be upset with yourself. Lots of people find silence disconcerting in therapy. I apologize for not making my approach clear to you before, but I have to commend you for doing so much with the space you were given."

Thinking back, she didn't really give the space. I took it. As soon as I sat down, I started talking. About Charlie and the dreams. About Cal and the post-nightmare showers. About Valinsky and my fear of being more like him than I thought.

"Thanks." I shrug awkwardly. "It felt easier to say this time."

"That's not uncommon especially if you had a positive experience the first time you disclose, which it seems you did with your partner, Cal." She glances at the notepad to make sure she got his name right. "Receiving acceptance once typically makes us feel confident that we can again, so we repeat the story with less shame, less doubt, less fear of judgment and rejection."

"Makes sense."

"It does, doesn't it?" she asks, laughing lightly at my flat response. "I'm afraid that's our time for today, but in our next session, I'd like to unpack some of the statements you made today."

"Which ones?" I quip. "Apparently, I've shared a lot today."

"That's not a bad thing, Agent Beckham." Dr. Pike runs her index finger down the side of the notepad, tapping it lightly on the page when she finds what she's looking for. "If you're comfortable, I'd like to start with you referring to yourself as a monster and discuss why you so easily accepted that as your truth."

I frown as I push to my feet. "Isn't it obvious?"

"Not to me."

"I wanted someone dead, and I acted on that desire without remorse."

She's standing now too, following me to the door which she holds ajar after I open it and step into her empty waiting room. "You think this belief was formed around Charlie's death?"

"You don't?"

In true therapist fashion, she sidesteps the yes or no question with an artful grace. "In my experience, the stories we tell ourselves about who we are shaped in our childhood and affirmed or disproven in our adult years. Usually, we tend to hold on to the things that support those beliefs and filter out anything that doesn't."

"So, you think I believed I was a monster before Charlie's death?"

Her lips are pursed together as she gives a reluctant nod. "Possibly. The question is why?"

I turn Dr. Pike's inquiry over in my mind several times on my way to the parking lot and find myself unreasonably frustrated when I can't find a suitable answer. Cal is waiting for me in the car, expectant eyes on my face when I slide into the passenger seat.

"How was it?"

"Good. I think."

He takes a slow inventory of my expression before backing out of the spot. "I'm proud of you," he says, easing into traffic and onto the road that will carry us to work. "I know going back wasn't easy."

"It was actually a lot easier than I expected."

Long fingers play a cadence of impatience on the steering wheel, and I laugh. "Do you want details, Drake?"

"Of course, I want details."

"Nosey motherfucker," I complain, but I give him exactly what he's asked for, recapping the entire session while he splits his attention between me and the road. When I'm done, he opens his mouth to respond, only to be interrupted by the sounds of an incoming call. According to the name displayed on the screen, it's his brother, Hunter, but when I click the green button to accept the call, it's not him on the other end of the line.

"Uncle Cal, can you please tell my daddy that you can give me a tour of the White House, and we don't have to sign up on the stupid website," Riley says, trampling all over pleasantries and getting straight to the point.

Cal and I share an amused but disbelieving look.

"What'd I tell you about calling things stupid, Nugget?"

The second voice belongs to Rae, Riley's mom and Hunter's fiancèe. She's a little further away from the phone than her daughter, leading me to believe that our headstrong niece has commandeered her father's phone and left whatever room they were in together to make the call in private.

Riley's exasperated breaths rush through the speakers. "Sorry, Mommy."

Rae's loving murmurs are unintelligible, but I can tell the apology has been accepted. Seconds later, Riley is back pushing the envelope.

"Can I have some privacy?" She requests, tone sweet as sugar and just as deadly.

"Girl, no. Get back in here with your daddy's phone, so we can all talk to Uncle Cal and Uncle Beck about this supposed White House visit together."

Another bemused look passes between Cal and I. We haven't actually said anything yet, so this talk is just as one sided as my therapy session was. Riley huffs, mumbling under her breath as she follows her mom back to wherever her dad is, and I bite back a laugh at this display of her newfound attitude. Hunter complains about it every time we speak, but this is our first time witnessing it. Even over the phone, the potency of her indignation is clear as if Rae's lack of patience when she warns her to get it under control immediately.

"You're not giving your mama attitude again are you, Ri?" Hunter asks when they finally make it back to him. Judging by how clearly we can hear him, he's the one holding the phone now.

"I just wanted some privacy," Riley says, sounding like she's got her lips poked out.

"And I'm sure your mom understands and appreciates that, baby, but just because you ask for something doesn't mean you're going to get it. Do you understand?"

"Yes, Daddy."

The line is quiet for a second, and then the car is filled with the sound of wet kisses and Riley's happy squeals.

"Well, this has been a delightful little after school special," Cal says. "But I'm just wondering where Beck and I fit in?"

"Damn, Little Drake, I forgot you were there."

Cal rolls his eyes at the nickname. "You're lucky your daughter's in the room, nigga."

"Riley, step out for a second."

"No!!! I want to talk to Uncle Cal and Uncle Beck about visiting the White House!"

"You can come visit whenever you want," I tell her, needing this chaotic phone call to come to an end so I can mentally prepare for being trapped inside the place Riley is so desperate to see.

She gasps. "Promise, Uncle Beck?"

"I promise, Nugget."

"But the timing of the visit is up to your mom and dad," Cal adds, turning onto the private drive that leads to the employee lot. "When you come, we'll roll the red carpet out for you. You can meet the First Lady and everything."

His eyes turn to pools of melted copper when he says that, and I smile at the thought of introducing Riley to Selene. The display of joy dies a painful death when Riley asks her next question.

"What about the President? And the Vice President? I heard they're best friends. Is that true?"

She's rambling now, and because we're approaching the gate where we'll have to identify ourselves and produce our IDs, Cal rushes to end the call, promising Riley and her parents that they're more than welcome to make the trip up anytime.

"It'll be nice to have them here," I say to Cal as we make our way to the office to debrief with Agent Granger before he ends his shift.

He adjusts his tie, tugging at the knot he must have made too tight. "I agree. I'd love to see them."

"Gotta keep Riley far away from Aubrey's bitch ass, though," I mutter under my breath, turning the knob to open the office door.

Cal grunts his agreement and grunts again when I stop abruptly and he runs into my back. "The fuck, Beckham?"

I step to the side, showing him the obstacle I've just encountered.

Jordan St. James stares back at us with wide green eyes that hold both contempt and the exhausted wariness that has become synonymous with her name in my head. There isn't a single hair out of place on her head or even a hint of a wrinkle on any of the designer items that make up her outfit for the day, yet she still reads as wild to me.

And it's not a dangerous kind of wildness; it's the other kind. One made of fear and the anger you feel when you're not used to being afraid.

Behind her, frozen in a crouch that suggests his brain hasn't decided if it wants him to sit or stand and come to Jordan's aid, is Sam Granger with the smallest smudge of lipstick on his face. He watches us watch Jordan, his own brand of fear filling the room with the scent of pleas that have yet to be spoken. I know the ask. After all, I've made the request a million times to Agent Shaw and the rest of her team: *don't say anything, don't do anything, just please, let us have this.*

Cal recognizes it too. He steps to the side creating a path for Jordan to pass between us, and she takes the out immediately, leaving the three of us behind without so much as a second glance.

13

SELENE

Very few things on my social calendar inspire legitimate excitement in me. Too often, I have to show up to events Allegra has thrust upon me with a forced smile stretching my lips and feigned interest lighting up my eyes for hours while I hold boredom at bay.

Surprisingly, today's engagement isn't like that at all.

From the moment Representative Mr. Jackson of Virginia's 11th Congressional District extended the invitation, I found myself genuinely thrilled by the idea of walking into a room where the doors were only opened because of my First Lady title. Of course, most of the positive feelings swirling around in my belly as I sit at the judge's table are related to the middle and high school aged children filling the rows of seats behind me. Each and every one dressed to the nines and chattering nervously as they wait for their turn on the stage Mr. Jackson is currently occupying.

"I won't be up here for long," he promises, pushing the glasses slipping down the bridge of his nose back up. It's an absent-minded gesture, one he probably does several times a day since his frames appear to be warped, that also has the benefit of making him seem less intimidating. Since he's well over six feet and easily three-hundred pounds with broad shoulders and a hard stare, he can use all the help he can get on that front.

He wraps his fingers around the edges of the podium and smiles. "First, I want to thank each of you for being here. Back in the day you couldn't pay me and my friends to give up a single minute of our summer break, so I'm impressed with the way y'all have packed this room out. Give yourselves a round of applause." Scattered claps come from different parts of the room, but it's a far cry from what Mr. Jackson has requested. He squints into the crowd, mouth pulled into a flat line of disapproval. "Now, I don't know if y'all know this, but we've got First Lady Selene Taylor in the building today. If you won't clap for yourselves, maybe you'll clap for her."

He gestures toward me, and I have no choice but to stand and face the sea of unfamiliar faces, smiling and waving even as the growing noise level in the room sets my teeth on edge. After the explosion at the polls, loud noises and tight spaces became even more difficult for me than they were before. On instinct, I look to the only source of comfort I have at the moment: Agent Shaw. There are four other agents in the auditorium, lining the walls and keeping a closed watch on the doors, but Agent Shaw is closest to me. She pulls her gaze away from the crowd and meets my eye, offering assurance of my safety in the form of a curt nod.

It doesn't give me the same level of comfort I would feel if it were coming from Cal and Beck, but it's more than enough to give me the strength to send the anxiety buzzing underneath my skin back where it came from. The crowd calms at Mr. Jackson's insistence, and I return to my seat, praying the ringing in my ears will subside before the children take the stage. For a moment, I think it won't happen because Mr. Jackson's speech is nothing more than muffled murmurs, but as soon as he starts talking about the Congressional App Challenge, everything clears up.

"As you all know, the CAC was established in 2013 to facilitate national appreciation and recognition of the computer sciences and STEM. This is a nation-wide competition, but it's not my job to worry about every kid in the nation. My job is to worry about you. The brilliant minds of the 11th Congressional District."

He slaps his hand over his chest, eyes brimming with pride.

"*My district.* As your representative, it's my job to give you every advantage I can, and there is no greater advantage than adequate preparation. At this stage in the challenge, you've already developed the concepts for your app and began building. You're work shopping and fine tuning and double checking every line of code, in hopes that one day your app will be the one displayed in the Capitol building, and that's great. But I'm here to tell you that none of it will matter if you don't know how to talk about your app. If you can't convince a consumer that they need it, they never download it, and all your hard work goes down the drain. That's the last thing any of us want to happen, which is why today you're going to stand up here on this stage and convince me and Mrs. Taylor that we need your app."

A short silence follows the explanation, and then Mr. Jackson's lifts a brow, an assessing gaze rolling over the crowd. "Think you can do it?"

The kids meet his question with resounding screams of affirmation that make him laugh as he makes his way to the judge's table to take a seat beside me. Once he's seated, members of his team move into the crowd, pulling students from the rows and lining them up next to the stage.

"I can't thank you enough for doing this," Mr. Jackson says, leaning in a bit too close. "None of the other reps will be able to compete with this Pitch a Pro event. They're all doing run of the mill stuff like coding boot camps."

"It's my pleasure. Thank you for thinking of me."

"Of course! It would have been a failure on my part to not include the First Lady when she's an expert in the field." One of the members of his team, a young Black girl with a pixie cut reminiscent of the ones Mama spent her days doing in the 90's approaches, handing Mr. Jackson a stack of papers.

"Rubrics," he explains, placing the stack in between us. There are already pens on the table along with bottles of water for us to share.

"Will we be getting a list of the participants as well? I'd love to have some prior understanding of the students and their projects before hearing the pitch."

Mr. Jackson pushes his glasses up again, shaking his head. "No, ma'am. We figured the less you know beforehand the better. This way the score given to the presentation is based solely on what is said on the stage."

"Interesting. Did you at least have them prepare pitch decks to be given out afterwards?"

"Yes, ma'am." He pulls a few papers from the top of the stack between us, sitting some in front of me and some in front of him. "They'll be available to you through my office."

Satisfied, I nod and offer him a genuine smile. The CAC is a great initiative, but it's still young and relatively unknown. That means a lot of the work to put together events like this falls on the shoulders of the individual district representatives. Not many take the kind of initiative Mr. Jackson has to provide support to the participants. It's actually inspiring.

"The work you've put into this day is admirable," I tell him, watching him light up.

"Thank you, ma'am."

"Please, call me Selene."

"Selene," he repeats, testing out the syllables hesitantly.

"May I call you Reed?"

"Ye-yes, of course," he stammers, nodding enthusiastically.

"Perfect. Reed, how were you planning to reward the kids for their participation today?"

Perplexed, he glances around the room like the answer is hidden in the walls somewhere. "Umm, I wasn't?"

He winces, and we share a laugh. His is nervous and full of self-consciousness. Mine is pure amusement because of course he thought exposure and experience was enough to make this event worthwhile.

"Guess I should have thought that through, huh?"

"I mean, not having a reward certainly hasn't hurt your turn out at all," I say. "But I think it'd be nice to give them something. As you so wisely pointed out in your speech earlier, they are giving up a day of their summer break to be here. Not to mention the time they spent preparing."

"Right. You're absolutely right." Slight panic has taken over his features. "Do you have any suggestions?"

My answer is immediate. "You can never go wrong with tech when it comes to kids like this." As I start to rattle off items I would have killed for as a child, Reed flips over one of the rubrics and scribbles it all down, handing the list off to the closest member of his team with instructions to secure the circled items before the end of the day.

"We should probably make an announcement about the prizes" Reed says. "I'm sure it'll give them an extra boost before they get on the stage."

"Absolutely," I agree, fighting the urge to make another suggestion and losing. "Before you do, I'd like to add something to the list."

"Oh, okay, let me just—" he stands, preparing to call back or go after the young woman he just sent off.

"Not to the actual list," I clarify, standing as well. Reed's head swings back in my direction, and I feel bad for confusing him. "The new laptop and NAS DiskStation will go over beautifully with the winners, but those are just two items and we've got fifty kids here. I think it would be beneficial to offer something everyone can take advantage of regardless of if their pitch is chosen or not."

"What did you have in mind?"

"A spot in my company's junior coding academy."

The idea started to take root the moment I walked into this room and saw it filled with the faces of the future of my chosen field. It sprouted into possibility when I heard Reed's speech about his responsibility to the children of his constituency and immediately began to think about what my obligation was to them and why I hadn't considered how to fulfill it sooner.

He tilts his head to he side, brow furrowed. "Culture Code has a junior coding academy?"

"It will by the end of the day," I promise him, knowing that Monique will get Nichelle on it as soon as I send in the request.

She'll probably be thrilled to see me using my company email for something other than declining meetings and scolding her for sending me links to the many interviews Sutton's parents have done in the weeks since her death. There's never anything else in the emails, just the links and layers upon layers of subtext that ask why I believe the Ellsworths won't speak with me if they're making a point of talking to everyone else.

Reed doesn't question my assertion. He just nods and takes to the stage one more time, hyping up the crowd with the news of the prizes. Of course, they're more excited about the computer and data storage system than anything else, but there's cheers of appreciation for the coding academy too, which is good enough for me. I don't expect them to see the value of a freshly formed thought, but I know when it's all said and done, they'll be grateful for the opportunity.

As Reed takes his seat, I hit send on the email to Monique and turn my phone face down, giving the stage my full attention. Some of the presentations fly by while others seem to drag on so long I find myself praying for the end long before it ever comes. The kids are a mix between overly confident and a ball of nerves stumbling over their words, and while they all try their best to, none of them are able to command the stage the way a person has to in order to make the world believe in what they've built.

The line has dwindled significantly. Instead of watching the last few groups fidget their way to the stage, I direct my attention to sorting through the rubrics I've already completed in hopes of finding some viable contenders for the winner's circle while Reed's assistant, Olive, reads off more names.

"Our final presenters are Isis and Imani Lincoln," she says, and my head snaps up so fast my neck starts to ache a little. The discomfort barely registers as all my senses attune themselves to the twin girls standing before me with the confidence and presence of adults, discussing their app Hope's Map. But it isn't just their unflappable demeanor or the thoroughly impressive concept of a community-based overdose response network meant to make accessing lifesaving drugs like Naloxone easy and fast in times of crisis that has my attention.

It's their faces.

It's their last name echoing in my mind.

It's the picture of the family they lost displayed on the screen that brings back memories of their older brother Isaiah following AJ through the front door of our house. And once that memory is unlocked, the floodgates fly open. I spend their entire presentation assailed by images of a past I didn't realize we shared. I attended Isaiah's funeral, which was the day after AJ's, and held his mother, Hope, in my arms while two little girls who grew into the beautiful young women in front of me clung to her dress and hid their faces from view.

Some years ago, I heard the news of Hope's unfortunate passing due to an opioid addiction that was made worse by grief. No one ever said what happened to the girls, and I hadn't bothered to ask. Now I know that like me, they turned their pain into purpose.

I don't fill out a rubric for Isis and Imani, but Reed still agrees with me when I name them as my top choice. He asks me to join him on stage to present the prizes and then refuses to take no for an answer when his team asks if they can get a picture of us with the winners and then with all the participants before the group disperses.

When the cameras are gone and the crowd has thinned, I find Isis and Imani just outside the auditorium with a woman I don't recognize. The cold stare she gives me doesn't stop me from approaching with Agents Shaw and Morgan at my back.

"I apologize for the interruption," I say, deferring to the woman who must be the foster mother the girls spoke about when we met at the high school. Hostility rolls off her in subtle waves, but she still takes my outstretched hand. "I'm Selene Taylor. It's a pleasure to meet you."

"Joanna West," she supplies, brown eyes hard with resentment and distrust.

"Ms. West, I just wanted to take a moment to congratulate Isis and Imani."

Her gaze is scathing as it roves down the length of my body and back up. "Didn't you already congratulate them when you were up on the stage?"

"Well, yes, but I—"

She snatches her hand back. "Then I don't know what more you need to say. Besides, I need to get them home, they have chores to do."

"Chores? Don't you at least want to celebrate what they accomplished today?"

Joanna's head rears back, and it's clear to me that she's about to take things to another level. Agent Shaw takes a step forward, but it's Isis who puts herself between us. Now that I know who she is, all I can see is Isaiah's face written into her features.

"It's okay, Mrs. Taylor." She forces a smile. That ever-present worry line wrinkling the skin between her brows. "We don't care about a celebration. Do we, Mani?"

"I mean, it would be nice to go out to eat or something," Imani says, causing panic to flare in her sister's eyes. Isis shoots her a pleading look, but she refuses to recant.

"A celebration dinner would be lovely," I agree, arching a brow at Joanna.

She waves a dismissive hand through the air. "Nobody don't got no money for no celebration dinner. I already burned up all my gas getting them up here. They'll be lucky if they get a bowl of cereal."

"*A bowl of cereal?*"

Rage burns its way through my veins, encouraged by thoughts of Hope Lincoln who never once sent her son to my home with an empty stomach or dirty clothes. It never stopped him or any of AJ's other friends from eating us out of house and home, but that's neither here nor there.

"Do you have any idea how gifted these girls are, Joanna? How much work they put into the app they pitched today? Do you even care?"

Her expression answers my question even when her mouth refuses to move, and I shake my head, reaching into my purse to give her whatever cash I have even though it's clear to me finances aren't the real issue here.

"I'm more than happy to cover the cost of a dinner," I say, forcing calm into each word despite the ball of anger swelling in my chest.

"We don't want your money," Joanna spits, ignoring the small burst of hope in Isis's eyes. It disappears immediately, chased away by her foster mother's words, and all my long dormant maternal instincts come online. The urge to fix, to soothe, to help rising high in my throat and stifling any response I could muster.

It's for the best.

The last thing I need is a video of me dragging Joanna West through the halls of this building by her hair going viral online.

"Let's just go, Ms. Jo," Isis pleads, placing a hand on the woman's arm and gently directing her away from me. Imani follows as well, tossing me a rueful look over her shoulder.

"Thank you," she mouths before disappearing into the crowd behind her sister and Joanna.

I watch them go, wondering what exactly she's thanking me for. All I've done is upset her foster mother and cause more trouble for her and her sister because there's no part of me that believes Joanna won't take her anger with me out on those girls. I take a small step forward, following the ridiculous thought that I should go after them, and Agent Shaw puts a staying hand on my shoulder.

"You can't, ma'am."

Knowing that she's right, I allow her to lead me through the back of the building and out to the car, stewing the whole way because Isis and Imani's faces won't leave my mind.

"How does someone like that end up taking care of kids?" I ask, directing the question at no one in particular. Agent Morgan is in the passenger seat while Shaw is behind the wheel, and she turns to look at me.

"You'd be surprised how often it happens, ma'am. My sister is a social worker, and she says the foster system is filled with awful people."

"There are some good ones too," Agent Shaw adds, meeting my eye through the rear-view mirror.

"Yes, but Joanna West is not one of them."

"No. She is not."

Shaw's tone is as dark as my mood, and the car goes quiet. I pull out my phone, hoping for a distraction from my thoughts of the girls and, thankfully getting one immediately. It comes in the form a text from Monique.

> Monique: Got your email. This sounds like a great idea. We can discuss it at length when you get back.

My brow furrows as I type out a response.

> Selene: Get back from where? I don't have any trips planned.

> Monique: Yes, you do. You're flying to Kentucky tomorrow night.

I open my calendar and see no changes to my schedule, which makes no sense given every move I make is tracked and documented by Allegra and Nichelle, then return to our messages.

> Selene: What's in Kentucky?

> Monique: Not what. Who.

> Selene: Who's in Kentucky, Monique?

Impatience flares in my gut as I wait for her response. After that interaction with Joanna, and the persistent worry lingering in my bones for Imani and Isis, I'm not in the mood for these kinds of games. Monique must sense my restlessness because she texts back immediately.

> Monique: Peter and Janice Ellsworth.

My jaw drops, and before I can recover from one bomb, she drops another.

Monique: They want to talk to you.

14

SELENE

Sutton's childhood home is nothing like I thought it would be.

In the one conversation we'd had about her upbringing, Aubrey made it sound like she grew up in a shack on the side of the road not in a large Colonial style house in the suburbs of Lexington, Kentucky with a picket fence and the American flag flying proudly from one of the white columns bracketing the red brick steps leading to the front door. He'd also said she had no one to fall back on, but after weeks of watching Peter and Janice Ellsworth gush over their daughter in interviews, I now know that's a lie as well. A warped reality presented to me for the sole purpose of inspiring pity for someone who never needed it.

Both of Sutton's parents stand inside the entryway welcoming me, Agent Shaw and Agent Morgan into their home, and as they lead us into the cozy den right off their kitchen, I wonder if this is the first time they've had this many Black people in their home.

If Monique were here, she'd laugh at the question and tell me they've probably never had a Black person in this house at all. The thought makes me smile even though I'm still annoyed at my best friend for going out of her way to facilitate this trip and then refusing to tag along. I'd had to jump through multiple hoops to get out of

Washington without anyone finding out. An impromptu trip to Camp David for Aubrey and his consorts that began yesterday plus a private jet chartered in Monique's name had made that incredibly easy, but now I have to do the hard part.

"You can take a seat here, Mrs. Taylor," Peter says, gesturing to the cream couch with American flag themed pillows perched in the colors. "Janice loves decorating for upcoming holidays," he adds, sitting down across from me in one of the armchairs on the opposite side of the coffee table.

Agent Shaw moves to the window to my right, peeking through the blinds into the blanket of darkness covering the backyard and then pulling the curtains closed tight. Morgan does the same thing on my left, and I take a small comfort in the calm they're both emanating. Janice enters the room carrying a tray of coffee and cookies.

She leaves it on the table between us and takes a seat next to her husband. "No one in the neighborhood is up at this hour, and we haven't had a news van parked outside in days."

Meeting this early in the morning had been my idea, and I'd been surprised when the Ellsworths agreed to host me before sunrise without so much as a question about why I'd flown to Kentucky only to spend a few hours on the ground. I was glad I didn't have to explain what might happen to them, and me, if word of this little fact finding mission made its way back to Aubrey.

In an effort to be polite, I take a cookie from the tray and place it on a napkin without taking a bite. "Thank you for agreeing to speak with me. I promise we won't stay long."

Peter casts anxious looks in Agent Shaw's direction as she shifts her weight from one foot to the other. It's not lost on me that everyone in the room seems to be ready to get this visit over with.

Janice brushes imaginary lint off her pants. "I'm surprised you wanted to speak with us given your…history…with Sutton."

"You're referring to her affair with my husband."

Candidness isn't something people come to expect from someone in my position, so I completely understand why my response makes

Peter choke on the coffee he's just taken a large sip of. Janice, who looks more like her daughter than I realized, nods.

"Yes. The affair. I want you to know Sutton was incredibly ashamed of her actions."

When the news broke, Aubrey did everything he could to keep me away from Sutton. I was fine with that because I had no true desire to share space with her again. Because of that, I never got to find out whether Sutton was actually sorry for fucking my husband. Nothing about her presence on social media after leaving the campaign suggested remorse, but I could see her doing or saying things to her parents that would make them believe otherwise. She wouldn't have had to work hard at it.

Parents always want to see the best in their kids.

"Does that mean she was no longer sleeping with my husband?"

This isn't the first time they've fielded this question. Every single interviewer they've sat down with has wanted to know the same thing. Each time, they've stated that Sutton's relationship with Aubrey ended when she left his employ. There's never been an ounce of hesitance to their delivery, but this time, it's there in the guilt creasing the corners of Peter's eyes and the resolve weaved throughout Janice's sigh as she slides to the edge of her seat, prepared to level with me.

Peter places a hand on his wife's shoulder. "Jan, we signed those papers."

She shrugs him off. "We also agreed to speak with her. What was the point of having her come all this way if we weren't going to tell her the truth, Pete?"

"You signed an NDA? But you've been speaking with the press."

Peter takes his hand from Janice's shoulder and links their fingers together, squeezing hard. "They said we can talk about Sutton as much as we want, but Aubrey is off limits."

"Who?"

"They didn't give us names," Janice says, using her free hand to drop cubes of sugar into her mug. "Just showed up on our door the day after Sutton died with paperwork for us to sign and a check for doing so."

I wrack my brain for possibilities, but the truth is it could have been anyone. Aubrey has an extensive network of people at his disposal, and I'm sure he deploys them without so much as a second thought. There's a likely chance he doesn't even know who came to Kentucky to silence the Ellsworths. Knowing trying to figure it out would be a waste of my time, I turn the conversation back to the original topic.

"So, the relationship hadn't ended."

Suspicion swirls in Janice's irises. "You really didn't know?"

It's as close to verbal confirmation as I'm going to get, but it's more than enough. My heart rate increases slightly as all the reasons Aubrey might want Sutton dead rush through my brain. I started crafting the list of possible motives the day I found out she was gone—threats to go public and demands for money to stay silent or a secret pregnancy were my first choices—but none of them worked if I couldn't prove they were still seeing each other.

"No," I say once it becomes clear my silence is making this so much more awkward. "I had no idea."

"She *was* sorry," Peter declares, attempting to defend his daughter's honor. "I could see the way it weighed on her. All the sneaking around and lying and hiding. I told her she deserved better than an adulterer, but she wouldn't listen."

Janice's hand shakes as she brings her coffee to her lips. "She was in love. You know how intoxicating it is to be caught in the snare of Aubrey's affection…or at least you did once."

I take a bite of the cookie I've been holding for a while now. It's a little on the crisp side, so crumbs sprinkle onto my lap as I laugh at her attempt to insult me even though the affection she's bragging about her daughter receiving are likely the reason she's dead.

"You're right. It not hard to imagine how someone like Sutton could be ensnared by a man like Aubrey."

"Someone like Sutton," she repeats. "What do you mean by that? What exactly are you insinuating about my daughter, Mrs. Taylor?"

Leaning forward, I set my napkin and half-eaten cookie on the coffee table. "It's not an insinuation, Mrs. Ellsworth. My personal belief is that women who sleep with married men grow up viewing other women as competition. Affairs aren't about love for them. They're acts of dominance, attempts to best women who are nothing more than surrogates for the mother who treated them as an opponent from the day they were born. If I had to guess, Sutton's inability to leave Aubrey's bed probably had more to do with who he is than the quality of his affection. After all, I'm sure none of the men you've fucked have possessed nuclear codes."

Agent Morgan hides a laugh in an unconvincing cough as Janice's face turns red.

"You dare to sit in my home and speak that way about me, my daughter, *our relationship*?!"

"You started this catty exchange, Mrs. Ellsworth, all I've done is finish it."

Her nostrils flare, but she doesn't respond, looking to her husband for defense. Something about Peter's expression suggests my assessment of Sutton and Janice's relationship isn't far off. When he doesn't say anything, Janice snatches her hand away from him and stands, huffing dramatically.

"I want you out of my house."

She storms out of the room, leaving me with a stressed out Peter. Since I have no desire to overstay my welcome, and no need for the awkward silence we've been left in, I push to my feet. "I'll see myself out."

Peter doesn't reply, remaining in his seat as Agent Shaw steps in front of me and Agent Morgan takes my back. We've made our way back to the door when he finally finds his voice.

"Mrs. Taylor, wait!" I turn to see him coming up the short hall with his phone in his hand. The screen is lit, displaying an image I can't quite make out. "I need to show you this."

I step around Agent Morgan, meeting him halfway. "What is it?"

"A photo." He pushes the phone into my hand, shame a hard shadow over his features. "Sutton sent it to me a few days before she died. She was convinced someone was following her. I told her she was just being paranoid, that the guilt of the affair was getting to her, but she was insistent."

My heart is pounding again, slapping against my ribcage so hard I'm scared the repeated collision of muscle and bone are audible. I study the photo. It's a blurry shot taken with Sutton's front camera somewhere on the streets of Lexington. Her face is mostly obscured, blonde hair blowing in the summer wind, and it's clear that she didn't care if anyone could make her out. What she wanted the viewer to see is the man a few steps behind her.

The top half of his body is cut off, so I can't see his face. I can't see anything but the dark wash of his jeans, the hem of his black t-shirt and the crescent moon shaped scar on his right hand. It could be anyone with any number of reasons for walking down the street at the same time as Sutton. I tell Peter as much when I give him back his phone.

"Why did you come here, Mrs. Taylor?"

"To find out if your daughter was still sleeping with my husband."

It's the only answer I feel comfortable giving. The only one that keeps me safe and the integrity of my investigation intact. As far as motivations for flying across the country and visiting a stranger's home in the middle of the night goes, it felt pretty solid to me. No one would have trouble believing that a public figure who's already been caught unawares once would do anything to avoid that embarrassment again. Peter doesn't believe me, though. He scrubs a hand down his face to temper his frustration.

"No, if it was just about the affair, you wouldn't have gone through all this trouble now that she's gone. It just doesn't make any sense. I know that's what you've told everyone else, but it's not the truth. Or at least not the whole truth."

"What exactly do you think the truth is, Mr. Ellsworth?"

His eyes bounce from my face to the expressionless masks of the agents behind me and then he leans in, voice low and urgent.

"The truth is, you think your husband had my daughter killed, and you came here hoping to find something to help you prove it." He holds his hand out, showing me the photo once more. "This is all I have. I'm sorry it's not more, but she was only brave enough to try and get a picture of him once."

"Wait, so she saw him before this?"

Peter nods, and I resist the desire to ream him out for burying the lead. "Multiple times in the week before she died. Outside of her apartment and a few times when she was leaving work. She was scared, Mrs. Taylor, and I know that might not mean much to you given your history, but it's true. She spent the last few days of her life paranoid and afraid, and when she came to me, I dismissed her because I was angry that she kept debasing herself for him. Maybe if I had listened—"

"No." I cut that line of reasoning short, placing a hand on his arm to get him to look at me. "Nothing you could have done would have stopped this, Peter."

Hope sparks in his eyes. "So you do believe there's more to her death than they're letting on?"

Folding my lips together to prevent myself from saying more, I step back from the grief-ridden man and turn back towards the door. This time he doesn't give chase or call for me to stop, he lets us go, holding the door open as we retreat into the pink, orange and red hues of a dawning day. Agent Morgan opens the back door for me while Shaw climbs behind the wheel and starts the engine of our rented SUV. I find myself lingering, one foot on the sidewalk and the other inside the safety of the car, all my attention on the person who just gave me the first real lead I've had in weeks.

"Mr. Ellsworth?" I call out to him, a sad smile of commiseration curving my lips ever so slightly. "I'm sorry for your loss."

15

BECK

The turning of the blades of Marine One are a rhythmic thrumming that echoes in my chest as the helicopter descends on the South Lawn. Cal and I share a glance from across the tight space, and the exhaustion weighing down his shoulders and extending the length of his blinks every time his eyes close is nothing more than a reflection of fatigue that's settled into my bones.

We'd been called on to join Aubrey for an unscheduled trip to Camp David right at the end of a shift. The last minute order left us with no time to do anything but grab our go bags and get on board the bird with Cordelia and the tyrant who, despite having six other men to choose from, requested Cal and I stand guard outside the lodge while he held court with an unknown number of people who arrived before we did and stayed behind to be entertained by Cordelia even when Aubrey had to go.

From what I can tell, the plan was to stay in Maryland for at least a day or two, but something changed. I don't know what, but I've spent the entire flight back praying to God that it has nothing to do with Selene. We haven't been in the same room since the night of the State Dinner almost a month ago. I've had to live off glimpses of her in the halls and brief updates from Agent Shaw that, up until yesterday, told us nothing more than she's alive and breathing. Her latest message stood out because it was longer than all the rest and made mention of flight to Kentucky leaving in the wee hours of the morning from a private airfield.

Cal and I have been on high alert since, spending what little free time we've had over the last twenty-four hours checking all her socials and asking Shaw for updates that never came. We're completely in the dark, with no idea of where she's gone, why she's left or if she's even made it back.

The metallic clang of bird's landing gear settling on top of the aluminum plates meant to protect the grass from damage signals the end of our descent. Aubrey is on his feet in an instant, rushing the flight crew through the deplaning procedure and offering a sloppy salute to the Marine at the bottom of the stairs as he hurries inside. Normally, this would be when Cal and I relinquish our responsibilities to the highest-ranking agent on duty and head home to recover from the overtime we've been forced to work, but neither of us are prepared to walk away just yet. Even without discussing it, we seem to be in agreement that Aubrey's abrupt departure from Camp David has something to do with Selene's trip to Kentucky.

It just doesn't make sense for it to be anything else.

Aubrey makes it inside before we do, and the speed at which he's moving sets my teeth on edge. I pick up the pace, hearing the hard slaps of Cal's feet against tile behind me as he does the same. We're not running, but it's definitely a brisk walk, enough to catch the attention of the staffers milling about and garner the interest of Sam Granger, who's lingering in the hallway with a cup of coffee in each of his hands.

He holds them out to us, completely oblivious to the fact that we're in pursuit. "Figured you would need these!"

I move past him without so much as a second glance, but seconds later I hear the splash of liquid hitting the floor and Cal's gruff voice as he says, "Fuck off, Granger."

No one else bothers trying to intercept us, which is a good thing because the responses would only get more hostile as we follow the trail of formal greetings and polite salutations Aubrey receives on his way up the stairs that lead to the private rooms he and Selene occupy.

"Do we even know if she's here?" I whisper to Cal when he falls into step beside me.

My question is answered when we reach the landing and immediately hear the sound of Aubrey's raised voice.

"WHAT THE FUCK WERE YOU THINKING?"

There is no one else on this floor. Agents aren't forbidden from operating in this space, but they only do so when given express permission by the President or First Lady. Cal and I have neither, and still, we allow Aubrey's vitriol to draw us in further, pulling us deeper and deeper into the sacred space until we're standing shoulder to shoulder inside the hallowed arch that welcomes guests to the East Sitting Hall.

Selene is on the couch in front of the window that overlooks the garden named after Jacqueline Kennedy years after her husband's assassination. Her eyes stretch into saucers when she sees us, and I know exactly what she's thinking. That we're risking our jobs by being here, but more importantly, we're risking our lives. Her life. Because the moment Aubrey realizes we've come to her rescue, he'll know we're not done. He'll know the love hasn't stopped, the want hasn't ended, the need hasn't ceased. And he will punish us for it.

None of it matters now, though. Nothing matters besides the fear in Selene's eyes and the way it washes away any traces of hope she felt at our appearance. Aubrey plants one hand on the arm of the couch and the other on the back of it, leaning in close to her face. Even from this distance, I can see the veins popping out of his forehead and throbbing in his neck as he screams at her.

"ANSWER MY FUCKING QUESTION, SELENE."

She plants both hands in the center of his chest and pushes him away, giving herself space to stand. Relief floods my system when she puts some distance between them, but my a wave of nausea hits me when I hear the tremor in her voice when she finally speaks.

"You need to calm down, Aubrey."

Her gaze slides in our direction, and she gives a subtle shake of her head, demanding us not to intervene. Aubrey hasn't noted our presence yet, and it would be for the best if we kept it that way. I doubt that will happen, though, because there's a frenzied, destructive energy running laps in the inches between Cal's body and mine. One wrong move by Aubrey. One shudder from Selene. That's all it'll take to sever the thread of control holding us in place and allow the frenzy to take over.

"Calm down?!" He growls, kicking the leg of a coffee table as he struggles to recover from the shove. "Don't tell me to calm down, Selene. Don't tell me anything besides the god damn truth."

She swallows, crossing her arms over her chest. "You haven't asked me a question yet."

"You're really going to make me lay it out for you?"

Aubrey is seething now, hands on his hips and shoulders high with tension. His back is to us, which puts all his focus on Selene when I'd much rather have the hate rolling off him pointed at me, or Cal, anyone but the woman I love who's half his size and too far out of my reach for my liking.

"If you would like me to participate in this conversation, it would be nice to have some context, yes."

"Context." Aubrey snarls, a derisive snort escaping him. "Here's some context for you. Late last night, you boarded a private jet chartered by Monique with two members of your security detail and flew to Lexington, Kentucky where you proceeded to make one stop and one stop only: the home of Peter and Janice Ellsworth."

Cal and I both pull in a sharp, but silent, breath through our noses. What the fuck was Selene doing visiting Sutton's parents, and how the hell did Aubrey find out so quickly?

"You tried to be smart about it," he says. "Got in and out of Kentucky in a matter of hours, made it back here before noon. Janice said you only stayed at the house for fifteen minutes. Honestly, I'd be impressed if it wasn't such a STUPID FUCKING THING TO DO!"

The sudden rise in volume catches Selene off guard. She jolts, shrinking away from him even though he's made no attempt to advance on her. I don't understand the reaction. Well, of course I do, I've seen the same skittish behavior exhibited in women who have experienced violence at the hands of the romantic partners, but to my knowledge, Aubrey has never laid a hand on Selene.

Red tints my vision as I turn the possibility over in my mind, knowing that a failure to witness something doesn't mean it hasn't taken place. I take a step forward, and Cal grabs me by the shoulder, preventing me from taking another.

"What exactly is so stupid about going to express my condolences to your girlfriend's parents?"

Double-layered shock rolls through me. I didn't expect Selene to come clean about the trip so easily, and I definitely didn't think she'd follow it up with an accusation about Aubrey still sleeping with Sutton. He doesn't bother to deny it, jumping straight into another anger fueled response that awakens something dark and deadly inside me.

"It's thinking you have anything to offer two people who have lost their child, who have had their entire world turned upside down—"

"Because of you!" Selene shouts, finishing the sentence for him. "Their daughter is dead because of you. Just go ahead and admit it. Save me the trouble of having to find proof. I already know about the man you sent to stalk her. Peter said she spent the last few days of her life constantly looking over her shoulder. What did she do to deserve that, Aubrey? Did she threaten to leave you? Did she get tired of sneaking around and ask you to make an honest woman out of her?"

Selene pauses, arching a brow as she tips her head to the side and levels him with a gaze. "Or maybe she came to her senses and realized what a piece of shit you are. Personally, I don't plan to get bogged down in the why. I don't even really need to know the how," she tells him, a humorless chuckle leaving her. "See, I've already read the coroner's report, Aubrey. I know exactly how long it took for her throat to completely close."

"SHUT UP," Aubrey screams, but Selene is on a roll, forging ahead despite the stench of his growing agitation filling the room.

"How she panicked and dumped out her purse looking for an Epi-Pen that wasn't there."

"SHUT. THE FUCK. UP!"

The hands on his hips turn into clenched fists he looks ready to put through a wall, and still, Selene persists.

"Do you know what it's like to die from anaphylactic shock, Aubrey? Did you look it up before you decided that was how you wanted her to go, or did you let the boots on the ground decide?"

"Stop fucking talking, Selene."

There's no more screaming. No more yelling. Only the quiet growl issued by a predator moments before it strikes. I recognize the sound in an instant, and Cal's body tensing beside me lets me know he does too. Selene, though, is blissfully unaware, or maybe she just doesn't care that she's in danger. Maybe she knows we'll get to her before anything bad can happen or maybe she's just too caught up explaining what happens to a person's body when they've ingested an allergen.

"You're aware of everything that's happening around you, but you just can't breathe. People say it's like having an elephant parked on your chest, that every time you try to pull in a breath, your body takes in a little bit less oxygen. And the whole time, you're just pouring sweat. Can you imagine, Aubrey? Just lying there in a puddle of your own making, limbs weak, lungs failing, knowing you're going to—"

He lunges at her. Arms outstretched, fingers splayed wide and aimed right at her throat. I'm not fast enough to stop them from making contact, so he's got a weak grip on her when I tackle him from the side, sending us both flying over delicate furniture that's older than the two of us combined. We land in a heap of flailing arms and curses with Aubrey underneath me, struggling to get away.

"Have you lost your goddamn mind?" he asks as I restrain him, wheezing his way through the question because my forearm is pressing into his windpipe. His eyes bulge, and there's genuine fear in his gaze as he stares up at me. I relish it for as long as possible.

"No, but you certainly lost yours if you thought you were going to get a chance to put your fucking hands on her."

"Knew you were…still..fucking her," he gasps, feet sliding uselessly against the carpet as he tries to gain enough traction to buck me off.

I have no plans of dignifying Aubrey's comment with a response, but the opportunity to do is taken when someone loops their arms around my middle and pull me off him.

It's not Cal.

I know this because when the bastard throws me on the floor face down and puts a foot in the middle of my back, he's on the carpet beside me.

16

SELENE

"What do you mean fired?"

"Pretty sure the word means the same thing everywhere, Mama."

I'm blinking back tears, thanking God that my mother opted for voice call instead of a FaceTime today. It's been a week since Cal and Beck were relieved of their duties, and I haven't gotten through a single conversation about them losing their jobs without crying.

I caused this.

Aubrey got under my skin, and I showed every card in my hand, ruining everything including the professional reputations of the men I love. The official reason given for their departure was insubordination and incompetence, which is worse than the truth because it makes them unemployable but also better because it keeps them out of federal prison. It could have easily come to that, and part of me is still surprised that it didn't. I guess when he weighed it out, Aubrey decided protecting his secrets was more important than extracting his pound of flesh.

Unfortunately for him, all I can seem to think about is getting mine.

Since I watched Cal and Beck be dragged through the halls of the Residence like criminals, I've had a craving for it. Sixteen ounces of rotting tissue squelching as I rip it from his body. Blood dripping down my fingers, arms and elbows when I hold it out for all the world to see, exposing him for the role I'm now certain he played in Sutton's death and destroying him before he devises a plan to get rid of me too.

Mama's tsk of disappointment snaps me out of my thoughts. "I just don't understand," she says. "Cal told me it was for the best, but it just doesn't sit right with me. You can't get Aubrey to reconsider?"

She doesn't sound the least bit hopeful, like she doesn't believe in my ability to persuade my husband to do anything. Of course, she's right to doubt me, so I don't bother pretending otherwise.

"No, ma'am."

A heavy sigh blankets the line. "Just don't make no sense," she mutters.

"I know, Mama, but Cal and Beck will land on their feet."

I infuse the statement with all the faith I can muster and send it up to the heavens, hoping the angels are listening. Getting another job is probably the last thing on their minds, but I know both of my men well enough to know that they need their work just like I need mine. They need purpose and the distraction of productivity. That's the only reason I'm at work today, to keep my mind off all the things spiraling out of my control.

Monique knocks on my door, opening it before I can tell her to come in. She's got a smile on her face that's as bright as the yellow silk blouse she's sporting today, and I do my best to soak up some of her sunshine.

"Mama, I've got to go. I'll call you later, okay?"

"Alright, baby. Have a good day. I love you."

"Love you too."

"I love you more," Monique chirps just as I'm ending the call. I roll my eyes at her.

"How you gone love my mama more than I do?"

She shrugs. "I'm just good like that."

I wave her off, rounding the desk to meet her at the door. "Is everyone here?"

We move into the hall, and Agent Morgan tracks our synchronized steps down the hall. She's in charge this morning because Shaw is at a mandatory meeting, and it's obvious by the way her eyes are constantly moving around the space that she's taking the job seriously.

"Yes," Monique confirms, double-checking the list of attendees on her phone. "All mentors and mentees have checked in. Everyone has their name tags and assigned seat." She presses the button for the elevator, and the doors slide open instantly. "No one skipped out on the catered breakfast, except you," she says, pressing the button for the first floor.

"I told you I wasn't hungry."

"Right, but I still put a sandwich to the side for you. If we're going to tell these kids they need food to fuel their brains, we have to be prepared to lead by example right?"

"Right," I agree.

The elevator dings, announcing our arrival on the co-working floor where the first meeting of the Junior Coding Academy is taking place. A swell of blended voices echoes inside the open space and surrounds us, pulling us into the fold like a pair of arms aware of your desperate need for an embrace. I take my time moving around the room, clutching the sandwich Monique shoved into my hands as soon as we were off the elevator but never managing to take a bite because I'm too caught up talking to everyone and listening to the Culture Code employees who volunteered to mentor a kid or two gush about how cool it is to be molding the minds that will shape the future of technology.

Since it's their first time meeting, Nichelle, Monique and I decided today would be all about connection. Every mentor has been seated with the child or children they've been tasked with guiding. I'm delighted by the ease with which conversation is flowing at all of the tables except for the one near the front where two girls in clothes that fit a little too tight and smell faintly of cigarette smoke sit with matching sour expressions on their faces as they watch everyone else.

I hadn't expected Isis and Imani to sign up, and even after I found their names on the registration list and agreed to be their mentor, I refused to let myself get excited because I knew their foster mother bringing them was a long shot. A pleasant kind of shock rolls down my spine as I approach and drop into the open chair between them.

"Why the long faces?"

"Mrs. Taylor!" Isis, who's on my right, squeals wrapping her arms around my neck in a hug that screams familiarity. I return her affection with no hesitation, delighted to find that holding her feels like holding AJ used to. It's an innocent, pure exchange of energy that leaves no room for the awkwardness I usually associate with physical contact from anyone outside of my small circle, and when Imani joins in, that perfect feeling doubles.

When they're both back in their seats, Imani sticks her tongue out at her sister. "I told you she'd be here."

Isis rolls her eyes. "*I* told *you* she'd be here."

"You were hoping to see me?"

"Of course! We wanted to thank you for standing up for us with Mama Jo," Isis says, eyes dropping to her hands in her lap. "No one ever does that."

There it is again, that swell of anger and protective instinct flaring in my gut, making me burn with the desire to knock Joanna West upside the head. Reaching over, I lift Isis's chin, splitting a serious, but hopefully, nurturing look between them as I let it go.

"I wish I could have done more. You two worked so hard on Hope's Map, and that moment shouldn't have been overshadowed by chores." I bite my lip when I realize how that might sound and then add, "Tending to your responsibilities at home is important, but sometimes our responsibility to ourselves has to take precedence. The only thing you two should have been required to do after that pitch was pat yourselves on the back and eat your favorite dessert."

They grin at that, and warmth spreads through my chest, prompting me to make a promise I hope Joanna won't stop me from keeping. "When we win this Congressional App Challenge, we'll have a proper celebration."

"We?" Isis asks.

"Yes, we." I waggle my brows at her. "Unless you want someone else to be your mentor?"

"Hel—I mean, heck no," Imani says, shaking her head wildly. Isis joins in, and soon their heads are a lovely blur of enthusiasm. I absolutely adore how excited they are about the prospect of learning from me, but I can't accept their answer without making sure they have a full understanding of the overlap between their lives and mine.

"Before you officially say yes, there's something you should know."

Disappointment wrestles with the remnants of exhilaration for control of their features.

Imani is the first to surrender, defeat evident in her words when she asks, "What is it?"

Isis is holding out hope, the wheels in her mind spinning into overdrive. "It's okay if you don't have the same amount of time as the other mentors. We know you're busy running a company and being the First Lady. We don't need a lot of help, Mrs. Taylor, really. And we won't get in your way."

With every word she speaks, my heart cracks and my hatred for Joanna West and everyone else who made these girls feel like a burden instead of a gift grows tenfold. I hold up a hand to stop Isis's devastating monologue.

"That's not what I was going to say at all, sweetheart."

Her shoulders drop. "Oh."

"Then what were you going to say?" Imani's neck rolls as she asks the question, all the softness from before now gone and replaced with the age-old defense mechanism of anger. I wish I could hug her again, but I doubt she'd welcome that right now.

"Every relationship you enter into, whether personal or professional, should be based on honesty," I tell them, my eyes on the ceiling because for whatever reason I'm a little nervous now. "If I'm going to be your mentor, and I hope you will let me, I have a responsibility to myself, and you, to make sure I am as transparent with you as possible. That's why I wanted to tell you that I knew your mother, Hope, and your brother, Isaiah."

A short silence follows my admission, and then both girls burst out laughing.

"Why are you laughing?" I ask, lips twitching because their amusement is contagious even when it's at my expense.

Imani giggles harder. "Because every time Mom gave Isaiah permission to go home with AJ after school we used to beg him to let us come too. He was always bragging about how nice your house was and how cool you were. He said whenever you came home from work, you always sat with them and asked about everyone's day. Not just AJ's."

"He also told us you used to let them order whatever food they wanted," Isis adds, a dreamy look glossing over her eyes. "One time, he said you got pizza AND Chinese, just because they wanted it."

"Sounds like something I would do," I whisper, voice wobbling at bit. It's strange to hear what parts of his experience in my care stuck out to their brother. Things that felt so insignificant in the moment but left an impression on him so strong they found new life in his sisters' memories, laying the foundation for the bond we're forging now.

Isis, Imani and I spend the rest of the day trading stories about our lost loved ones. Some stories make me laugh, and others make me cry, but no matter what the resulting emotion is, I never forget to feel grateful. For their candor and insight, for their laughter and sass that even gives Monique a run for her money. For the hugs they give me when Joanna's car pulls up to the curb, engine sputtering, brakes squealing. The woman clearly has better things to worry about than me, but she still manages to toss a nasty glare in my direction before she peels out of the parking lot.

"I can have my sister pull her file," Agent Morgan offers.

She's been so quiet all day, I almost forgot she's been shadowing me. I watch Joanna breeze through the stop sign without even tapping her brakes and sigh.

"What good would it do? It's not like I could use anything in there to have them removed from her care."

I hadn't even realized that was something I might want until the words leave my mouth and leave the flavor of truth on my lips. Everything I've seen of Joanna West tells me the desire is justifiable, but I'm also aware of how naive it is to think taking her out of the equation would automatically make things better for Imani and Isis.

"True, but it would give you an idea of who you're dealing with. Maybe help you build some kind of relationship with her, so she doesn't become an obstacle between you and the girls."

I nod, impressed at how the agent's thoughts complement mine. "You're right. Any information your sister could provide would be greatly appreciated."

"I'll ask her tonight."

"What are you two doing out here?"

Both Agent Morgan and I turn to find Agent Shaw approaching from the left. She's got her hands tucked in her pockets and a frown marring her features.

"You're completely exposed out here," she says to Morgan, shaking her head as she herds us back inside the building like wayward sheep. "You know better."

"It's not her fault. I wanted to see the girls out."

My defense barely registers as the senior agent begins to reprimand her second-in-command.

"No cover. No backup. The protectee standing in front of you, poised to take a bullet you're sworn to jump in front of...." She rants the entire way back up to my office, and Agent Morgan takes the critique beautifully, nodding when appropriate and only responding verbally when absolutely necessary. Despite her easy acquiescence, Agent Shaw keeps going, turning what should have been a quick moment for correction and redirection into something else entirely.

I slam my purse on my desk. "Enough!"

Her mouth snaps shut, but resentment at being silenced shines in her eyes. I pinch the bridge of my nose and try to hunt down a hint of calm in a body buzzing with second-hand embarrassment and anxiety.

"Ma'am—" Shaw starts, but I refuse to hear anything else from her right now.

"Agent Morgan has done an amazing job leading your team today. She has demonstrated a level of competence, dedication and flexibility most agents at her level wouldn't even dream of possessing, and most importantly, she has remained respectful and patient in the face of what is, quite frankly, an obvious case of punching down."

"It's okay, ma'am," Agent Morgan says. "I should have known better."

"And maybe you should have, but that doesn't make it okay for her to come in here and take what has clearly been a bad day out on you."

Shaw mutters a curse, head hanging heavy with shame. "You're right. I'm sorry, Morgan."

The other agent shrugs. "It's okay."

I gesture to the armchairs in front of my desk. "Sit down and take a load off, Shaw. You too, Morgan."

Within seconds, we're all seated and staring at the ceiling. I'm thinking about how awful it'll be to go back to the White House knowing there's not even the slightest chance I'll catch a glimpse of Cal's broad shoulders or Beck's bald head in the halls. I miss them so much it hurts, and today, for the few hours I spent with Isis and Imani, that ache was bearable. Now it's back in full effect.

"What happened in your meeting that put you in such a bad mood?" I ask Shaw, hoping that hearing her problems will distract me from mine.

Of course, I'm not that lucky.

"I was formally reprimanded for taking the trip to Kentucky without clearing it with the higher-ups," she mutters.

"Shit. I'm sorry." The apology is genuine as is the worry that slices through me seconds later. "Is your job in jeopardy?"

I wouldn't be able to live with myself if I were the reason for someone else losing their job. Especially if that someone is Agent Shaw. She's been nothing but a source of support for me since taking over my security, and I would feel awful if her kindness was rewarded with a trip to the unemployment line.

"No." She sinks further down into her seat. "At least not yet."

"What does that mean?" Morgan asks, stealing the question straight from my mind.

Shaw blows out a harsh breath. "It means they've started

outsourcing our jobs, Morgan. Can you believe that?" She laughs, but the sound is bitter and full of anger. "I work my ass off for twenty years to get here, and as soon as the world is used to the idea of a Black, female Secret Service agent, they decide to change the rules so any motherfucker who knows how to hold a gun can walk in off the street and guard the President of the United fucking States."

I'm trying my best to follow her rant, but there aren't enough details. I rest my elbows on the edge of the desk, squinting at Shaw like the context I need is going to appear in a bubble over her head.

"Elaborate, please."

She rights herself in the chair, sitting up straight and linking her fingers together over her stomach. "Your husband has a new security detail. They carry our government-issued weapons and wear our fucking badges, but they are not Secret Service agents."

"That doesn't make any sense," Morgan says. "We hold federal positions. Anyone tasked with guarding the President would have to go through the hiring requirements and training protocols."

"Right, and according to Director Evans, they have."

Sal Evans—the director of the Secret Service—has never struck me as a particularly honest man. His dark hair is always greasy and he has the kind of smile that warns you to never leave a drink unattended when he's around.

"But you don't believe him?"

Shaw stares at me for a long second, contemplating the question, then shakes her head. "No. I talked to the new heads of Aubrey's detail, and I've only seen them once before: on the day Drake and Beckham were fired."

Images of strange men rushing into the sitting hall and pinning Cal and Beck to the floor flash in my mind. My stomach turns when I remember the way light reflected off leather boots as they dug into skin and muscle, threatening to crack bone. I'd put that part out of my mind, forcing myself to forget the way the fibers of the carpet bit into my skin when I got on my knees and begged two strangers for the lives of the men I love.

Agent Shaw had been the one to lift me from the ground, and it was her team that came in and deescalated the situation Aubrey was content to let turn deadly. Shaw stayed with me, escorting me to my room, while Morgan and the rest of the team separated Beck and Cal from Aubrey and his henchmen.

"You're sure it's the same men?"

There's a hint of desperation in my tone. I would give anything not to be in the same room with those men again, but if Shaw is right and Aubrey has hired them, then I won't have a choice.

"I'm sure," she says. "They even remembered me, thanked me for helping them 'take out the trash'."

Morgan visibly bristles. "What'd you say to that?"

"Nothing. I changed the subject, asked them how they managed to score the Presidential detail when I've never heard of them."

I've always enjoyed Shaw's bluntness and find myself releasing a small huff of amusement. "Did they tell you?"

"Of course not. They just spouted off some bullshit about me never hearing of them because I wasn't on the short list for the President's detail."

"The short list?"

Both agents look at me, confused by my confusion.

"It's exactly what it sounds like," Shaw explains. "A list of names compiled by the Director that includes the best agents to lead a specific detail."

"The more prestigious the detail, the shorter the list," Morgan adds.

I rub my chin, interest more than a little piqued. "Who has access to the list?"

Shaw yawns, either bored with the conversation or done with this day. "The Director and the protectee, so in this case, Aubrey."

"And no one else ever sees it?"

"Nope," Morgan says.

Shaw's brows fold in on each other. "Well, that's not true."

Now the other agent's brows are furrowed as well. "It's not?"

"No, when I was selected as the head of this detail, the Director gave me the list. He suggested I use my competition to build my team.

I got access to entire personnel files, psych exams, credit reports, the whole nine."

Morgan looks a bit dismayed by her superior's confession, but I'm too distracted by the spark lighting up the edges of a path in my mind that starts at Shaw's revelation and ends at the only place we can find answers to the questions we have about the men who are now in charge of Aubrey's safety.

17

CAL

Beck shuffles and reshuffles the deck of UNO cards while I carefully stack the small wooden blocks from the Jenga set inside the box. It feels kind of pointless to be cleaning everything up when Riley is just going to want to tear it all out again as soon as she wakes up in the morning, but we both know that Rae or Hunter will do it if we don't, and we're not having that.

Since they've arrived, Beck and I have done everything we can to keep Riley occupied so her parents can have some actual downtime. They've managed to sneak out of the house every day this week to try restaurants their picky eating daughter won't enjoy and see movies she isn't old enough to watch while we've kept her distracted with museum visits, ice cream cones and pool days. Tonight, though, we all decided to stay in and let Riley beat us at literally everything.

"I'm tired," Beck says, resting his forehead on the dining table next to a half-empty pizza box. The UNO cards have been returned to their box, and he's clutching it in his left hand like a lifeline.

Laughing, I reach over and rub his back. "Buck up, Beckham, we're almost done cleaning up."

He groans softly but rallies, scooping up the pizza boxes as he rises from the table. "What's on the agenda for tomorrow?" he asks, transferring all the uneaten slices to a large zip lock bag and tossing them in the fridge.

At least once a day for the last week, we've found ourselves asking each other this question. Neither of us knows what to do with all the free time we now have, so I guess this is our way of coping, of prompting one another to find something to look forward to. It's been easy with Hunter and his family here, but they're leaving the day after tomorrow, which means eventually we're going to have to face the uncertainty of our future without Riley's constant requests for activities to distract us.

I slide the top of last block into the box and close it, turning to face Beck. "All I've got is running with Hunter in the morning and taking Riley to the Air and Space Museum in the afternoon."

Nodding, he folds the pizza boxes in half and presses them into the trash can. "She's still mad the White House visit isn't happening. I hate disappointing her."

A grimace twists my features into something dark and ugly. These days, I can't think about that fucking place without it happening. When I think about Selene still being there, surrounded by people like Aubrey and the men who treated us like animals, it gets worse. I force myself to relax, pushing the thoughts away. "Yeah, me too."

"It's for the best, though," Beck concludes. "Because if they ever let me back in that motherfucker, I'll be coming out in cuffs."

"A body bag," I correct him, knowing there's no way he'd make it out alive.

"Yeah, you're probably right."

Several pieces of balled up paper towel fall out of the trash bag when Beck lifts it out of the bin. He throws his head back and lets out a long groan that's wrapped in exhaustion. I cross the room, picking the paper towels on my way over to him, and take the bag from his hand.

"Go to bed, love. I've got this."

Red-rimmed onyx eyes meet mine. "I don't want to leave you down here alone."

One of my favorite versions of Beck is the tired one because it always comes with a side of clinginess. An indulgent smile tugs at the corners of my mouth, and I press a kiss to his cheek.

"Then wait for me on the couch."

He accepts the compromise gladly, trudging over to the couch and plopping down on it face first. Shaking my head, I tie off the trash bag and leave it by the garage door. By the time I'm done straightening up, there are three bags in total waiting to be carried to the bins. I'm contemplating whether I want to take them out to the big bins now or leave them until the morning when the sound of timid knocking reaches my ears.

Beck, who was snoring softly just a second ago, wakes immediately when I pass the couch on the way to the front door. "Who is it?" he asks, moving to his feet. I understand why he's on high alert. The last time we had an unannounced visitor late at night, it was Aubrey.

"No idea."

I look through the peephole, wishing I had my gun on me when I see a dark figure standing on the other side of the door with their head down. My lips part to issue a warning to Beck but think better of it, turning on the porch light instead. They look up, shielding their eyes from the bright light and revealing familiar features to me.

Immediately, I undo the locks and yank the door, wrapping my arms around the person and hauling her across the threshold.

"*Selene.*"

My nostrils are flooded with her scent. There are berries and flowers and the nectar of the sweetest summer fruit and *her*. Soft and supple and sweet and, somehow, mine. I can't stop touching her.

Even as I back us into the living room, crashing into Beck as I go.

Even as she pulls back and arches over me to meet his pleading lips.

Even when I drop down on the couch and she's straddling me.

My hands have a mind of their own, and I'm powerless to stop their thorough, yet modest exploration. Passing over her shoulders and back, ghosting over her arms and finally cupping her cheeks, lifting her head so my eyes can run anxious lines over the column of her neck.

"Are you hurt?" Beck asks, sinking onto the couch beside us with his mind in the same place as mine. "I thought I got him off of you before he got a good grip."

We've replayed the moment a million times in the last week. At first, Beck was confident he had stopped Aubrey from doing any real damage, but as time has gone by, he's been less and less sure. I know the dip in his degree of certainty is directly related to not being able to see Selene with his own eyes. I release her, allowing her to turn to Beck and show him the same flawless skin I was relieved to see.

"I'm fine," she says, grabbing one of his hands and bringing it to her lips. He pulls in a sharp breath when she kisses his knuckles. "Thanks to the two of you." Her voice breaks and suddenly she's blinking back tears. *"I'm so sorry."*

"Sorry? You don't have anything to be sorry for, gorgeous."

"I got you fired," she says, insistent and sorrowful. "I almost got you killed."

I don't know if this is what she came here for, knowing the risk it carries, I doubt it. Something much more important led her to our door, some question or concern or need, but this is the thing on her heart. The heavy weight of guilt, of actions she didn't take or condone, sit on her shoulders, completely at home among the delicate lines. I'll give her whatever else she came here for, but first, I have to take this burden from her.

My fingers grip her chin, gently turning her focus back to me. "You didn't get us fired. We went up those stairs knowing exactly what the risks were, and we didn't care. Leaving you alone to fend for yourself when we knew Aubrey was on a warpath wasn't an option." A tear breaks free from her right eye, and I brush it away. "I would gladly die a million deaths for you, Selene. Meeting my end doesn't scare me, but knowing a world without you in it is a reality I would do anything, *give* anything, to avoid."

"So don't ever worry about what loving you or protecting you will cost us," Beck whispers. "Because whatever the price is, we're prepared to pay it."

Selene shakes her head, refusing the comfort we're attempting to offer. "Love isn't supposed to have a cost, especially not a mortal one."

"And if you were anyone else, if we had met under different circumstances or led different lives before we found each other, that might not be the case, but that isn't our reality, pet, *this is*. And we have to live it. We have to fight our way through it. We have to do the work to change it, and none of that happens if we're too busy questioning what we're worth."

Insulting her wasn't my intention, but it still happens. She rears back. "I'm not questioning anything."

"Aren't you, though?" Beck's voice is soft as he puts his hand on her back to hold her in place when she tries to leave my lap. "No one is saying you don't see our value, gorgeous. I think right now, you're struggling to see your own, because it sounds like to me you're trying to tell us you're not worth all this trouble."

"Because I'm not!" Selene hisses, lips quivering as wild eyes bounce between Beck's face and mine. "You didn't see yourselves on that floor. You didn't see the joy those men took in holding you down, in causing you pain, in hearing you struggle for your next breath, but I did. I saw it all, I heard it all, and I will forever be haunted by the knowledge that I caused it."

"*Caused* it?" Disbelief coats my words.

"Yes, I provoked Aubrey. I kept badgering him about Sutton even though I could see how agitated he was. I should have stopped, but I didn't, and that put us all in danger."

"Gorgeous. You have to know that Aubrey was always going to escalate the situation. He was livid when we left Camp David, and by the time he got to you, he was completely out of control. You could have given him the silent treatment, and he still would have reacted the same way because in his mind, you had already done the worst thing you could do: step out of line."

Relief floods me when Beck's words penetrate the bubble of self-loathing surrounding Selene. Her shoulders drop, and the wrinkle of doubt between her brows smooths. I use the moment of calm as an opportunity to broach the topic of the Kentucky trip.

"Why didn't you tell us you thought Aubrey was involved with Sutton's death?"

I'd be lying if I said I hadn't considered the possibility, but I didn't know Selene had taken it upon herself to try and connect those dots. Apparently, she's done a hell of a job because everything she said seemed to strike a chord with Aubrey.

"Because I wasn't even sure they were still seeing each other."

"So, you didn't know if there was a motive."

"I still don't," she says to Beck, sliding off my lap to curl up between us with her back to his chest. "I wasn't certain he had anything to do with it until I saw the way he reacted. There's no way he would have come at me that way if there wasn't some truth to what I was saying."

I pull her feet into my lap, noticing that she's still wearing heels. "Did you come here from work?"

A small whimper leaves her when I slip her shoes off and start massaging her feet. We probably don't have time for this. She's here without security and operating outside of her normal schedule which means it won't be long before red flags are raised and alarms are sounded. Regardless, I'm not going to miss out on an opportunity to touch her, to care for her in some small way.

"Who's on you tonight?" Beck asks, nuzzling into her hair. It's bone straight today, the silk black strands shining under the glow of the light from the kitchen.

"Morgan and Shaw," Selene moans when I hit a pressure point. "They're in the car waiting for me."

Instinctively, I look toward the door as if the two women will magically appear. "They brought you here?"

"Yes, they didn't want to wait to find out if you had the information we needed."

I can't help but smile at how well I know her. "I knew you were after more than a foot massage. What kind of information do you need, pet?"

Her teeth sink into her lower lip as her breathing grows ragged. "Don't make it sound like I'm using you."

"Oh, but you are, gorgeous, and it's okay, as long as we get to use you too."

Beck's grin is silky and dark. It disappears into the curve of Selene's neck as his lips ghost over her skin, sending shivers through her body. Her eyes start to disappear into the back of her head as the air grows thick with a desire that dissipates as quickly as it came when heavy footfalls sound out above us. Selene jumps up, attempting to right herself even though nothing is really out of place. She's still fidgeting with her clothes when Hunter reaches the bottom step.

I turn to witness the rare sight of my brother at a loss for words. He's staring at Selene, clearly aware of who she is but unable to greet her. Needing to end the awkward silence, I stand gesturing between the two of them.

"Selene, this is my baby brother, Hunter. Hunter, this is Selene Taylor."

The ease with which Selene goes from being sensual and soft to professional and polite never ceases to amaze me. She rolls her shoulders back, stepping around me to meet Hunter in the middle of the floor and taking his outstretched hand.

"It's so nice to meet you, Hunter."

He looks to me and Beck, eyes wide. "Riley is going to be so pissed."

Now Selene's staring at us, notes of accusation in her voice when she says, "Riley's here?"

Hunter's brows shoot up. "You know Riley?"

"I've heard about her from her loving uncles," Selene explains, offering him a genuine smile. "She sounds like an amazing kid."

Pride causes Hunter's already inflated chest to swell. "She is. She was really hoping to get a chance to meet you while we were here, but...."

"Next time," Selene jumps in, sparing Hunter from the awkwardness of speaking on a topic he doesn't know much about. "Just have Cal and Beck let me know when you're coming, and I'll clear my schedule for her."

"That's....wow...she'd really love that."

"We'll set it up," I say, bouncing on the tips of my toes, ready for Hunter to get the fuck on because I don't know how long it'll be before

Shaw and Morgan come beating down my door, and I want to make the most of the little time we have together.

Thankfully, Hunter takes the hint, making his excuses and heading back up the stairs without getting whatever it was he came down here for in the first place. When we're alone again, Beck reaches for Selene, trying to get her back on the couch, but she dodges him and then me when I try to pull her into my arms.

She wags a finger at both of us, turning the space behind an armchair into a sanctuary. "I can't let you distract me again."

"But distraction is so fun," I argue, sitting down on the edge of the coffee table closest to Beck. He hums his agreement, and Selene rolls her eyes.

"You two are the worst."

"You love us," Beck counters, smiling.

She melts a little. "I do."

"And we love you," I remind her. "Tell us what you need."

Her request is simple, and we're able to grant it in a matter of minutes, moving Selene into the office so she can comfortably sort through the personnel files of all the agents who were on the short list for the lead of Aubrey's detail when Beck and I were tapped for the roles. He's leaning over Selene's shoulder, reading the files along with her even though we've already told her neither of the men from that day were in the stack.

"Shaw is sure it was them?" he asks, handing her the last folder.

"Yes, she was positive. She said Garrison was the one who referred to you as trash. His partner, Woodard, just stood there and laughed. "

"Have you seen them with Aubrey?"

"No." She slams the last folder closed, pushing it away when it doesn't provide what she's looking for. "They just announced their addition to his detail today."

I steeple my fingers, turning everything Selene told us over in my head. "But they're not on the short list, and no one has heard of them."

"They weren't in the disciplinary report either," Beck adds, hands on his head as he paces behind Selene. "I thought that was weird. If they were agents, they would have had to sign witness statements with their badge numbers and all."

"Hard to do when you don't have a badge," I growl, frustration ripping through me at the thought of being the predecessor of frauds.

Selene rubs her temples. "How could they do that, though? Move freely around the White House with no clearance? Embed themselves in the Secret Service AND put themselves in a position to guard a President?"

"There isn't anything or anyone money can't buy in this country."

Beck pauses, glancing at me. "You think someone bought off Evans?"

"Aubrey." Resentment wraps around Selene's vocal cords. "Aubrey paid off Evans."

She says it with so much conviction, I'm inclined to believe her, but the facts aren't meshing. "But why would he need to do that? There's no shortage of morally corrupt agents within the Service who would do whatever he wanted with no questions asked. Paying Evans to shoehorn Garrison and Woodard in would be expensive and unnecessary."

Even though I've taken a sledgehammer to her theory, Selene follows my line of reasoning readily, arriving at the conclusion I've yet to verbalize.

"So Garrison and Woodard don't...work...for Aubrey?"

Beck is right there with us, shaking his head. "No, I don't think they do."

A loaded silence envelops us. The idea of Garrison and Woodard was already off putting when it seemed they were doing Aubrey's bidding, but the thought of them operating at the behest of some nameless, faceless entity whose motivations are currently unclear is nothing short of horrific.

18

BECK

When I was six, I developed a fear of the dark.

I remember exactly how it happened. I'd just moved into a new foster home where I was one of five children vying for the limited resources of the adults' time, attention and affection. One day, I'd gotten a little too much of one of the three, and Brett, the kid who'd been there longer than anyone else, pulled me out of my bed in the middle of the night and forced me into a small, dank room inside the basement that no one ever went into. He left me in there overnight and was doubled over laughing when our foster dad pulled me out of the closet the next morning and spanked me for wetting my pants.

As an adult, I don't have an issue with the dark anymore.

Unless, of course, I'm being kept in it.

Selene left our house four days ago and took all the light with her, leaving Cal and me with nothing but each other and the constant worry for her safety. Every second that passes, every day that goes by, we sink a little further into the abyss of ignorance, never knowing where she is, who she's with, or if she's any closer to finding out who paid Evans off to get Woodard and Garrison into the Service, and why they want them in Aubrey's orbit, because we certainly aren't.

And how could we when we're so far outside of her world? Disconnected from everything and everyone who might have been able to offer even a little insight because, as Selene so brilliantly put it, our professional reputations are now ruined. I throw the burner down on the couch, and it bounces into Cal's hand. He's reading the newspaper with those annoyingly sexy glasses on, and he glances at the discarded device over the black rims, scanning the text thread between me and Agent Shaw. It's filled with the uninterrupted steam of bubbles representing my outgoing messages.

"Still no reply?"

"Nope." My leg bounces anxiously. "I guess she finally realized staying in contact with us is career suicide."

"Doubtful," Cal says, scooping up my phone and scrolling back to the last reply I got from Shaw. It was around noon yesterday, and she had just confirmed Selene's arrival at another high school for one of her AJ's Promise forums. After that, it's been nothing but radio silence. "Maybe she had a family emergency?"

I take the phone from his outstretched hand and flip it closed. "Or maybe something's wrong."

"Beck." He folds his paper and sets it aside. "You can't go to the worst-case scenario every time Shaw goes quiet. We knew she wouldn't be able to be in constant contact."

We decided months ago that any and all contact related to or for Selene would go through Shaw. When we were still employed through the Service, we sent coded messages using our work phones because we couldn't risk being caught with burners. Even on the busiest days, she was good about keeping us in Selene's loop. Going this long without hearing from her is completely out of the ordinary.

"I don't need constant contact, Cal, but I do need *something*."

"And you'll get it," he says, certainty I even laced in the words. "You just have to be patient."

"Patience is the one thing I don't have."

"What's it going to take for you to acquire some?"

My jaw clenches. It's a subconscious attempt to stop the request I know Cal won't grant from hitting the air. It doesn't work. "I want to see her."

Now that I've lent my voice to the desire, I'm powerless to stop it from taking over my mind, from stoking a restless fire in my veins that makes my muscles twitch with the need to move. I'm on my feet before I've actually decided to stand, grabbing my keys from the hook beside the front door and pausing just long enough to pose a question to Cal.

"You coming?"

It might have turned into an argument if he wasn't as desperate to see Selene as I am. Since he is, the drive to Culture Code is tense but brimming with an excitement that makes me wonder why we hadn't thought of coming to her office before. I guess we've just been playing it safe, keeping our distance because the last time we took it upon ourselves to get close it fucked everything up.

"There aren't any agents covering the door," Cal observes as I maneuver into one of the spots on the street across from the building.

"Shaw's vehicle isn't here."

The blacked-out, bulletproof tank of an SUV wasn't on any of the side streets or at the back either. I made sure to look for it when we did a reconnaissance lap to make sure there weren't any paparazzi camped out in the area. Thankfully, the press has lost interest in the mundanity of the First Lady's participation in the corporate world. They've moved on to much more interesting things like her husband opting to return to the table with the leader of Qatar to discuss the military base they want to build on US soil. Apparently, things are going much better than expected, and everyone wants to know what led to Aubrey's sudden change of heart.

I kill the engine, conducting a visual sweep of the area and finding nothing out of the ordinary. There are people moving in and out of the building, computer bags on their backs or slung over their shoulders and headphones in their ears. Everything looks normal, except it's not because today is one of Selene's scheduled office days, and she's not here.

I've completely dismissed the possibility of her being anywhere her detail is not because we agreed before she left the house the other night that she would stick close to Shaw and her team. Cal's fingers drum lightly on the arm of the door, and I don't have to ask to know what he's thinking.

"Two possibilities," I say, unhooking my seat belt. "They're all taking a sick day or something's wrong."

Cal scrubs a hand over his face, a dark resignation rippling in puddles of brass and copper as he pops open the passenger door. "Maybe it's a stomach bug," he offers as we cross the street.

"What like some virus they all happen to have at the same time?"

"Or a case of food poisoning," he suggests, following me through the automatic doors. It's been months since I've stepped inside this building, and everything looks pretty much the same. Outside of the youthful members of the Junior Coding Academy, there aren't really any new faces either, and because everyone knows us they make it annoyingly easy to get to Selene. Even Nichelle, her assistant, just smiles and waves us through the doors, not even bothering to leave her desk to announce our arrival.

I'm vibrating with anger by the time we make it to her, so my tone is sharp and close to cutting when I ask, *"Where the fuck is your security?"*

Selene is standing near the conference table with her back to us and all of her focus on the white board before her. She's not writing on it, just staring at it with her hands on her hips and a black marker clutched in her left hand. The TV, which she usually keeps on to provide ambient noise, is off, so the sudden sound of my voice interrupting her silence scares the fuck out of her.

"JESUS!" she screams, almost jumping out of her skin.

The marker flies out of her hand, landing near her feet as she turns to face us with a palm pressed over her heart. When she sees that it's Cal and me, the fear fades, transforming into joy laced annoyance that, thankfully, doesn't stop her from letting us both take her in our arms and steal a few kisses.

"What are you two doing here?"

Cal passes a soothing hand over her back. "We came to check on you."

I move over to the whiteboard, curious about what exactly she's mapping out. "And it's a good thing we did since you're here with no protection."

"The building has a dedicated security team," she protests, the edge in her voice reminding me of the first time I came to this office and we argued about the deficiencies of her security set up.

"The team that let Cal and I through without asking for identification or making us get visitor's badges?"

"They know who you are. That wouldn't have been necessary."

My jaw is clenched when I face her. "They know who Aubrey is, too. Does that mean you would have been safe if they had let him waltz through those doors? Because the last time I saw you two in a room together—"

"*Beck.*"

There's no mistaking the warning Cal has just turned my name into or the cracks spreading across Selene's face thanks to my callous words. My heart twists in on itself.

"I'm sorry, gorgeous." I hold out a hand as I start to close the distance between us, hoping she'll meet me halfway. She does. Our fingers lock together, and I use the connection to pull her into me, sliding my free hand through the hair at the nape of her neck and kneading her scalp.

She rests her head on my chest, wrapping her arms around my waist. "It's okay."

"It's not. I could have made my point without bringing Aubrey into it."

"You're right. You could have, or you could have considered that you didn't need to make the point at all."

Cal laughs softly at that, and I glare at him, only cutting the death stare short when Selene tilts her head back to see my face. "I'll have Monique talk to security about consistent protocols as it relates to visitors, even the ones they know. It won't happen again."

My brow furrows. "Why would Monique need to have that conversation?"

"That would be more Shaw's wheelhouse," Cal adds.

I already knew. When we pulled up and saw no agents in or around the building, when Shaw went quiet on her work phone, when I walked in here and saw Selene alone, unattended, *abandoned*. I knew. And still, it doesn't feel real until her gaze slides away from mine and lands on the ceiling the way it does when she has something uncomfortable to say.

"Agent Shaw is no longer a part of my detail," she explains, lips twisting into a ball that only stays for a second before it smooths out and she continues. "Actually, I don't have a detail anymore. Aubrey took them away."

The last thing I want to do is let her go, but I'm left with no choice when she starts to pull away. I follow her anxious steps as she walks the length of floor between me and Cal. He's finally parted with any notion of calm and positivity. Thick brows drawn together to form a harsh, angry line that matches the fury boiling inside of me.

"He did *what*?" Cal growls.

"He recalled them," Selene says, panic evident in her voice and in the flicking of her fingers. "He just took them away. No one even notified me. I spent the entire morning searching for someone on the team, but they were all gone. Sam Granger finally took pity on me and explained that a memo went out saying I was refusing protection. Shaw and Morgan were fired, and the rest of their team was reassigned."

I want to hit something. No, I need to hit someone. Suddenly, I'm filled with the strongest sense of regret for not having caved Aubrey's skull in when I had the chance. Even with dark figures lingering in the shadows around him and unknown entities spending mind-boggling amounts of money to infiltrate his inner circle, he's still carving out time to fuck with Selene.

I should have known she'd bear the brunt of it. Firing us was pretty much all he could do to Cal and me without risking dragging his own shit out into the streets, but with Selene there are so many more options. And because he thinks he owns her, because he resents her for having the audacity to disobey him by going to Kentucky and still being involved with us, it appears he's hellbent on exploring them all, starting with mental warfare.

"He's punishing you, taking away your only source of comfort and support, so you're vulnerable and afraid."

Her chin wobbles as she nods. "I know."

"But what's the goal?" Cal asks, wrapping an arm around Selene. She leans into his embrace, soothed by the touch. "Does he want her too afraid to leave the White House? Is he hoping she'll get desperate enough out here on her own to try to come back into the fold?"

Selene scoffs. "I would never do that. I know too much about that depraved bastard."

My gaze snaps to Cal's, and we fall into one of those exchanges where no words are spoken but understanding is easily found. What we've both come to understand over the course of our careers is that knowledge isn't just power, sometimes it's a death sentence.

The icy, skeletal fingers of fear pierce my chest as I replay every accusation Selene launched at Aubrey in the sitting hall that day. Each word was wrapped in conviction, drenched in certainty, delivered with the kind of authority that could shape minds and sway juries. Her knowing is more than enough on its own, but when you pair the allegations with a violent attempt to silence the person making them, it's as good as an admission of guilt. I know. Cal knows it. And Aubrey does too, which is why he can't risk Selene standing in front of a camera or sitting down with a reporter to share a theory that, by the time she's done, will be accepted as fact.

"He wants you dead."

Bile rises in my throat. The first time Valinsky made a threat against Diana, I heard the distant thunk of metal grooves sliding into place. Cogs groaning as gears began turning, marching us slowly toward death. I'd done everything I could to stop it, but Valinsky's machine was bigger than I could ever be, built with fail safes and auxiliary power sources I couldn't find or kill fast enough. It was insurmountable. He was insurmountable, and he didn't have a fraction of Aubrey's power or influence. I stare at Selene, this urgent need to take her, to hold her, to hide her building inside of me so fast, I can't stop the words from coming.

"We need to run."

Cal and Selene both look at me like I've lost it, and maybe I have. Maybe I'm doing the thing Dr. Payne says I shouldn't do and obsessing over things outside of my control. Or maybe I'm just the only one who hears the churning of gears and the ticking of a clock counting down the hours until we lose everything.

"I'm not running, Beck," Selene says, her chin lifted in defiance.

"Why not? You have done everything you set out to do, Selene. Your promise to AJ has been fulfilled, and the work will continue to happen well after you've left the White House. You can walk away. You can be free. You can be with us."

She'd asked me for it before. Prior to the kidnapping and the election and the threats from Aubrey, she wanted to run away. I see the moment so clearly now. A stunning gown, two stolen kisses, a bracelet meant to keep her safe, and an unspoken request to pick her up and take her away from all of this when she knew she couldn't go. I wish like hell I hadn't talked her out of it.

"We're not cut out for a life on the run," she murmurs, her voice softened by memory as she returns to the circle of my arms. "That's what you told me that night, and you were right to say it to me then, just like I'm right to say it to you now." She smiles, but the upturned line is riddled with sadness. "I want to be free. I want to be with you and Cal. I want those things more than I want my next breath. If you're right, and Aubrey wants me dead—"

The tips of my fingers dig into her waist. "I am," I tell her without an ounce of doubt in my body.

She takes my face in her hands. "I believe you. It's exactly where my mind went this morning, but Beck, you know just as well as I do that running won't stop that desire in its tracks."

"It'll make it stronger," Cal says, shrugging when I frown at him. "It's the truth, Beck. Running makes the chase more enticing."

"And staying is the same as locking yourself inside a trap," I shoot back. "I don't understand how you two don't see where we are right now. This is dire straits. You have no security, no protection, no one in that fucking place that's in your corner. We're on the outside of everything, if something happens...." My voice breaks, images of Selene falling over the railing in Charlie's place flashing through my mind. Tears burn at the back of my eyes. *"I can't save you."*

Selene lifts up on the tips of her toes, offering me solace in the form of a sweet, licking kiss that does nothing but make me more desperate to pick her up, sling her over my shoulder and run away. When she pulls back, there's a world of tender understanding in her eyes.

"You've already saved me, Beck. From Jacob, Charlie and Leigh Anne. From guilt and grief and loneliness and even from myself. I know there isn't a battle you wouldn't fight for me or a sanctuary you would keep me from, but I don't want shelter, Beck, and I don't need you to grab your sword and ride off to slay the dragon."

"But I will."

"I know, baby, and I love you for it. Believe me. But Aubrey is *my* dragon, and I don't want anyone else cutting off his fucking head."

In the time that I've known her, Selene has given me a million different reasons not to bet against her. When her top lip curls and the purest form of hatred hardens her eyes as she talks about ending her husband, I know that I've found reason one million and one. Selene isn't scared; she's determined. She's a general with a battle plan in hand that, hopefully, includes two soldiers prepared to die and kill for her.

A quiet sigh of resolve leaves me, and a victorious smile curves her lips when I say, "Read me in."

19

SELENE

Bringing Beck and Cal up to speed doesn't take long.

Mainly because they're quick studies, but also because I don't have a lot in the way of actual proof. My whiteboard—which Monique has taken to calling a 'murder board'—is divided in half. One side dedicated to the things I know for certain, and the other filled with theories, questions and, towards the bottom, names and other single word phrases I haven't figured out where to place.

"Mistook peanut butter for tahini?" Beck gapes at the witness statement from the sous chef who made the fatal swap. "Isn't tahini white?"

"It's more beige or deep brown, depends on how the sesame seeds are processed," Cal says, leaning in close to my computer screen to get a good look at the pictures of Sutton's planner that her father sent to me.

Several dates marked 'CD' with little hearts around the letters corresponded with times Aubrey was at Camp David. Cal and Beck were always with him on those trips, but they said if she was there, they never saw her. It doesn't surprise me since they never got to see or vet a lot of the people who visited Aubrey there.

While they've pored over all things related to Sutton, I've tasked myself with rescuing at least one thing from the side of the board that represents obscurity and insignificance. So far, I've had no luck.

Beck appears at my side suddenly, the frustration rolling off me as I gaze at the board a beacon he can't resist. "Why do you have President Sanders up there?"

In an instant, Cal is on my other side, and then I'm wrapped in the bubble of their warmth and familiar scents. Despite the stressful circumstances that made this moment possible, I'm nothing but grateful to be standing here with them looking at the pieces of a puzzle and figuring out how they all fit together.

"He died in the middle of the campaign, and his death guaranteed Aubrey's win."

"So did the sympathy he garnered from your kidnapping," Cal points out. "Why isn't that up there?"

"You think Aubrey was involved with my kidnapping?"

I never even considered it. Some things, like the kidnapping and AJ's death, felt so clear to me in terms of responsibility. Jacob was responsible for my kidnapping. He recruited Leigh Anne and flipped Charlie and Agent Harris. He introduced my temple to the barrel of a gun. He was bred in hate and fed pain from the time he could walk and talk. That same thing was true for the child who ended AJ's life. None of those things had anything to do with Aubrey, or, at least, I didn't think so.

Beck plucks the marker from my hand and walks over to the board, adding the kidnapping under the half-erased note about the military base. "We've never found any links between Aubrey and Jacob that didn't include you. Personally, I don't think he was involved, but when you're conducting an investigation, everything matters until you're able to determine that it doesn't."

My core clenches, something primal in me reacting to the display of competence. Cal's gaze is warm on the side of my face, but his knowing chuckle is an open flame that threatens to melt me.

"Did that turn you on, pet?"

I bite back a smile, wondering how it's possible to be wet when we're talking about one of the scariest days of my life. "Shut up, Drake."

"Are you two even listening?"

"Of course we are, love."

Beck is clearly skeptical, twisting his lips up at Cal's overenthusiastic answer. "What did I just say then?"

"Yeah, what did he say, Cal?"

We both stare at him, waiting for him to say something. When he throws his hands up in surrender, we all share a laugh. It's short lived, this moment of levity, but it's a nice glimpse into the future we're working towards.

"Anyway," Beck says eventually, ready to get back to work. "I was asking if you had anything on Sanders's death, Selene."

"Nothing outside of what was readily available to the public," I tell him, moving over to the conference table to find the file. "I had Nichelle put it together, but I never really got around to looking through it because I've been so focused on Sutton."

"It was probably the better use of your time."

Cal hums his agreement with Beck's statement. They join me at the table, watching as I lay all the items out. There's the printed history of Sanders's health, which he made public record after his hospitalization during the campaign. Multiple articles about his death, including an emotional tribute by his oldest daughter that was published in the Times. Lastly, and to my complete surprise, there's a copy of his autopsy accompanied by photos taken outside of the Sanders' Chesapeake Bay home from the day he died.

Press descended on the waterfront home within minutes of the 911 call Deborah Sanders made when she found her husband unresponsive on the patio where he'd been having his morning coffee, so there are plenty of angles to work with. I take the stack of photos and split it between me and Cal while Beck takes the autopsy.

"How did Nichelle even get this? I thought these didn't become public record for years."

"They don't," Cal says. "But they're always available somewhere if you know the right place to look."

He's right. The internet is a vast and extremely dark place some-times. I heard once that photos of the report written by the coroner who examined AJ's body ended up there, free and available for the whole world to see. I don't find it shocking at all that the same thing has happened here. Sanders died in the midst of an election, so there were bound to be questions and impatient constituents unwilling to wait twelve years for the documents to be released by the National Archives and Records Association.

Both men go quiet, disappearing into their work, and I do the same, walking the length of the room as I shuffle through the pictures. Even though Cal has half the stack, I still have close to fifty photos in my hand. Some of them are basically the same photo just with minute differences like a person's hand moving from inside their jacket pocket to running a finger over the yellow tape billowing in the late October wind.

It's an odd thing to do.

Touch a line that's not meant to be touched.

That's what catches my eye. The audacity. The disregard. The flirting with the idea of crossing a clearly defined boundary. But what keeps my attention, what steals my breath and makes my skin vibrate over my bones is the scar. Thin and silver in the shape of a crescent moon and attached to the hand of a man whose face I couldn't make out in Sutton's photo but see clear as day now.

"Oh my God."

The rest of the stack falls away, landing in a messy heap at my feet, and I slip on them as I rush over to my desk, clutching the only one that matters to my chest. My outburst has, of course, drawn the atten-tion of the men in the room. They're on me in an instant, large bodies curved over my desk and crouching by my chair, wild eyes watching my fingers fly across the keyboard.

Cal gazes up at me from his perch on the floor. "What is it?"

Beck scoops up the photo I've left beside the keyboard, onyx eyes roving over the photo trying to see what I saw. "Did you find something?"

"Please, just hold on a second."

They both go quiet, barely breathing while I click through several pages of Google links looking for the article I need. It's buried deep. I should have been more specific with the search terms, but I wasn't thinking straight. I don't even think I spelled his name right. Glancing up, I see there are three f's in officer instead of two and an extra 'l' in his last name. None of it matters though, because after just a few minutes, I've found it. The article published just over a week after AJ died, the one that shows Officer Travis Langham in his dress blues standing next to me and Aubrey at our son's funeral. I'd remembered it as the one with the clearest view of his face, and I was right.

It's him.

The officer who stood on the other side of a line of caution tape and told me my son was gone is the same man in the photo Beck is holding. With a few clicks of my mouse, I pull up the email Sutton's dad sent, opening the image he showed me that day in his home. I refused to take it then, but I'm glad I have it now because it's a tangible link between Aubrey, Sutton and Sanders.

I fall back into my chair, staring blankly at the screen until Cal and Beck block it out with their bodies, and I'm left with no choice but to look somewhere else.

"He didn't have the scar back then," I mumble, studying the skin on the top of my right hand while they compare the man in the photo they're holding to the ones on the screen.

"It's definitely him," Cal confirms. He glances at me over his shoulder. "How well do you know this Langham character?"

"He was the officer in charge of the scene at Beaumont High. I haven't seen him since the funeral. I don't know him at all."

"But you did," Beck insists, shifting around to sit on the edge of my desk. Cal mirrors his stance, and suddenly I'm the subject of an interrogation. They don't mean for it to come across that way, I know, but it still does. It's their expectant gazes and perked ears open and ready to receive information I don't have to give. It's the questions that roll into each other.

Did Aubrey and Langham seem friendly?

Did he ever mention Langham in the years after AJ's death?

Do you think it's strange Langham is the only thread outside of Aubrey connecting three separate instances of suspicious deaths?

That one gives me pause. I hold my hand up to stop them both from speaking.

"Three?" I shake my head, ticking the names off on my fingers. "Sutton and Sanders. Those are the only suspicious deaths we've connected Langham to."

I don't miss it. The pity that passes between them or the silent conversation that happens after they've tucked it away that determines who's going to say the hard thing to me. Beck's lips part on a sigh, and I want to stop him, to tell him he doesn't need to say it because the connection has already been formed in my mind. It's been there since Beck lectured me about looking at everything with fresh eyes, but I've refused to acknowledge it, to give any credence to the idea that my son's name belongs on that murder board.

"Selene," Beck starts, Adam's apple bobbing when he swallows. "We have to consider the possibility…"

No part of me is able to sit here and withstand this. I stand suddenly, storming out of the room with tears clouding my vision. They don't stop me from seeing anything, but when I run into Monique in the hallway just outside my office with Isis and Imani in tow, they are a little blurry. I stop short, put off by Monique's sudden appearance and the fact that Imani and Isis are still here when they were supposed to be picked up over an hour ago.

"Hey!" I force a smile, hoping to ease the tension lining both girls' shoulders. "What are you two still doing here?"

Isis throws herself into my arms, and Mo's eyes stretch wide when I hug her back instead of cringing or shying away. The truth is, I wouldn't deny either of these girls anything, especially the physical affection I'm sure they're not getting at home.

"Mama Jo is running late," she explains, voice muffled because her face is in my chest.

Monique gives me a look that suggest there's more to the story. Imani is happy to provide that context, crossing her arms over her chest and pursing her lips.

"She forgot about us."

Isis twists around, breaking our embrace. "No, she didn't! When Ms. Monique called her, she said she was on the way."

"That was an hour ago, dummy. We only live twenty minutes away."

"An hour?" I aim my confusion in Monique's direction. "Why didn't you come get me?"

"Because you were occupied, girl." She waggles her brows, and I roll my eyes. I texted her earlier to let her know Cal and Beck were on the premises, and she's been making inappropriate jokes through text all day.

"We were working."

"Sureeee," she drawls teasingly, making the girls giggle.

Ignoring her childish antics, I turn back towards my office doors and wave a hand for them to follow. "Come in and sit down. I'll see if I can get Joanna on the phone."

Cal and Beck are shocked by me reappearing with company in tow, but they adjust easily. We make a silent agreement to revisit the conversation I walked out on the moment they see Monique, Isis and Imani behind me, and I couldn't be more grateful for that.

"Oh, y'all have been busy," Mo exclaims, taking in the mess we've made of my office.

Imani looks around too, her interest clearly piqued. She starts to creep over to the conference table where Sanders's autopsy is sitting on the top of a pile with the word CONFIDENTIAL written in bright red letters. I open my mouth to tell her to stop, but Beck swoops in first, managing to keep his distance and avoid startling her even as he puts himself between her and the table.

She jerks back, glaring slightly at him, and my heart starts to sink. I didn't realize it until this very moment, but I really want Isis and Imani to get along with Cal and Beck. I had the same desire with them and Monique, and they hit it off instantly, but I know it won't always be that simple when it comes to bringing people together from different parts of my world.

Imani hooks a thumb in Beck's direction, eyes bouncing from him to Isis. "Did this man just hit the Naruto run?"

Isis snorts. "He really did!"

"Like he was using Flying Raijin," Cal quips, laughing when Beck flips him off. Pretty soon, all four of them are lost in a conversation about the fastest characters in anime while Cal and Beck clear the table, and Monique and I stand by the desk, completely lost.

"Well, that's sexy as hell," she whispers.

"What?"

"Them being good with kids."

"Yeah," I muse, catching glimpses of a future I didn't plan for or even know I wanted in the laughter and easy conversation flowing between four people who were just perfect strangers.

                                20

                             SELENE

It happens six more times.

Joanna missing pick up by hours and refusing to answer the phone when the girls or I call. Hours will pass in the wake of her silence, and then eventually she'll show up without so much as an apology or an excuse, blowing her horn and rushing Isis and Imani into the car she refuses to get out of. Each time it happens, I watch Isis go from calm and relaxed to anxious and soothing, apologizing for taking too long, while Imani goes from cracking jokes to clenching her jaw to avoid saying something that might further break what her sister is trying to fix.

The first night it happened, I wanted to snatch Joanna out of her car and ask what the hell was wrong with her. Cal and Beck stopped me, and because they've taken it upon themselves to act as my personal security now that I have no protective detail, they've been there to stop me from confronting the woman over the last month and a half as well, but there's no one on Earth who can stop me from giving her a piece of my mind tonight.

All four people in the car with me know that.

Cal is driving, his hand on my thigh in an attempt to calm the storm brewing inside of me. Beck is in the back with the girls, his long legs bumping against the console because he let them talk him into getting in the middle. He has to be uncomfortable, but he hasn't uttered a word of complaint or attempted to shift a muscle because there's a head of a sleeping child resting on each of his shoulders.

It's a beautiful picture, a groundbreaking display of the trust that he, Cal and I have worked our asses off to earn from Isis and Imani, and I can't even appreciate it because I'm too busy counting down the minutes until we arrive at Joanna's house. I don't know if Beck is fully appreciating it either, or if the heartwarming image has even registered on Cal's radar, because they're both preoccupied with monitoring my energy.

"I'm not going to say anything that doesn't need to be said," I whisper, not wanting to wake the girls because they've had a long day. We attended a code-a-thon put on by Representative Reed. He convinced his fellow Virginia reps to invite the children in their districts who were also participating in the CAC, so they could have one last hurrah before the school year begins. The day started at eight this morning and went until five this evening, so my company provided catered meals, volunteers to guide and support the students, and transportation to and from the venue for everyone who needed it.

Overall, it was a great day.

Some of our parents didn't feel comfortable having their kids using the provided transportation and asked to pick their kids up from the office, so we brought them back to Culture Code. By seven o'clock, everyone was gone except for Isis and Imani. As usual, we brought them back up to my office, so they could have somewhere comfortable to wait for their foster mom. Tonight, the girls whooped Cal and Beck's asses at some video game while I ordered dinner and considered the wisdom of letting them set up a gaming console in my office.

It was nice. For a minute.

And it always goes that way. The shared excitement of having a few more minutes with them. The laughter and meals and trash talking. The far too familiar feel of family that had deserted me when my son died. It's a lovely little bubble to lose yourself in, but it only lasts for so long. Most of the time, I pop it on my own, forcing myself to call

Joanna or shoot her a text just so I can tell anyone who asks that I did my due diligence, that I did everything in my power to return the girls I've grown to love to the person who can't seem to bother to even care for them.

When I pop the bubble, it's only a matter of time before everyone else comes tumbling out of the sky behind me. Cal and Beck always hit the ground first, adjusting easily because they know what it's like to have to let go of things you really want to hold on to. Then it's Isis, who lands on her feet but wobbles a little bit, her balance weighed down by the misplaced shame of being neglected. Imani is the last to let go. She always waits until the fall is inevitable, until the edges of our shared dream disintegrate between her fingertips, sending her plummeting to the ground where, probably for the first time in a long time, someone other than her sister is waiting to catch her.

Though, necessary, the cycle is cruel and completely unavoidable. *That* is what I'm going to say to Joanna. What I'm going to try my level best to explain in a way that won't lead to her pulling the girls out of the coding academy, that won't result in her taking them away from me forever because they need me, and for whatever reason, I need them as well.

"Maybe you shouldn't say anything at all," Cal hedges quietly. "The girls need rest, not to be caught up in an argument between you and their foster mom."

Beck's gaze snags on mine in the rearview mirror, and I can tell he agrees. I fold my arms, hating the fact that they're so calm and reasonable when I feel like I could tear the roof off that lady's house with my bare hands.

"It's almost eleven," I hiss, pointing at the time displayed on the screen in Cal's dashboard. "She didn't even bother to answer the phone this time. She hasn't read any of Imani's messages. Isis looked at her location, and it said she's at home. What kind of person, what kind of *mother*, sits at home twiddling her fucking thumbs while her kids are calling and texting her asking when she's going to pick them up?"

A muscle in Cal's jaw jumps. "I hear you, Sel. When my dad used to pull shit like this, my mom would be furious too. She'd pull me in off the porch, help me unpack my bag, fix me a snack and then leave me in the living room with cartoons playing to mask the sound of her cursing him out over the phone."

My chest feels like it might cave in. That's how angry I am, for Isis and Imani and now for little Cal. Nick Drake better be glad he's dead, or else he would be on my shit list right next to Joanna.

"You deserved better than that," I say softly, laying my hand over the one he has resting on my thigh. He flips his over, pressing his palm to mine.

"I know, and I know they deserve better too. I'm just asking you to consider if going off on Joanna is the best way to make sure they get it."

He glances at me as he pulls in front of a red brick house with a small front porch, blue shutters and a white front door. The porch light is on, illuminating the numbers on the door that match the address listed in the girls' file. Another bead of agitation rolls down my spine at that. My mama only ever left the porch light on when one of us was out somewhere that she wouldn't be retrieving us from. Seeing it here, and now, makes me feel like Joanna was never planning to be a part of Isis and Imani's journey home, and when she opens the door in a robe with her hair tied up, that theory is confirmed.

The girls are in front of me, with Cal and Beck standing at my back, and she eyes us all with narrowed eyes and a curled lip. "What have I told y'all about bringing strangers to my house?"

"Mama Jo, we—" Isis starts, but I put a hand on her shoulder to silence her.

Remembering Cal's words, I force a calm and kindness I don't feel into my voice when I speak. "Joanna, please don't be angry with the girls. We insisted on bringing them home. It wasn't our intention to invade your privacy."

And we wouldn't have had to if you had answered your damn phone.

Those words don't leave my mouth, but I feel like she can see them bouncing around my head. She purses her lips and leans against the door jamb, blocking the girls from entering.

"Hmmph."

That's it. That's her entire response. Frustration claws at my chest, and I push out a breath, trying to expel it from my body.

"Are you going to let us in?" Imani asks, voice coated in sleep and sass.

It's a sensible question, but Joanna glares at her like she's just demanded access to the moon and all the stars in the sky instead of the house she's lived in for years now.

"What time is your curfew, Imani?"

The girls look at each other, confusion radiating between their bodies.

"Ten," Imani grumbles.

"And what happens when you miss curfew, Isis?" Joanna asks.

Although the line of questioning makes no sense, I wait for Isis to answer, needing to know what the punishment for the crime they haven't committed is.

Isis's gaze drops to her feet. "We have to spend the night wherever we were."

"That's right, so as of," Joanna glances at her watching, noting the time. "An hour and two minutes ago, your access to my house was revoked for the night."

My jaw drops as a shocked and angry scoff sounds behind me. I'm not sure if it's from Cal or Beck, but it draws Joanna's attention. She leans to the side, looking around me and the girls to the men at our backs. When she returns to her former stance, there's something nasty dancing in her eyes.

"Oh, I see," she says, waving a finger between Isis and Imani. "Y'all been out being grown, huh? And where do you fit in this?" That question is directed at me, and she takes delight in my offense. "You get off on watching little girls with grown men?"

I push the girls to the side, needing them out of the way so I can get in Joanna's face. A flicker of fear pierces the cloud of loathing around her when I invade her personal space, all thoughts of decorum out the window because of that disgusting allegation.

"What the fuck is wrong with you?"

"Does the press know you speak that way in front of children, *Madame First Lady?*"

The title falls from her lips and hits the ground, dripping with censure and an unsuccessful attempt to dangle the press over my head. I laugh, dragging my tongue over my teeth before I lean in even more, close enough now that I'm able to smell the alcohol on her breath.

"Is that your attempt at threatening me? I live under constant scrutiny, Joanna. There are cameras around me at all times and lies written about me for no reason almost every day. The world finding out that I cursed at you after you accused me and the men kind enough to bring home the children who have been entrusted to your care child molesters wouldn't even stay in the news cycle for a full twenty-four hours. You know what would stick? Maybe not in the press, but at the very least with the Department of Social Services? The story of a foster mom repeatedly abandoning her foster daughters and refusing to let them into her home after she got too drunk to come and pick them up from an event that's been on their schedule for weeks now."

She rears back. "I'm not drunk!"

Of course, that's the only part of my statement she deigns to respond to. Unsurprised, I glance over her shoulder, noting the presence of a half empty bottle of vodka on the coffee table, and then look back to her, arching a brow but saying nothing else on the topic.

"You're going to let them in this house, Joanna. And you are never going to so much as suggest that they have come to any harm while in my care because unlike you, I would die before I let anything happen to them."

Her jaw works, the desire to respond evident in the flare of her nostrils. I tilt my head to the side, daring her to utter another word, to do anything but step aside and let the girls in. When she does, Isis and Imani let out a collective sigh and step forward, waving goodnight to Cal and Beck before giving me hugs I wish lasted longer.

"I'll see you next week," I call out to them as they disappear down the dark hall. It's as much a promise to them as it is a warning to Joanna that her disliking me won't get in the way of my relationship with the girls or all the things they're learning through the coding academy.

Joanna puts her hand on the door, starting to close it even though I'm still standing in the doorway. I step back, letting her have this small win because it's really all she's got.

"And I'll see you too," I tell her. "At the allotted pick up time, not a second later."

Malice warps her features, turning them into a mask of hate. "You're not helping them, you know."

"What?"

"Isis and Imani, you're not helping them. All this coddling you're doing and all these dreams you're feeding them about going to college and having fancy jobs and big paychecks is just hurting them. They need to know that life is hard and this world is harder."

"They've lost their home, their brother and their mom all before they hit puberty. You don't think they know that life is hard?"

"I think every time they go to your office, they forget what it's like to live in the real world. They come in here talking and acting like they're better than me, too good for the house I raised them in, for the food I feed them and the clothes I put on their back."

"And you leaving them stranded and refusing to answer the phone for hours on end is what? Payback?"

She shrugs. "I just want them to see what it's going to be like for them when I'm not around. It's an important lesson for them to learn before they age out of the system and have to go into the real world with nothing and no one."

"That won't ever happen."

"Yes, it will. It happened to me, and every other kid I know that grew up in foster care. Isis and Imani aren't special, girl. The same thing is going to happen to them, and when it does, they'll wish they had listened to me instead of believing all the shit you're putting in their heads."

"Everything I've told them about what their lives can be has been rooted in truth and based on my observation of their skills and work ethic. They are exceptional girls, Joanna, and they are better than you in every way. The sad, miserable life you lead could never be their future. I would never let that happen."

"You're talking like you planning on sticking around or something."

"That's the first thing you've gotten right all night, Joanna." I bring both hands together, treating her to the applause she seems so desperate for. "You might not care enough to see them past a certain point, but I have no intention of ever walking away from them. As long as they want me in their lives, I'll be there."

It's a sacred vow. One I've sworn without consulting the people it centers around or the men I plan to spend my life with. And still, the words only feel right coming out of my mouth. A truth that tastes like destiny. A pledge that scares the fuck out of Joanna and leads to her slamming the door in my face. A promise that could shake the foundation of what Cal, Beck and I are trying to build.

I turn to face them, heart pounding and sticky tendrils of fear wrapping around my insides because we never discussed dedicating ourselves to anyone but each other. They both stare at me, and I'm hit with the memory of standing on another porch being held in their gazes. This time, there's no Aubrey and no pretense, only the open channels of love flowing freely and resolute expressions that tell me nothing I've said to Joanna scares them because they adore those two girls as much as I do.

21

BECK

"And how does that make you feel?"

The most well known therapy question slips past Dr. Pike's lips with ease, and I can't stop myself from laughing. She gives me an odd look, gazing heavenward to recall the last thing she said. Then she cringes and laughs too.

"Sometimes there's just no avoiding the classics," she says, smiling. "And I still need an answer."

We were discussing Selene's argument with Joanna, particularly the way it ended, before I got distracted. I take a second to gather my thoughts, making sure that my answer is thorough and truthful while still maintaining the privacy of Selene and the girls. So far, I've only mentioned Cal by name in our sessions, and I'll keep it that way for the foreseeable future. I trust Dr. Pike, but I can't have my romantic involvement with Selene documented in any way because I don't know who might have access to her files. Especially the ones in her home office where she sees clients who aren't employed by the federal government.

Just looking around, I can spot several ways someone would half a brain could get in and out of here undetected. She follows my gaze around the room. "Something wrong?"

"You should really think about upgrading your security system," I say, smoothing my hands over the fabric of my sweats.

Dr. Pike frowns. "I'll consider that. Let's stay on topic, though, Lance. Your partner expressed a desire to establish an ongoing relationship with these girls. This means that they will be a part of your life as well, might even require you to act as something of a paternal figure to them to some degree. That's a big commitment for her to make without first discussing it with you and Cal. Tell me what you were feeling."

I think back to that moment. It's been a week, but I still remember the steel infused in Selene's words. The fear in her eyes when she turned around and looked at me and Cal, clearly worried that she'd promised more than we'd be willing to give. The hugs she gave us when we told her that we'd been talking about the future and what it might look like to have a family. The hope we all felt at the thought of potentially building that family around two amazing kids like Isis and Imani.

"Excited," I admit, pulse kicking up a bit. "And scared."

"Fear is understandable. The girls seem to have a complicated home life."

"Their foster mom is….something."

Joanna's suggestion that Cal and I were…I can't say the words, can't even think them, that's how fucking sick they make me. When I was done being angry though, I felt kind of sad for Joanna. She said she grew up in foster care too. I can only imagine what kind of horrors she must have lived through to have such a warped view of the world. Still, it doesn't give her the right to draw conclusions like that about me or Cal.

"Do you think she'll pose a threat to the bond you and your partners are trying to establish with the girls?"

"Absolutely."

There's not a bit of doubt in my mind about that. Joanna has been dealt a bad hand, and she can't imagine an outcome for Isis and Imani that's any different than her current reality. Because of that, she's determined to keep them from anything and anyone that might bring them any joy or hope.

Dr. Pike's brows raise like her interest has been piqued by my certainty. I'm prepared to elaborate, but then she shifts in her seat, signifying a change in subject. "Is the fear you feel rooted in the potential obstacle? Or is it related to something else?"

I fight the urge to analyze, to look past the brick she's just laid in my path in search of the destination. That's the hardest part of therapy for me, staying present and being mindful. I'm always putting the outcome before the process, trying to mold my answers to fit whatever point I think Dr. Pike is trying to make instead of just answering honestly and letting the chips fall where they may.

"Mostly, the obstacle." I say. "I'm worried about what it might do to my partner if the foster mom doesn't allow her to see the girls anymore. That's a real possibility since legally she's not obligated to do so. My partner would be devastated though. She loves those girls. We all do."

The words feel almost foreign on my tongue, but they're true. Imani and Isis are easy to love, innocent in that way children are but also full of wisdom that reflects the pain and loss they've experienced too early in life.

She nods. "Those are valid concerns. Let's imagine for a second that it all works out. The foster mother is not an issue. The girls are in the care of you and your partners. What fears come up for you then?"

Knowing it helps me envision things, I allow my eyes to fall shut and breathe, listening for the honest answer to her question. "Normal things like if I'm doing a good job and setting a good example. If I'm too hard on them or too impatient. If they know that I only want what's best for them. If the love we give them will be enough to heal whatever has been broken in them."

"Good," she says, voice soft. "And beyond that? Are there any concerns about worthiness? Any doubts about whether you deserve this life with your partners and the girls?"

If I would have followed my original desire to try and map the conversation, I would have known that we were going to end up here. Because I didn't, I'm a little caught off guard. I shouldn't be, though. We've been doing this work since I returned to therapy, following the thread that started with my belief that I am a monster all the way back to being given up by my birth parents. Apparently, I'd internalized that early trauma, allowing it and the neglect and abuse that followed to make me believe I was unlovable. Some bad, broken, monstrous thing that was rotten from the start.

From that point on, every loss, every hurt, everything I did and even the things that were done to me became proof of that fact. I've held tight to that belief for so long, allowing it to send me into spirals of shame and feelings of unworthiness. Once we unpacked that, Dr. Pike introduced EMDR into our sessions, walking me through reprocessing specific memories related to the negative belief so we could install new, positive ones. I reach for that belief now, holding tight to the affirming words that tell me I deserve good things.

"Some," I admit, knowing better than to lie and pretend I'm fully healed. "But those thoughts aren't louder than the love."

A smile curves my lips, and I open my eyes, watching Dr. Pike watch me. "Diana used to say that," I tell her. "She'd get mad at me for something and still want to hold my hand or cook dinner together. I could never understand it. When I asked her why, she'd just smile and say 'the anger isn't louder than the love'."

I rub at my chest as a pang of fondness hits me. "God, I miss that woman."

"Do you find yourself thinking of her and Cameron more or less often now?"

"I think of them every day. They never leave me."

"That's not in question. I asked if you think of them more now that you're on the verge of building this new life with your partners and, potentially, these young ladies you've all grown to care for." She crosses her legs, assessing me. I'm sure she sees the discomfort knotting my muscles. "There's no right or wrong answer here, Lance."

"So, it would be okay if I said it's less?"

"As long as it's true," she says.

"It is." I swallow, feeling sick to my stomach. "That doesn't feel right, though."

"Why not?"

"Because it feels like I'm forgetting, and I don't get to do that."

"*Is* that what you're doing? In the last few minutes, you've shared something of your wife that I'm going to take into my own marriage and told me that you think of her and your son every day. That doesn't sound like forgetting to me."

"But it's not like it was before," I protest. "I used to spend hours lost in memories of Dianna or daydreams of Cameron. Now, I get so caught up in Cal and Sel—" I follow the rest of the syllables in Selene's name and start again. "In Cal and our other partner, the challenges we're facing and the life we want to have together. It feels like forgetting."

"Or maybe it's simply moving on."

"Isn't that the same thing?"

"No, Lance, it's not. Forgetting would mean wiping them from your mind. It would mean you don't think of them at all, and you've just told me that isn't true. What you're doing is crafting a life for yourself that honors new love while holding space for the love that's been lost. That is a beautiful, brave thing to do, and you shouldn't feel guilty about that, only proud."

* * *

AN HOUR LATER, I'm standing shoulder-to-shoulder in the packed deli Selene is currently obsessed with to pick up the lunch order I called in for me, her, Cal and Monique *before* I made the thirty minute drive across town from Dr. Pike's office. I was hoping to beat the lunch hour rush, but apparently it started early today. It was packed when I walked in here, but I was lucky enough to grab a spot right by the door, which is where I've been for the last thirty minutes, turning the pearl of wisdom the good doctor gave me before the session ended over in my mind. Her even tone and genuine expression left me with no choice but to believe she was being sincere, but I'm still having trouble accepting her assessment.

"Order for Beckham!"

Eager to get out of the crowded space, I rush to the counter, grab the food and drop a tip in the jar at the register for the clearly over-worked staff. I push through the crowd, sorting through the bodies that stepped into the space I cleared when I approached, and find myself face-to-face with Mason Woodard and Patrick Garrison. I only know their first names because Agent Shaw sent us the internal memo that went out about their 'promotion' just before her access to her email was revoked.

They're dressed for work, but Aubrey would never come this far out for lunch, and if he was around the entire block would be shut down. Neither of them seem to recognize me at first, so for a second, we're just staring at each other. Me, seething and murderous. Them, entitled, mediocre and confused.

"Can we help you?" Garrison asks. He's taller than his counterpart with blonde hair that hugs his scalp.

Woodard sizes me up and then grins, bumping Garrison with his elbow. "It's one of the boys we had to throw out of the White House on their ass. Which one are you? Beckham or Drake?"

"I'm the one who'll put his foot up your ass if you keep talking."

Garrison whoops loudly, drawing the attention of the other customers. "You hear that, Woody? Fucker thinks he can handle us both all on his own. You couldn't even take us when your sorry ass partner was around."

"Let's step outside and see."

He balks, clearly expecting me to be intimidated by being outnum-bered. Cal being here would certainly make it easier to lay them both out, but his absence doesn't impact my confidence nor my ability to do so. Garrison tries to step forward, but Woodard stops him with an arm across his chest, shaking his head in warning.

"Not here. Not now."

I look between them, smiling when Garrison steps back. "Soon," I promise him, bumping his shoulder on my way out the door.

When I get to my car, I'm still put off by their appearance. I don't know anything about the men, but they hardly seem the type to be wearing suits in the middle of August when they don't have to. Thinking back to the discussion Selene, Cal, and I had about their spots in the Service being funded by someone other than Aubrey, I decide to do a mini stake out and see if they'll lead me to the unidentified benefactor.

They emerge from the deli twenty minutes after me, climbing into a sleek, black Audi with DC plates. I snap pictures from afar even though I've already committed the plate to memory, making sure to capture the two assholes getting into the vehicle so the link between them and whoever owns the car is concrete. When they pull away from the curb, I wait a beat before following and then get into the same lane they're in, just a few cars behind.

As we approach a stoplight, my phone starts to ring. I use the button on my steering wheel to accept the call, smiling even though Cal's about to rip me a new one for taking so long with lunch.

"I know. I know. I should have been there already, but I ran into Garrison and Woodard and—"

"*Beck.*"

The smile falls off my face immediately. "What's wrong?"

Any thoughts of following the lead that fell into my lap were pushed to the side the moment I heard the graveness in his tone, but when Cal starts speaking, detailing the development of an old threat finding fresh life while we were focused on untangling the web that is Aubrey Taylor, they dissolve completely.

All that's left is the familiar clang of metal dropping into place. The grinding of gears. The churning of an engine. The awakening of a machine made for destruction. The pending promise of certain doom.

22

CAL

"*Marsh, who went viral earlier this year in a video where he can be seen blaming First Lady Selene Taylor for her role in his son's death, was one of fifteen prisoners unaccounted for after a riot broke out at the federal prison in Florence, Colorado yesterday afternoon. While all the other inmates were eventually found and returned back to their cells, Marsh has yet to be located...*"

Beck presses the power button on the side of the flat screen TV as he walks by, phone in one hand while the other sweeps over his bare scalp over and over again. He's been trying to wear a hole in the floor ever since he got here. I understand his need to move, to do something to work off the anxious energy bursting out of him and spilling into the room. I want to be moving too, but ever since the news of Marsh's escape broke, Selene has refused to leave my arms.

She wasn't afraid at first, watching the breaking news story with a distant kind of interest as she worked through compiling a list of people who could afford to pay off the Director of the Secret Service, but when they showed the video from earlier this year and followed it up with footage of Marsh's cell, she wandered over to the couch she ordered when the girls talked her into putting an Xbox in her office and sat down beside me, inching closer and closer as the broadcast went on, showing the pictures of her papering one of the cell walls. By the time the cameraman got around to zooming in on the ones with the eyes carved out or half the face slashed through, she was pressed into my side.

That's when I called Beck.

I didn't need him to do any particular thing besides be here, but from the moment he walked through the door, he's been in constant motion. Calling everyone we know, including the warden of Leland's prison to figure out what the fuck happened. Of course, Bennett stonewalled him, but he took the punch and kept right on rolling, ending the call and moving on to some of our contacts in the FBI. So far, no one has been able to give him anything useful.

"Fuck!" He tosses his phone on the end table next to the couch, and Selene jumps. His entire demeanor changes. "I'm sorry, gorgeous," he murmurs, sinking into the cushion beside her and scooting in close.

"It's okay," Selene says, slipping out of my hold to move into his open arms. I stand, grateful for the opportunity to get my blood flowing so I can think. Selene watches me, her expression flat. "Are you two going to take turns pacing?"

"Maybe," Beck replies, pressing his nose into her hair. It's grown out now. The blunt ends of the bob she sported in January now soft layers that frame her face and graze the top of her back.

"Is it bothering you?" I ask, not wanting to add to her stress.

She nuzzles into Beck's chest. "No, I don't care as long as someone is holding me."

"Perks of having two boyfriends," Monique muses, breezing into the room without knocking. She's been in and out of the office since the news broke, fielding questions from staff and briefing security on the situation. Perching on the arm of the couch, she looks at Selene and Beck and sighs dreamily. "I have *got* to get me a man."

My favorite thing about Monique is her ability to make Selene smile in just about any situation. This one is no different. Her random, and ill timed, comment pulls some of the tension out of the air, replacing it with humor for just a second. She looks at me and winks, silently communicating that that was her intention all along.

"Any word on Marsh?"

I shake my head. "Nothing but what's already circulating on the news. Beck put some feelers out, but no one's talking."

"And we're certain he's coming for her?"

Selene raises a limp arm, waving it in the air. "Hello? I'm right here. If you're going to talk about me, you might as well talk *to* me."

Monique's head swivels in her direction. "Okay, do we know for sure that Marsh is coming for *you*, Selene?"

The color that had faded from Selene's sable skin earlier is starting to come back. I guess she needed a little verbal sparring session to pull her out of the state of shock. She tries to sit up, but the muscles in Beck's arm flex, indicating his refusal to let her go. With a sigh, she relaxes into him again.

"No, we can't be certain about that, *Monique*," she says, emphasizing her best friend's full name. To my knowledge, she never calls her by it unless she's annoyed with her or truly upset.

"Okay, so maybe we don't need to worry. For all we know, the man could be sipping Mai Tais in one of those countries we don't have an extradition treaty with and laughing because everyone was too busy checking under the beds of the White House for him while he was crossing the boarder."

It's a pleasant thought, truly it is, but I know Leland Marsh. I looked into his eyes and heard the vitriol in his voice when he told us that he'd rain hell down on all of us if something happened to his son. Now Jacob is dead, and he's stolen his freedom back. I'd bet my last dollar that he's planning on using this time to make good on that promise.

Monique splits a woeful gaze between me and Beck, reading our faces easily. "Wishful thinking, huh?"

I nod. "Running would be the smart thing to do, but I've never met a man in the Marsh family that's been acquainted with common sense."

"Ohhh. Can I use that?" Monique asks. We all look at her like she's lost her mind, and she frowns. "What? I'm always looking for new ways to call men stupid."

"Can you be serious for once in your life, Mo?"

"Girl, it's serious enough in here. I'm trying to keep everyone off the train to death and despair." Selene narrows her eyes, and Monique rolls hers, conceding. "Fine. I'll be serious."

She squares her shoulders and sits up even straighter, aiming a severe look in my direction.

"I've authorized overtime for our security team indefinitely. They've all agreed to work around the clock, but Dean wants to know if we'll give the okay for him to bring in contractors."

Beck shakes his head. "No. We don't have time to properly vet or train them."

"That's what I told him you'd say," Monique says, pulling out her phone and typing out a message. "I'll let him know it's a no go."

"Thanks, Mo."

She waves Selene's expression of gratitude off, moving on to the next thing. "Mama J keeps calling me. She's mad that you're not answering your phone. I told her Cal and Beck were taking care of you, but she'll want to hear from you sooner rather than later."

Once again, Selene tries to escape Beck's grasp, and once again, he denies her.

"I need to find my phone, Beck."

"You said you needed to be held," he reminds her. "Monique just said she spoke to your parents. They're fine. We can call them once we're somewhere safe and have a plan in place."

She starts to protest, but I cut her off. "He's right. If you call them now, they'll just have a million questions you don't have the answers to, which will add to your stress."

A resigned sigh passes through her lips as I try to read her. I know that she's afraid, but there's also this eerie kind of calm around her that makes me think she's dissociating a little. I can't tell if it's an intentionally deployed protective measure or a subconscious result of lingering shock, but it worries me.

"So, what's the plan?" she asks, lashes fluttering as she blinks up at me.

"You can't go back to the White House."

Her brows dip together. "Don't be ridiculous. I can't just disappear. Aubrey—"

"Who gives a fuck about Aubrey?" Monique interjects.

"He threatened to have me killed, Mo. He told Cal and Beck if we continued our relationship, he'd make sure one of the awful things people fantasize about doing to me online became a reality."

"Girl, these men have been here with you every day for almost two months. I'm sure he already knows that you're still involved."

"He came right out and said it the day we got fired," Beck says. "I don't know if we were on his radar before that, but when we came into the room, that was all the confirmation he needed."

"But this would be different," Selene argues, finally managing to break free of his hold so she can stand. "This would be giving him the ammunition he needs to load a gun and point it in my direction. In *our* direction."

I approach her with slow cautious steps, grabbing her chin to make her face me. "You loaded the gun when you accused him of murdering his mistress, Selene. Taking away your security detail was him clicking off the safety. For all we know, Marsh was the bullet waiting in the chamber, and Aubrey just pulled the trigger."

Fear flickers in her irises, but she's following my logic. "He wants me dead."

"He wants you dead," I confirm, tightening my grasp marginally when her chin starts to wobble. "But he won't get to have that, baby. We will keep you safe until you have everything you need to fucking destroy him, and when it's done, when you've vanquished every demon and slain every dragon, we will build a life so beautiful, so full of happiness, you'll forget you ever spent a single second being afraid."

She closes her eyes, letting the words soak into her skin. When she opens them again, the fear is gone, replaced by the fire of determination. It's the most she's looked like herself in hours, and I'm glad to have her back. I lower my hand, setting her free to do whatever it is she needs to do right now.

Move.

Sit.

Pace.

Hover.

Curl into a ball.

To my surprise, she goes to sit behind her desk, clasping her fingers together, signaling to us that she's ready to get down to business. Between the four of us, we're able to develop a plan fairly quickly. Monique calls one of her many exes, this one a New York based real estate tycoon with properties up and down the East Coast. With a few giggles and a vague promise to let him take her out to dinner the next time he's in town, she's got several options for us to choose from. We go with a secluded estate in Bethesda that was once owned by a paranoid recluse who paid a pretty penny to turn the property into a fortress.

With the largest problem out of the way, we divide the rest of the tasks among ourselves. Selene steps away to call her parents. Beck volunteers to take Monique by her place as well as Aubrey and Selene's home in McLean to pack clothes. Both women are annoyed to learn that we're in the habit of keeping go bags for both of us in each of our cars, so there's no need for us to return home.

While everyone is off doing what's necessary to disappear from their lives at a moment's notice, I drop into Selene's desk chair and call Hunter. For some reason, my heart rate kicks up as I wait for the call to connect. It's not until he answers and I bypass a greeting to blurt the words out, that I realize why.

"I need a favor."

The pause on his end of the line tells me he's just as shocked as I am by what I've just said. Never in the history of our lives have I asked Hunter for a favor. Because of his history with addiction and the strain our asshole of a father put on our relationship, I've never known or trusted him enough to do so. But today I need something only he can give.

"What is it?"

Selene walks slow laps around the room, whispering urgently to her mother. I track her steps, counting how many it takes to get her from the head of the conference table where we shared our first meal to the window that displays the city below us.

"Cal?" Hunter asks, pulling me out of my head. "You still there?"

"Yeah." I clear my throat, averting my gaze from the lovely and distracting creature I'm currently sharing air with.

"What did you need?"

"We've got a, uh, developing situation here."

"You're talking about the Marsh thing? It's been all over the news. They said he's coming for the First Lady. Is that true?"

"We don't know yet, but we're taking precautions."

Another pause. This one a little longer than the last. "We? Did you get your job back?"

I snort, humor laced frustration running through me. "No, but Beck and I are still handling the situation, just in a more personal capacity."

"In a more personal capacity," he says, like repeating the words will help him decipher their meaning. Apparently, it does because in seconds the slow drawl of realization is filling the line. *"Ohhhh."*

"Yeah, so I—"

"Does Beck know?!"

"Of course, Hunter. He's…they're…we're all together."

"Shit," he says, and I imagine him rubbing his head in confusion. "That sounds…complicated. She's married to the President, Cal."

I pinch the bridge of my nose. "I'm aware. Just like I'm sure you were aware that Rae was in a committed relationship when she fell back in love with you."

"She never fell out of love with me, asshole," he snaps, and then in a softer, amused tone, he says, "I guess we are our father's sons."

"Dad cheated on his wives. We're just stealing other people's," I muse, enjoying the inappropriate exchange more than I should.

"Rae wasn't married when we got back together."

"She was engaged."

"For two damn seconds," he retorts. "Are you going to tell me what you called for or are we just going to keep commiserating about being homewreckers?"

Needing to get him off the line before we start arguing about whether or not homewrecker is the right term for us, I give him the rundown on the Marsh situation and ask him to put me in touch with the guy he used to work security with so I can make sure Selene's parents, siblings and their families are protected. Men like Marsh and Aubrey tend to thrive in your blind spots, and I'm determined to make sure we don't have any. I've already gotten Dean to agree to keep an eye on Isis and Imani from a distance, so if Hunter comes through for me on this, we'll be well on our way to safeguarding all our vulnerabilities.

"It'll be quicker if I call him," Hunter says. "Russ will make sure they're straight."

My brother's confidence in his friend and former supervisor's willingness to help is all I need. I breathe a sigh of relief, knowing Selene's family will be safe, then steel myself to a final set of requests, one I know Hunter will buck against.

"Does he have enough men to cover you, Riley and Rae? I'd also need someone on Beck's mother-in-law, Erin."

"Of course, we can make sure Erin is good, but I've got Riley and Rae."

"Hunter."

"Cal."

"I just want you safe."

"And I will be. You make sure you are."

The office door opens, and Beck and Monique appear moments later. I sigh, knowing I don't have time to push Hunter further on this.

"I've gotta go. Take care of yourself," I order, heart twisting in on itself at the thought of anything happening to him or his family because of me. "I love you."

"I love you too, bro. I'll text you when everyone is in place."

"I trust you to come through. Make sure you tell Russ I owe him one."

"You owe him more than one," Hunter quips before he hangs up.

Everyone's eyes are on me as I push to my feet. I meet each of their gazes, projecting confidence and strength even as the weight of the world starts to press down on my shoulders. I'm worried for everyone. For Selene, for Beck, for Monique, for me. For our families that are too far away to hold close. That fear has a vice grip on my throat, but still, I hold my head high, refusing to let them see.

How hard the hold makes it for me to pull air into my lungs.

How my knees are buckling under the weight.

How *fucking* afraid I am of failing.

"Are we ready to go?"

23

SELENE

Thankful is the last thing I should be feeling towards Leland Marsh and whoever broke him out of federal prison, but when I wake up in a bed that's something beyond a standard king with Cal's warmth pressed to my back and my head on Beck's chest, that's the only emotion that makes sense in the moment.

Which isn't to say that I want to be here in this big house that belonged to a paranoid man with more money than sense and a panic room larger than the house I grew up in because I don't. I don't want to be running. I don't want to be hiding. I don't want to be looking over my shoulder and jumping up out of my sleep every time I hear a branch brush a window or see the motion sensor lights pop on because a baby deer is grazing on one of the berry bushes at the edge of the yard where the landscaping turns into acres of sprawling woods that butt up against the Potomac river.

I don't want any of those things, but I do want to be with Cal and Beck. I want the comfort of their bodies on either side of mine. I want the weight of their arms over my hip and around my stomach. I want Beck's soft snores and one of Cal's long legs peeking out from underneath the cover because he got too warm. I want the kisses on my bare shoulders in the middle of the night, and someone putting my bonnet back on my head when it slips off again.

But most of all, I want the constant reassurance their presence provides. The persistent reminder that bleeds through my subconscious when I'm sleeping, telling me that I am not alone.

It's been so long since I've had that, since I've found myself between them and didn't have to rush to end the moment, compiling lies as I fixed my clothes and prepared my heart for another indefinite amount of time where I would be without them. So long, in fact, that I had to stop myself from jumping out of bed in a panic, afraid I'd fallen asleep somewhere I shouldn't have. I came to my senses as soon as I stared up at the white curtains of the canopy bed, settling back into the mattress and marveling at the fact that I woke up before both of my men.

Five minutes have passed with them still deep in their slumbers and me reveling in the novelty of this experience. I'm content to just lie here, but Cal tightens his grip on me, pulling me back into his chest. My ass brushes against the swell of a generous erection, and my core clenches, a sudden and desperate hunger rushing through me at the feel of it through the thin fabric of my nightie. Unsure if he's awake, I tentatively roll my hips into him and bite my lip when I'm instantly met with a thrust.

"Good morning, pet."

Gravel coated sin. That's what his voice is when he's fresh out of the depths of sleep. I close my eyes, memorizing the sound of it along with the gentle press of his lips on my neck. He follows it up with a graze of his teeth, and I whimper.

"I said good morning, pet."

"*Good morning.*"

His lips curve against my skin, as he tosses the covers back. "How did you sleep?" he whispers, fingers sliding over my hip to find the lace hem of the silk dress and drag it up.

"Fine," I gasp when the cool air hits me, inciting goosebumps along my thighs and ass. Cal runs a warm palm over the pebbled skin, cupping my knee and lifting my leg.

"Keep that there, please."

I nod, too worried about what he's going to do next to speak. He nips at my neck, sending small sparks of pain and pleasure shooting down my spine. I arch into him, moaning softly because I don't want to wake Beck.

"He's not going to sleep through this, pet," Cal warns, fingers ghosting over my sex, parting the lips and teasing my clit before dipping into my soaked channel. It's been so, so long, and the burn of the stretch from what has to be multiple fingers has tears glazing my eyes. It's not painful, not really, but Cal stops anyway, kissing my shoulder. "Are you okay? Did I go too fast?"

"I'm fine. Please don't stop."

To prove my point, I grind down on his hand, crying out when he starts to massage my front wall and my entire body lights up. Beck shifts from his side to his back, not awake but definitely on his way to consciousness.

"I bet he's already hard, pet. He probably thinks the sexy little noises you're making are only happening in his dreams. Do you want to show him what it's like to greet a brand new day with his dick in your mouth?"

My pussy pulsates at the thought, and Cal releases a dark chuckle into the air. "Yeah, you want that, don't you, baby? Go ahead and pull that beautiful dick out. I don't think I've ever seen those lips wrapped around him."

His filthy words are accompanied by shallow thrusts of his fingers that are setting me for the greatest fall of my life. My entire body is a live wire, all sensation and need and the desperate desire to give him everything he wants. But even in the haze of lust, I'm still concerned about crossing some sort of line. Logically, I know that Cal wouldn't suggest that I do anything Beck wouldn't be okay with, but I need to hear it from him.

I glance over my shoulder at him, taking in those stunning features and dark eyes. For a second, I forget what I'm supposed to be asking him, but it comes back to me when he leans in and bites my bottom lip.

"What is it, pet?"

"He's sleeping…" I start, but the sentence falls apart, dissolving into a moan because he's repositioned his hand so his thumb can rub my clit in maddening circles.

He kisses me again, this one involving a plundering of my mouth by his tongue, and only pulls away once I'm breathless. "You want permission?"

"*Yes.*"

Sweat blooms on my skin, a ball of heat gathering low in my belly as Cal calls Beck's name softly. He startles awake, onyx eyes wide and unseeing. I reach for him, laying my hand over his heart, hoping my touch is enough to soothe him because, thanks to Cal, I can't fucking speak. Beck covers my hand with his own, still blinking away sleep.

"Wake up, love," Cal says. "Our girl wants permission to put your dick in her mouth."

Beck's brows shoot up, a smile spreading across his face as he takes in the scene in front of him. The air, which was already heavy with need, grows even more charged as he slides closer, cupping my jaw and running a thumb over my lips.

"Anything you want, gorgeous."

I'm salivating, watching him slide down the briefs he slept in so the magnificent length of his manhood can spring forth. It stands proudly, the tip glistening with precum I remove with a flick of my tongue as soon as he's within reach. I'm on my knees now, kneeling between his splayed legs with Cal behind me, the flared tip of his dick notched at my entrance. He spreads my ass cheeks, sliding into me just as I take Beck to the back of my throat. I moan around him, jaw already aching from the stretch required to accommodate his girth, and his hands go into my hair.

"*Fuck*, Selene."

His grip tightens, sending pinpricks of pain reverberating through my scalp. It's a lovely compliment to the pleasure rolling through me due to Cal's strokes, and I'm so stunned by the dueling sensations, that I can't move, can't think, can't do anything but feel. Which is just as well, because the men behind and below me are content to take control. Beck uses his hold on my hair to guide my mouth up and down his shaft, cursing loudly while Cal's balls slap my ass repeatedly.

My eyes roll into the back of my head as I give myself over to the moment, surrendering to the sensation of being used for their pleasure while they spoon feed me mine. As the pressure builds inside of me, the room fills with loud moans and muffled cries that melt into contented sighs in the minutes after we all find our release.

I collapse in the center of the bed, cum leaking down my thighs and lingering on my tongue, but that doesn't stop Cal or Beck from treating me to sweet, reverent kisses before they tuck me back into bed, promising to return with breakfast and coffee so we can do it all over again. I don't know if they keep the promise because there's no coffee or food when I wake up again, tangled in sheets that smell like the men who are nowhere to be found.

My first instinct is to march through this big ass house, find them and ream them out for letting me sleep through breakfast, but I decide to shower and brush my teeth first. I'll already have to deal with Monique making suggestive comments, I don't need to give her any new material to pull from. Once I'm presentable, I make my way to the first floor, surprised to find Monique in the living room with a white board identical to the one in my office in the middle of the floor and all the files I brought with me stacked in neat piles on the oversized coffee table.

"Umm, good morning?"

"Morning, babe," she says, giving me a sideways hug as she sips on an iced coffee in front of the board.

"Where'd you get that?"

"I made it. You want one?"

"Sure."

I follow her into the kitchen, looking around the large and incredibly open floor plan. When we arrived last night, I was suffering from a headache and bone deep exhaustion, so I hadn't bothered to take in my surroundings. Now, I'm able to fully appreciate the sleek appliances and warm finishes that help the home toe the line between modern and traditional.

"This house is seriously stunning."

Monique hums her agreement, pulling out the items she needs for the coffee. I'm shocked to find that includes an espresso machine that she works with ease. I prop my hip against the edge of the marble countertop and cross my arms.

"Since when do you know how to pull espresso shots?"

The bold notes of ground caffeine permeate the air between us as Monique arches a brow at me. "Since when do you let men call you *pet*?"

I search her tone for any sign of judgment and come up empty, finding only humor and intrigue. "You heard that?"

"Oh, I heard everythinggggg." She bounces on her tip toes, twisting the long handle on the basket to disengage it from the machine now that my shot is done. "They fuck you good, huh?"

Heat sweeps over my cheeks. "Monique!"

"What?! Y'all had me ready to go back to my room and rub one out."

I cover my face with my hand. "Please stop."

"Fine. I'll leave it alone, but all I'm saying is you deserve it."

"Deserve what?"

The question comes from behind me, and I turn to find Cal and Beck entering the room. In their dark jeans and plain t-shirts, they look so casual I can almost make myself believe we're here on a vacation of sorts, unplugged from the world and focused on each other. The presence of the guns on their hips dispels that notion, though, reminding me of our current reality. It's a hard pill to swallow, but I manage to scarf it down, pushing away the lightness from joking with Monique and the joy of morning sex with Cal and Beck.

"Perimeter check?" I ask, accepting my freshly made coffee from Monique.

Both men nod, coming in for chaste kisses before heading to the sink to wash their hands. Beck grabs a towel from inside one of the drawers, drying his hands and then tossing it to Cal.

"We're all good," he assures us. "Did you two eat?"

I take a sip of my coffee. "I just woke up, but I do seem to recall the promise of breakfast in bed that never came true."

Cal moves to the stocked fridge, pulling out a tray of cut fruit, a carton of eggs and a pack of sausage. "You were sleeping so soundly. We didn't want to wake you."

He sets everything down, crouching low to search for pans, bowls and whatever else he needs in the cabinets beneath the large slab of stone.

"I'm sure she needed the rest too," Monique quips, dancing out of my reach when I try to swat her for making dirty jokes again.

Beck folds a laugh between his lips, bringing the eggs and one of the small bowls Cal produced from the cabinet to the spot in front of him. "The board looks good, Monique."

She preens. "Thank you! It's not done yet, but I figured we could work on it after we eat."

"Sounds like a plan," Cal says, turning on the stove with his eyes on me. "How are you feeling?"

"I'm okay," I tell him, and for the most part I am. The thought of Leland Marsh in the free world hunting me down is still scary, but it's not as terrifying as it was yesterday. Especially now that I know everyone we care about is being guarded by people we trust. Having Monique here is helping too. Initially, she'd balked at the idea of coming with us, but when we explained that anyone looking for me would more than likely start with her, it wasn't a hard sell. I'm glad she came to her senses because I would probably feel a lot less like myself without her.

Cal and Beck study me, measuring my tone and expression. At some point, Monique joins in too, and then everyone in the room is just staring at me, waiting for me to fall apart. I bring the coffee to my lips, taking another sip.

"You can stop staring at me whenever you're ready."

Beck is the first to break, turning his focus to cracking the eggs. "Did you check the app for messages from Aubrey?"

My heart sinks at the mention of my husband's name, and I shake my head. "Not yet."

Before we left Culture Code, I uploaded a digital monitoring soft-ware to all our devices, knowing it wasn't safe to bring them with us in case Marsh has the help we think he does and could track them, but also needing to be aware of what was happening on them in case of emergencies. The plan was to have the app up and running constantly, keeping us plugged into the world from the safety of our little bubble, but I'd been avoiding setting it up because I didn't want Aubrey present in this space in any way.

Beck frowns, capturing me in pools of glittering onyx. "After we eat?"

His offer for compromise in the face of clear disappointment sends warmth skittering down my spine. I hold his gaze, fighting the urge to bite my lip as I nod.

"After we eat."

The preparation and consumption of our first meal of the day goes by far too quickly, and not even thirty minutes after accepting the delay to check the app, I'm left with no choice but to follow through on my promise. I sit cross legged on the couch with a fresh laptop from Culture Code's inventory on my lap while Monique, Cal and Beck collaborate on the board. It's nothing like the one I kept in my office despite me giving Monique reference photos for the rebuild, but I don't have the authority to question her right now, not when my task for the day is yet to be completed.

With a few clicks of my fingers, I'm looking at the phone calls that have come to my phone in the last twelve hours. Most of the calls are from my sisters, Robin and Jessica, who I assume heard the news from Mama. One is from my hairdresser, Ms. Diane, and the other two came from Imani's phone, but I know she and Isis were on the line together. Their missed calls and the accompanying texts send guilt slicing through me, making it almost impossible for me to appreciate the fact that Aubrey hasn't reached out to me at all.

I slam the laptop shut and leave it on the couch while I join the others at the board.

"He hasn't called or texted."

Cal wraps an arm around me, kissing my forehead. "So, he doesn't care where you are or who you're with."

"Because now that Marsh is out, he thinks I'll be dead soon."

"Possibly."

I shift out of his hold, needing to face him head on. "Possibly? Are you walking back your theory that Aubrey helped Marsh escape, so he can kill me?"

Secretly, I'd been hoping he and Beck would walk back another theory, but I haven't been brave enough to bring AJ up in conversation with them since the day they planted the awful seed of suggestion in my mind.

Cal catches my fingers in his grip, tugging me back into him. "Of course not. I just want us to consider all the possibilities before we lay this at Aubrey's feet."

I'm fairly certain it belongs there, but I decide to follow Cal's lead, deferring to his investigative experience. "Okay, so the question would be who else does Leland know that would have the motive and means to break him out of a federal institution?"

It wouldn't have been a small feat, not by any stretch of the imagination, and I doubt there are any people in the world who would risk their lives and freedom to spring a waste of space such as Leland.

"The Brothers?" Beck suggests, handing Monique a sticky note with the words 'military base' written on it. She places it above Sutton's name, and I squint, trying to see the connection.

"Doubtful," Cal says. "They're weaker now than ever. If they were going to break Leland out, they would've done it when Jacob was leading and Charlie was there to lend insight and support."

Silence pools between us while Mo keeps muttering to herself.

"Anyone else?" I ask, anxious to turn my full attention to what she's doing.

Beck shakes his head. "Not that I can think of."

"Then it must be Aubrey," I conclude. "He definitely has the means, and his motive is to silence me just like he silenced Sutton. Only this time he's using someone I have history with to make the story more salacious, which will ensure that he'll be able to profit off of it for years to come."

Monique spins on her heels, hands on her hips. "Why didn't he do the same thing with Sutton?"

My brows dip together, forming a line of confusion. "What?"

"Why didn't he spin Sutton's death into something he could make money or gain power from?"

"Because it's kind of hard to do when he wasn't even supposed to be speaking to the girl anymore, let alone fucking her. Besides, why would he want to draw attention to her death when he's responsible for it?"

She gives me a quizzical look. "You believe he had President Sanders killed and then attended his funeral, holding the man's grand-babies and crying and shit."

"He didn't cry."

But I'm pretty sure there's a photo or two out there of him holding the most recent addition to the Sanders clan. Monique dismisses my comment with a wave of her hand.

"I know he'll do it with you. There will be press conferences, interviews and photos of him kneeling at your grave. He'll milk it for all it's worth, so why would Sutton be any different? I mean, it's not like orchestrating the murder of your mistress carries more weight than that of the President or your wife, so why wouldn't he look at her death through the same opportunistic lens as everyone else we think he's had a hand in killing?"

The line of questioning shakes something free inside my brain. An alternative theory floating up from the trenches slowly, appearing on the surface just as Cal's warning about considering every angle during an investigation echoes in my mind. From the moment I heard about Sutton's death, I'd decided that Aubrey was responsible. I didn't look past him, just *at* him, and even when I couldn't find a single reason why he might want her dead, I kept my focus on him, missing the key difference between her death and all the rest.

I see it now, though.

The hollow look in his eyes. The despair that cracked his features when I described her death. The pure hatred when he tried to choke me for mocking her.

"Aubrey didn't kill Sutton," I whisper, disbelief coating my tongue. "He loved her."

24

BECK

There's no hurt on Selene's face when she speaks about her husband being in love with another woman. Only shock. Like she can't imagine the man being capable of that depth of emotion. I can't imagine it either though I suspect he did love Selene once. As much as a narcissistic asshole can love someone besides themselves, anyway. He must have been damn good at playing the part to have convinced her to bear him a son and stick by his side for so many years.

But now his mask is off, and I couldn't be more thankful for the sudden alienation of affection he subjected Selene to because it very well may have saved her life.

Monique taps the board with her nail repeatedly, eyes lit with excitement because of Selene's sudden realization. "Exactly," she exclaims. "Aubrey was in love with Sutton and someone used her to hurt him."

Selene slips out from under Cal's arm, striding over to the board. "Not to hurt him," she murmurs, picking up one of the markers and circling the 'military base' sticky note three times. "To get him back in line."

Cal snaps his fingers. "Of course. The news broke about him pulling out of talks for the Qatar base on the day of the State Dinner."

"But that was just when it was announced publicly," I add. "He met with the Cabinet to notify them two weeks prior. I remember because Cordelia was *pissed.* No one else seemed to think it was a good idea anyway, so they didn't care."

"That's right," Cal says. "She did that whole 'I implore you to reconsider' thing that she always does when he tells her no. It's weird. Like she's genuinely offended that he would disobey her."

"I don't think it's weird at all." Selene tosses the words over her shoulder as she writes a list of dates and events on the board. "Before Aubrey was elected, Cordelia essentially told me he would be the head of the operation, but she would be the neck, turning it in whatever direction she likes. She thinks she owns him."

Monique passes behind Selene, grabbing another marker from the cup on one of the end tables. "Maybe she does."

I rub my chin, considering the theory. There's a definite imbalance of power at the heart of Aubrey and Cordelia's relationship. She obviously holds more influence over him than he does over her, but I'm not quite ready to accept that she's the person at the heart of all of this.

"What do you know about serial killer teams?"

Everything in the room stops. Monique and Selene gawk at me, their hands hovering above the board where a timeline that starts in February and ends on the day Sutton died is starting to fill out. Cal, who's standing beside me watching the ladies work, cuts an eye at me.

"Where are you going with this, Beckham?"

"Okay. This isn't going to be a perfect analogy," I warn them, gazing heavenward to gather my thoughts. "Most of the time, serial killers work alone. In fact, teams are usually more likely to get caught because internal dynamics and shifting power structures can lead to instability and betrayal."

"Why team up if you have a better chance of getting away with your crimes if you work alone?" Monique asks.

"For the same reason anyone joins a team," Selene says. "To gain something you couldn't achieve on your own."

"Cordelia wanted the power of the Oval, but she failed to convince her party that she was a viable candidate. They cheat her out of the nomination and put up Sanders, probably making it clear that she won't ever have their full support."

Selene taps her lips with the marker, considering my point. "She takes Aubrey under her wing, promises to help him achieve his lifelong dream of becoming the first President with true bi-partisan support. They kill Sanders when he poses a threat to their shared goal."

Cal shifts his weight from one foot to the other. "Was he an actual threat though? I mean dropping those last photos of Aubrey and Sutton after the debate seemed like a last ditch effort to me. It wasn't going to secure the election for him."

Something sparks in Selene's eyes, a memory she hasn't shared. "They weren't even upset about the photos," she says. "I mean, not really. Aubrey screamed at me over them, accusing me of giving them to Sanders to destroy him, but Jordan calmed him down, telling him the pictures hadn't changed anything on our front. He seemed content after that, like everything was settled, but I just kept wondering what would happen when Sanders realized the photos didn't have the intended effect and decided to keep digging."

Cal studies her, concern furrowing his brows at the faraway look in Selene's eyes. "Did you ask them?"

Selene nods. "Jordan said there was nothing left to find, but when she said it, Aubrey and Cordelia shared this look that made me think that wasn't true. Not too long after, Sanders was dead." Her eyes fly to mine, wide and panicked. "Did I get that man killed? I mean, if I hadn't asked the question, if I had just let them think it was settled—"

I rush to reassure her. "They would have came to the conclusion that he needed to die anyway because the two of them are hiding something bigger than an affair. Something dark enough to warrant the assassination of a President."

Silence envelops the room, and we all sit in it, letting our minds wander. After a full minute passes by, Monique clasps her fingers and lifts her arms, resting them on top of her head.

"So, they worked together to kill Sanders to protect some big secret, but just a few months later, they're so far out of alignment Cordelia has Sutton killed to bring Aubrey back in line?"

Her question brings me back to the original point I was trying to make when I brought up serial killer teams. Duos are already unstable, but the dynamics that deteriorate the quickest are triads. When a third person is added into an already chaotic mix, what was once a relationship based on symbiosis and shared, but imbalanced, power becomes a dysfunctional hierarchy where alliances between two of the members leaves the other floundering to find their place in the organization.

I've seen Cordelia bide her time, waiting Aubrey out until he eventually comes around. She did it a few months ago when they were at odds about the AI-enhanced video cameras in schools. Cal witnessed their disagreement, but I was the one in his office when he finally folded. If she knew giving him some time to see things her way was a successful approach, why would Cordelia go to such extreme lengths where the military base is concerned?

The simple answer is, she wouldn't.

"I don't think Cordelia had Sutton killed."

Everyone looks at me like I've lost it, but by the time I finish explaining that impatience and strong arming isn't Cordelia's M.O., we're all in agreement.

"There's someone else involved," Selene says, sinking back into the spot she abandoned on the couch. Monique takes a seat too, laying her head in Selene's lap. They both look exhausted, and I can't say that I feel any different. It's taken a lot of mental space to connect these dots, and we're still not certain of anything. It's all just conjecture, nothing concrete enough to take Aubrey down but more than enough to keep the target on our backs.

Cal and I remain standing. He's at the board, taking a closer look at the timeline Selene and Monique put together, while I look at things from afar. Despite the stakes being high and the problem hitting so close to home, there's the familiar thrum of excited energy running between us. It's been present in every investigation we've ever run together, guiding us through obstacle after obstacle until we found the answers we needed.

This investigation will be no different.

I step to the board, shoulder brushing his as I begin reading off the dates.

"February 3rd, an article is published detailing Aubrey's January 29th meeting at the Embassy of the State of Qatar. He speaks with Ambassador Moustafa, and it's rumored that Emir Karim attends via video. Jordan confirms the military base was the topic of discussion in a press conference later that day."

Racking my brain for any further details and coming up empty, I move on to the next date which is all the way in May.

"May 26th, morning news reports that Aubrey has officially dropped out of talks with Qatar about the military base, returning to his original stance about foreign forces on U.S soil."

Cal picks up a marker, drawing a small line between the February and May dates. "May 12th, Aubrey notifies his Cabinet of the decision. Cordelia urges him to reconsider."

"Somewhere around that time, maybe a few days later, Langham arrives in Kentucky and begins following Sutton," Selene calls from the couch. "She takes a photo of him on the street on the 20th."

He adds that date too, and then another, explaining his reasoning as he does. "May 23rd, Cordelia shows up at Dahlia's with a group of unidentified men. Aubrey is clearly afraid of them."

"Which makes sense if they were there to shake him down. A final warning to fall in line before they had Langham pull the proverbial trigger on Sutton."

"Does that mean he was there?" Cal asks me, tilting his head to the side. "I mean he had to have been right? Cordelia wouldn't have needed muscle to threaten Aubrey. She could have done that on her own."

"It's possible. If he was there, his presence wasn't enough to sway Aubrey."

Cal shakes his head. "Dumb motherfucker. He gets in bed with these people and then thinks he can just say no whenever he wants? What did he think was going to happen?"

Aubrey Taylor is not the kind of man I'll ever relate to. He is selfish and needlessly cruel. He takes pleasure in inflicting pain and will do anything for power. I don't know what it's like to be any of those things, to do any of those things, so I can't even begin to make sense of his mindset. There's nothing I wouldn't do to save Selene and Cal, nothing I wouldn't give to see them happy and healthy.

I would rip a hole in the sky, dig a tunnel to hell with my bare hands, *end my own fucking life*, before I let someone lay a finger on either of their heads, so it makes no sense to me that he would allow Sutton to be a pawn in a power struggle he went on to lose.

"I don't know," I say finally. "But it looks like he learned his lesson because a month after Sutton's death, he's back at the table with Qatar and the military base is all but guaranteed to happen."

Cal folds his arms, stepping back to observe the altered timeline. "The only question now is who stands to gain the most from that? If we figure that out, then we've got our third man."

A WEEK PASSES with us exploring and eliminating possibilities in our hunt for the point at the top of the power triangle Cordelia and Aubrey are a part of. We turn our focus to the forces outside of the U.S. first, knowing that owning an American President would be worth a lot to many international players. That line of thought gets pushed aside quickly when we factor in the military base angle because we can't figure out what another country would stand to gain from it.

Qatari leaders, of course, remain on the list simply because of the circumstances, but there's no real motive there since we're already their allies and it'll be their country paying for the building of the base, not ours. When Cal makes that point, the conversation changes, shifting from international considerations to domestic speculation that centers around the one percent because the richest people are always willing to do the foulest things to get richer.

From there, we turn our attention to the list of billionaires Selene compiled when the most important question to us was who could afford to buy not one, but two, spots within the Secret Service and have those fraudulent agents put in charge of the President's detail. That's where we find him. The third man. The mastermind. Cordelia's bene-factor and Aubrey's boogey man.

Phineas Gambit.

Cal stares at his picture displayed on Selene's computer screen and sighs incredulously.

"That's the man who was with Cordelia at Dahlia's," he says, leaning in for a closer look. "He's got more gray in his temples now, but those spooky ass green eyes are the same."

"No wonder Aubrey was so scared when he showed up."

Cal snorts a laugh, returning to his spot on the couch. We've been up since five this morning, and now, nearly twelve hours later, neither one of us is showing any signs of slowing down. Selene and Monique were up with us, but they left the living room within minutes of each other, both yawning and mumbling about naps. After the early dinner Cal put together—a mushroom pasta reminiscent of the one he made when we were in Texas with Selene—I was ready to succumb to a post-meal nap as well, but I decided to work instead.

Now, I'm extremely glad that I did.

We've been at this for days with nothing to really show for it. Every moment that passed with Leland still on the loose and no tangible proof that the third man existed felt like the tightening of a noose around my neck. With Cal's confident identification of Gambit, I can feel the rope slackening just a little.

"What do we know about him?" Cal asks just as I'm clicking the link to the man's biography on what I'm sure is one of the many company websites he's featured on. I scroll past another picture of him, scanning the paragraphs underneath that lay out what I'm sure Gambit believes is a pick-yourself-up-by-your-bootstraps origin story but in reality is nothing more than a tale of a boy who grew up rich and got a loan from his daddy that he used to become even more rich by starting a slew of businesses that are all linked below the last paragraph.

"Gambit Construction," Cal says the company name just as I click the link, opening the web page in a new tab.

I guide the mouse across the screen, scanning for any pertinent information. What jumps out at me is the section near the center of the page. I highlight the section, making sure Cal sees where I am when I start reading. "Gambit's Federal Division has worked on many government contracts for projects such as dams, wind farms, transit systems. We also provide *military construction services…*"

Cal grins. "We got him."

Disbelief bubbles in my chest, and I shake my head, wondering how such a complex web of events could come down to something as simple as a fucking government contract. Granted, due to the scope of the proposed project, we're talking about a multi-billion dollar contract, but still. It feels ridiculous to know that a woman has lost her life all because Phineas Gambit wanted a job he probably could have gotten anyway if he had just thrown his hat in the ring.

That probably hadn't even occurred to him though, to earn something based on merit alone. I'm sure in his warped mind it was faster and easier to put a man you owned in the most powerful office in the land and force your lackey to look after him and make sure that he did your bidding.

It's certainly more lucrative.

Whatever he spent getting Aubrey into the Oval and keeping his hold on him, he'll make back tenfold over the course of his term or terms. Because of course it won't stop at the Qatari military base. There will always be something else. A waste treatment plant to build in Idaho. An oil field to restore in Kuwait. A reactor that needs to be enclosed in the Ukraine.

An endless stream of money all flowing in Gambit's direction.

Disgusted, I close the computer. "We need to tell Selene."

Cal follows me up the stairs to the room we've been sharing. The curtains are drawn, and the TV is on, the volume low but not inaudible. My intention is to head straight for the bed and scoop her up in my arms, but I stop short when I see Jordan's face. She's behind the podium I've seen her stand at so many times before. The Presidential seal hovering above her head and a slew of reporters and cameras at her feet. She should look at home up there, but she seems nervous. She has a white-knuckled grip on the edges of the stand that matches the pale skin of her face and shadows underneath her sunken eyes.

I glance at Cal, who's closest to the nightstand where the remote is. "Turn it up."

He ups the volume just a bit, so as not to wake Selene, and I inch closer to the TV to make sure I'm hearing everything. The press corps is relentless today, hounding her with question after question about Leland Marsh and the approval of Qatar's military plans, and despite looking ready to go home and crawl into bed, Jordan fields each one with ease.

She doesn't stumble until they start to ask about Selene.

"It's been days since First Lady Taylor has been seen in public," one reporter says. "Is she sick?"

"No, Mrs. Taylor is not sick. Next ques—"

"Then has she gone into hiding, perhaps been placed on lockdown due to fear of Leland Marsh targeting her?"

Jordan's eye twitches. "As I've stated before, we have no reason to believe Mr. Marsh is a threat to Mrs. Taylor, and we have every faith in the U.S. Marshall's ability to capture him before he can harm anyone. Next question." Hands fly up, and she points to someone on her left. "You."

"It's been reported several times that Mrs. Taylor has moved out of the White House and her marriage to President Taylor is once again on shaky ground. Can you speak to the validity of that?"

"There is no validity to those reports," Jordan replies, forcing a brittle smile as she selects another reporter from the center, clearly hoping someone will throw her a bone and ask a question she won't have to lie to answer. A spark illuminates her eye when she makes her next choice. "How can I help you, Mr. Landry?"

"Fucking Landry," I mutter under my breath, remembering the one time I met the man speaking on the television in person. He'd crashed the last real date Aubrey had taken Selene on and been bribed by Jordan to kill a story about Sutton still working for the campaign after she was reportedly fired. I guess his reward is the occasional spot in the White House press corps.

"Is President Taylor looking forward to his golfing trip this week-end?" Landry asks, a smile evident in his voice even though I can't see his face. He must be proud of himself for offering Jordan a reprieve in the midst of the frenzy.

Her appreciation is evident in the sinking of her shoulders. "Yes, he is ready for a much needed break. I hear the weather in Florida is going to be lovely as well."

Unfortunately for Jordan and Landry, the reporter who asked about Selene going into hiding is starved, and she came here ready to make anything, including Landry's marshmallow of a question, into a meal.

"Will the First Lady be joining President Taylor on his trip?"

Annoyance dances across Jordan's features as she faces the woman again. "No, Mrs. Taylor will not be in attendance. She is not a fan of golf."

"But it's their anniversary," the reporter says. "Why are they spending their wedding anniversary apart? I thought you said there was no validity to the claims that their marriage was on the rocks."

Jordan's lips part, but no sound comes out for several long seconds.

"Is she short circuiting?"

Cal has been so quiet, I forgot he was even in the room.

"That's what it looks like."

Finally, she finds her voice again, but when she starts to speak, I think it might have been better for her to have stayed quiet. "Oh my God, Freda. Will you get off it? The President and First Lady are fine. Everything is fine! Everything is fine. *Everything. Is. Fine.*"

The rest of the room is stunned into silence, and the same shocked quietness sweeps over me and Cal. I don't think I've ever seen Jordan this way. It's like she's a rock and the reporter, who's name I still don't know, is a hammer, cracking her over the head until she breaks apart and reveals whatever is at her center.

"Why aren't the Taylors spending their anniversary together?" the reporter asks, voice raised to ensure she's heard over Jordan's continued screeching. "Is Selene Taylor in hiding because Leland Marsh is a threat to her safety? The people in this country have a right to know the answer these questions. The well-being of the First couple is a matter of national security," she reminds everyone in the room.

Most of the other reporters can be seen nodding, but none of them speak, letting her continue hounding Jordan.

"Has Mr. Marsh made any attempts to contact Mrs. Taylor?"

"I don't know," Jordan whispers, sagging against the podium.

Flashes from several cameras light up the room, documenting the unraveling of a once formidable woman. Still, the reporter keeps going.

"Where will Mrs. Taylor be this weekend if not in Florida with her husband?"

Jordan raises a hand to her face, fingers shaking as she wipes sweat from her brow. "I don't know," she says again. The reporter stands, allowing the camera to capture her side profile. I'm impressed and proud to find that it's a young Black woman with a short, puffy afro and earrings shaped like Africa swinging from her ears.

"Will she be in DC? At their home in McLean? Will she be out of the country or back home in Georgia visiting her family?"

"I don't—"

"Where is Mrs. Taylor right now, Jordan?" She shakes her head, but the reporter isn't having it. "She hasn't been seen in days. All her public appearances have been canceled with no explanation. It is your job to explain to the American people what is happening with the leader of this country and his family, so you need to tell us right now, Ms. St. James, *where is the First Lady?*"

Jordan stands up suddenly, mustering all of her strength to run away from the podium just after she shouts, "I DON'T KNOW!" a final time.

25

SELENE

Monique slaps my ass on her way to the kitchen. "Up and at 'em, Gone Girl, time for our walk."

She's been calling me by that since we watched the playback of the press conference where Jordan fell apart, taking pleasure in how much I hate it. I glare at her from my very cozy spot on the couch and let out a groan because of the stupid nickname but also because moving feels like something of an impossibility for me at the moment.

I'm nestled between the two men who took turns folding me like a pretzel last night. My head is resting on Cal's thigh and my hands are tucked under my chin. He's running his fingers through my hair while he reads the paper with a pair of black framed glasses resting on his nose. Beck has my feet in his lap, gentle callused hands rubbing small circles into my soles while he watches the Hallmark movie playing on the screen because we're all tired of the news.

It's a perfectly lazy afternoon, and I'm more content than I should be, laying here with a full heart and the sunlight streaming in from the windows kissing my skin, learning things about the men I love that I would have known before if we'd ever had the kind of time we have now. This is the most we've been around each other since we met, and now I have another name to add to the list of monsters I have to thank for this bittersweet gift.

Phineas Gambit.

Beck and Cal identified him four days ago, and since then we've learned everything there is to know about him online, including the fact that he's had Mason Woodard and Patrick Garrison on his payroll for over a decade. We did a deep dive on his limited social media and found them lurking in the background of a lot of photos, guns on their hips, comms in their ears, determined expressions on both of their faces as they scanned the crowds on red carpets and inside galas for any threat to their employer.

Tying Gambit to Garrison and Woodard was a definite win, proving our theory that their addition to Aubrey's detail was a way for the person who owns him to keep an eye on him while remaining in the shadows. What's been harder to do, is tie the corrupt billionaire to Officer Travis Langham. Obviously, we know they're both involved in this web of deception, but it's unclear when Langham was brought into all of this and if he was recruited by Gambit personally or contracted by someone on his payroll.

The timing of it all matters most to me because if Langham was in bed with Gambit on the day that we met…

A shiver runs through me, and I push the thought away, refusing to go there.

"You know she's coming back for you," Cal murmurs, the strokes of his fingers growing even more intoxicating.

"I know. I know. I'm going."

But my eyes are falling shut, and there are these lovely little ripples of warmth and pleasure radiating from the places they're touching me.

"You didn't move a muscle, gorgeous."

"Shhhh."

I don't have to be looking at him to know when his demeanor goes from relaxed and teasing to mischievous. I feel it. In the span of a heartbeat, he shifts gears, fingers turning torturous as he begins to tickle my feet.

"Did you just shush me?"

"Beck!" I squeal, thrashing against the cushions to try to get away from him. It's no use. He's got a death grip on my ankle, so I try to kick away with the other foot, squirming and pleading even as hysterical laughter pours from me. "Seriously, Beck!" Giggle, gasp. "Stop!" More giggles and a jerk that results in my head slapping against Cal's thigh. I look to him for help, but he's useless, watching the whole thing with an amused glimmer in his eye.

"Apologize," Beck orders, using his hold on me to pull me down the couch toward him. At first I don't know what his goal is, but then, quick as a flash, he's on top of me, fingers digging into my ribs while I scream bloody murder.

"MONIQUE!!!"

"SHOULD HAVE GOTTEN YOUR ASS UP WHEN I TOLD YOU TO," she shouts from the kitchen, the sounds of ice dropping into a glass accompanying her pettiness.

Beck is hovering over me. His chest against my chest. His nose against my nose. His body a solid wall of muscle that doesn't so much as budge when I try to buck him off.

"You know how to end this, Selene," he whispers, lips curved in an annoyingly adorable smile. It's so good to see him like this even if it's while he's attempting to murder me.

"I'm sorry," I gasp, beating at his back and sides. "I'm sorry. I'm sorry. *I'm sorryyyyy.*"

He drops a kiss on my lips, fingers going still as the show of affection tries to turn into something more. Monique clears her throat, and he pulls away. "You're forgiven."

I scramble off the couch, narrowing my eyes at Cal, who just blows me a kiss, and then Monique who taps her foot and says, "We're late."

There's not really a way to be late for a walk that consists of laps around the large backyard while Cal and/or Beck sit on the patio and keep watch, but I don't argue with her because I know she needs the open air. We're all going a little stir crazy now. Marsh is still on the run and everything has been quiet. Too quiet. Normally, I'd say quiet is good, that it's safe, but this is different. It's the kind of silence that makes you question yourself, that has you relaxing back into your bed, telling yourself that you're in the house alone even though you definitely heard the steps creak under the weight of a full-grown person.

"How are you doing?"

I pose the question when we're halfway through our second lap, taking a sip of water from the bottle Monique was gracious enough to fix for me while Beck was killing me on the couch.

She shrugs. "Ready to go home."

"I know. I'm sorry."

"Selene, please stop apologizing to me for things that are out of your control. We're here because of Aubrey and all his nonsense. The only thing you did wrong was trust a white man."

Her steps falter when I bump her with my shoulder. "I hate you."

She recovers with ease, elongating her stride to catch up with me. "You do not."

"I don't," I admit, looping an arm around her shoulder and pulling her into me because I know she likes when I'm all touchy feely. "I love you so much, and I'm glad you're here. Thank you for coming on the run with me."

"I love you too, and there's nowhere else I'd be than by your side. Besides, it's not like I had much of a choice," she gripes, leaning into me. "Cal said I was going to end up being waterboarded for your location if I didn't."

"You're exaggerating, as usual."

"That might have been what he said verbatim," she says, shoving me away. "But that was definitely what he wanted me to take from the conversation."

I don't bother dignifying her ridiculousness with a response, opting to guide us back to the original topic of conversation. "Seriously, though, how are you? I know it can't be easy putting your whole life on hold to hide out here with us. You've been cracking a lot of jokes and contributing so much to the investigation, so please don't think I don't appreciate you. I just need to know what's happening underneath all of that, so I can try to take care of you how you've been taking care of me."

She stops walking, grabbing hold of my arm to force me to pause too. Then she takes both of my hands in hers and squeezes hard. "Sel, the only thing you can do for me is what. you have been doing. Keep living, keep loving those gorgeous men of yours and keep letting them love you. Keep looking forward to the future you're going to have after you get the proof you need to take Aubrey down once and for all."

My heart clenches at the mention of the future. An empty ache building inside of me, inspiring the urge to grab hold of something that is so far out of reach. "What if I can't do it? What if I never find the proof? What if we're just here, hiding forever?"

Her head jerks back as if she's been hit. "Girl, that's not even an option. I mean my pussy is good, but it's not good enough to get a man I haven't fucked in years to give me this big ass house for forever."

The words combined with the sheer seriousness of her expression surprises a laugh out of me. "Oh, my God. I really need you to stop talking," I wheeze, holding my sides.

"You're laughing, but I'm so for real right now. We can't stay here forever, Selene, and we won't need to. Marsh is going back to prison. Aubrey is going to end up in a cell right next to him. Cordelia and Gambit and whoever the hell else is in on this little conspiracy theory, is going to get what's coming to them, and then you're going to live happily ever after with Cal and Beck. There is no other acceptable outcome, do you hear me?"

"Well there is one other outcome I'd accept," I say tentatively.

"And what exactly would that look like?"

"Adopting Isis and Imani?"

My eyes run in frenzied lines over her face, trying to gauge her thoughts before she can fully process what I've said. There's shock, and the small flickers of cautious excitement pulling at the corners of her lips.

"I didn't realize you wanted more kids."

"I didn't, and I don't want just any kid. I want the chance to raise them, to show them what it feels like to grow up with people in your corner who'll always have your back and stand at your side. They deserve to know the love and safety of a home again, and I think that when all of this is said and done, I can give them that."

I bite my lower lip as hope swells in my chest. It's accompanied by sharp pangs of guilt that come from having to leave the girls without saying a word. They know what it's like to be left behind, and I know that kind of pain has left them with scars, I just hate that I might be the person reopening those wounds for them now.

"Do you think they'll want me?"

Monique frowns. "What?! Of course, they'll want you, Selene. Those girls are obsessed with you. They talk about you, Cal and Beck all the time. I don't think there's anything you could do to change that."

"Except disappear for days with no explanation."

"Sel, Isis and Imani are smart girls. They are aware of what's happening right now. The hunt for Leland and his obsession with you are all anyone is talking about. I'm sure they're more worried about you than anything else."

Despite the strength of her conviction, I struggle to accept her reassurance. The guilt and anxiety are just too much for Monique to break through. I still thank her, though, accepting her reassuring smile and allowing her to set the pace as we resume our walk.

"I assume Cal and Beck are on the same page as you?"

"Yes. Beck said he even talked to his therapist about it."

She fans herself with her hand, swooning. "A Black man in therapy, we *love* to see it."

I shake my head, exhausted from her silliness and the walk. We're nearing the patio now, and I'm deciding if I should grab a seat next to Cal and convince him to use the grill for the chicken he has marinating in the fridge for dinner tonight or do another lap with Mo when I notice Beck stepping outside with the laptop in hand.

His brows are furrowed, and there's a grim tilt to his lips that makes continuing the walk a distant thought. Monique follows me up onto the teak wood deck, both of us pausing opposite the men.

"What's wrong?" I ask.

Beck turns the computer to me, showing me the digital monitoring app. It takes a moment for me to realize the messages displayed on the screen are coming from my phone. There's one text selected, and the content of it shocks me just as much as the name of the sender.

> Jordan St. James: I need to see you.

* * *

WE ARGUE for what feels like hours about whether it's safe for me to meet with Jordan. Monique is team, do whatever the hell gets us out of this house and back to our lives quicker while Cal and Beck are steadfast in their refusal to entertain the idea for even a second. They each make their points known while I listen intently, allowing them all to speak even though I knew what I was going to do the moment I saw the text.

"This is a bad idea," Cal says, pressing the button to open the gate and allow Jordan through. Beck volunteered to meet her on the road and inspect her vehicle, so now he's in her backseat. I'm almost certain he has a gun pointed at her even though the video footage doesn't allow me to see that much.

"The meeting or the location?" I ask, leaning against the wall near the front door.

"Both," he mutters as he flips the deadbolt.

"We need to know what she has to say, Cal."

"We also need to keep you safe."

"She is safe," Monique reminds him from her spot inside the grand arch that leads into the main living area. There's a flare of agitation lacing her words. "Beck searched the car. He confirmed that no one else is in the vehicle–"

Cal grimaces. "Besides Sam Granger."

"What's that about anyway?"

"I don't know, Selene. I think they're sleeping together, but I don't know. I don't know anything right now except that bringing them here was a bad fucking idea."

"Hey." I close the space between us, taking his chin between my fingers. "You're scared. I get that. You're allowed to be scared. You're allowed to be whatever you need to be in this moment, but you are not allowed to take any of that out on me."

Remorse softens the hard lines of his expression. He closes his eyes, pushing out a breath that's meant to soothe him but calms me too. "I'm sorry."

I steal a kiss from his lips as the headlights of Jordan's car send streams of light passing through the windows of the foyer. Cal urges me to step back, and I don't argue, taking up residence at Monique's side. When Beck knocks on the door using the specific cadence he and Cal came up with, she reaches for my hand, an irrational wave of fear thrumming through each of us. My heart smacks against my rib cage as Cal cocks his gun with one hand and pulls open the door with the other, and I nearly pass out from relief when I see that everything is as it should be.

Beck is at the back with his gun out and plenty of distance between him and the rest of the unlikely trio. Jordan and Sam are in front, and she throws her hands up when she finds herself staring down the barrel of another weapon.

"I don't think the guns are necessary," Sam says, hands raised in surrender. "We're not here to hurt anyone. We want to help."

Since Jordan is already staring at me, I step forward. "You've spent years in Aubrey's corner, lying and scheming right alongside him. Why should I believe you're ready to turn on him now?"

Suddenly, she's not afraid of the gun anymore. She shoves past Cal, ignoring all three men as they shout for her to stop. I hold a hand up to calm them, almost certain she means me no harm. Jordan stops just a few feet away from me and Monique, and I don't realize she's wearing a turtleneck in this August heat until she reaches for her collar, hands trembling as she yanks it down to reveal angry red marks around her throat.

Her eyes shine with unshed tears that emphasize the ruptured blood vessels, and when she speaks, her voice is nothing more than a hoarse rasp. "Because the bastard tried to have me killed."

The revelation should change something for me. It should make me less skeptical or at the very least sympathetic, but as I stare at Jordan, I feel nothing more than the faint twinges of satisfaction that come from seeing someone get what they deserve. She is not a victim. She is not an ally. She's a minnow who got dropped into the ocean and found out she wasn't a shark. I don't feel bad for her, but I will hear her out.

"Let's talk in here."

Everyone follows me through the house, and when I take a seat at the head of the table, Jordan choose the one to my left while Monique takes the one to my right. Cal and Beck remain standing, keeping a close eye on Sam, who's on his feet as well, rubbing Jordan's shoulders.

"Do you have any tea?" he asks. "Talking hurts her throat."

"This isn't a social call, Granger," Beck growls.

He starts to defend his request, but Jordan lays her hand over his. "It's okay, Sam. I'll be fine."

"You've survived worse," Monique quips.

Jordan dips her chin. "I deserved that."

"You did," I confirm. "But I'm not interested in what you deserve, I'm interested in what you know and whether you have any proof to back it up."

"Of course I have proof. I've recorded every meeting I've had with Aubrey from the day we met up until he fired me four days ago"

"Where are they?"

"Some place safe. I wanted to talk to you before I handed them over."

My mind begins to race at the mere thought of what could be in those files. Impatience becomes a nagging pain at the back of my skull that has me blurting out words instead of listening.

"We already know everything," I tell her. "Aubrey and Cordelia are in bed with a man named Phineas Gambit who is using his money and influence, and a whole lot of coercion, to ensure that his construction company makes a shit ton of money off of government contracts. Gambit is a psychopath who eliminates weak links without a second thought which is why he sent one of his men to kill you when you fell apart during the press conference." I tilt my head to the side. "How am I doing so far?"

She swallows and then winces in pain. "You know more than I thought you did, but that's not everything."

"It's everything that matters."

"No." Jordan shakes her head, emerald eyes wide and imploring. "No, Selene. If you knew everything that mattered, you wouldn't be here building a case; you wouldn't be looking for proof to have Aubrey impeached and arrested. You'd be figuring out how to get away with his murder."

26

AUBREY

A*pril 28, 2009*

"Phineas, have you met my son, *Senator* Taylor?"

Dad slaps me on the shoulder. His heavy hand landing with a dull thwack that agitates an old baseball injury. He knows about my torn rotator cuff. He was there, screaming at me about accuracy and control, when the tendons pulled away from the bone in the fourth inning. You would think that knowledge would stop him from pounding on it with those clubs he calls hands or squeezing it when he needs my attention, but it doesn't. In fact, I'm half convinced he does it on purpose, using the pain to direct my focus to whatever person or thing he wants it on at the moment.

And right now he wants on this man.

Or rather, he wants this man's attention on me.

Phineas? I think that's what his name is, squints in my direction. Disdain curling his upper lip and suggesting that he isn't as familiar with my father as my father is with him.

"And you are?" His voice is as smooth as the whiskey in cup, but his eyes are cutting. Shattered jade with sharp, jagged edges that snag on your skin as they rip through.

Dad's grip on my shoulder loosens, and I slip out of his hold, extending a hand to the only man I've ever seen humble my father. "I'm Aubrey Taylor."

"*Senator* Aubrey Taylor," he replies, flicking his gaze to my father as he mocks him. Then he looks back at me, disgust dripping off his tongue when he says, "I do not shake hands."

Immediately, I drop my hand, shoving it into my pocket to hide the evidence of my blunder and then cursing myself for being so fucking nervous. One glance over my shoulder reveals that my father has abandoned me. My jaw clenches as I turn back to the stranger who's still staring at me.

"I apologize for my father's interruption."

He dragged me over to the private corner at the edge of the balcony overlooking the D.C.'s skyline, telling me Phineas was the only person at this party I needed to meet. The way he spoke, I thought they were acquainted, but now I know this was just another one of his ham-handed approaches to networking. He's always complaining about how people pussy foot around each other, waiting for a friend of a friend of a friend to come along and give them a way in when what they should be doing is making it happen for themselves. I've told him repeatedly how embarrassing that approach is, but he never listens.

"You are still standing here, so it is now your interruption, is it not?"

"Right, well I guess I'll just—"

I hook a thumb over my shoulder, indicating my intention to leave him alone, and he turns his back, moving toward a door I failed to notice when I was making an ass of myself. He grips the handle and glances at me, boredom floating in those freaky green eyes.

"Are you coming, Senator Taylor?"

Shock and intrigue move me forward, and soon I'm following Phineas up a flight of stairs that leads to the roof. We were already up pretty damn high when we were on the balcony, but the air is different up here. Dense with possibility, but light enough to make you feel like you're floating.

Phineas strides right up the edge and takes a seat, feet dangling over the city streets from thirty stories up.

"Must I invite you to engage in every interaction we have tonight?"

The impatient lilt to his otherwise docile tone pushes me into action. Soon, my feet are dangling over the edge too, and Phineas is handing me a cigar he produced out of thin air then cut and lit while I was thinking about what it might feel like to jump.

I take a long pull, relishing the flavor of singed earth and sweet wood on my tongue. "My wife would kill me if she knew I was up here."

"Strict, is she?"

"Doesn't even begin to describe it," I admit, huffing circles of smoke that linger in the air, tangling with the ones Phineas makes. Selene has always been…particular, but the last few years have exacerbated things. "She's worse since the kid was born. He's four God-damn years old, and she still acts like he needs her for everything. I don't think I even saw my mother until I was ten."

"Nannies?"

"Nannies."

"I do not have the desire to procreate," he announces, holding his cigar off to the side and rolling it between his fingers gently to dislodge the ash. "But if I did, I would enlist the help of caregivers. Is your wife opposed?"

"Strongly. She grew up poor, so she doesn't understand how much easier parenting is when you have money. It's like she's determined to struggle the same way her parents did, make the same kind of sacrifices they did even though we don't have to."

Truthfully, I can't tell if Phineas is interested in this conversation or simply entertaining the ramblings of madman, but I don't think it really matters. It's nice to get this shit off my chest. I can't say any of it to my mom because she'll just bring it up to Selene, and if I mention it to my dad, he'll go off on a tangent about letting a woman control my life.

He pushes a stream of billowing smoke out between his clenched teeth. "What kind of sacrifices?"

"Sleep, time, sex, our careers. I'm serving my first term in the fucking Senate, and she's making me promise not to even think about a run for the Oval until 2028." I brush ash from my cigar off my lap and try to squash the anger rolling through me. I'm not successful. "Can you believe that shit? That's twenty fucking years from now."

"I am aware of how math works, Senator."

For the first time since we met, I look at him. I mean, really look at him, trying to make sense of his whole…vibe, but instead getting stuck at the gray hairs overtaking the dark brown strands at his temples.

"How old are you?"

A vein pulses in the center of his forehead as he stares at me, giving me the sense that he gets this question for this reason all the time. "Thirty-five."

"Do you know why my father wanted me to meet you?"

He runs his tongue across his teeth, breaking eye contact to look back out at the sky.

"Perhaps because it is my birthday, and you are a guest at my party."

My jaw drops. "Holy shit. I'm sorry, Mr.—"

"Gambit," he supplies, turning his head slowly and offering me his hand, which I take with my mouth agape.

"I thought you didn't shake hands, Mr. Gambit."

"With strangers," he clarifies. "I do not shake hands with strangers, but you and I are not strangers, Senator Taylor. We are very good friends."

* * *

June 3, 2015

The goddamn air in this office is broken again.

Beads of sweat roll down my back, soaking into my shirt and making my skin crawl. The fan in the corner spins uselessly, blowing hot air in my direction that causes the edges of the papers I'm reading through to flutter.

I slam my hand down on the stack, trying to stop them from being picked up and carried away but it's no use. The pages on the top lift up and take off, floating around the room while I watch with resentment simmering in my bones. Not just for the papers, but for the fucked up air conditioning unit connected to the offices at this end of the hall that never seems to function the way it's supposed to, leaving me and the other junior members of the Senate to freeze in the winter and sweat through multiple sets of clothes in the summer while the bastards with more seniority and notoriety live in the lap of luxury.

Most of all, the resentment is for the woman and child smiling at me from the frame on my desk. Their happy faces mock my suffering, which is ironic considering they're the cause of it. Their demands for my time and attention devour every morsel of my energy, keeping me from committee assignments that would raise my profile and help me ascend from the hellish ranks of the Cannon House.

A low whistle pierces the silence of my reverie, and I jolt, brows shooting toward my hairline when I see Phineas Gambit standing in my doorway. I'm on my feet in an instant, rushing around the desk to pick up the pages of the prospectus now scattered all over the floor.

He looks down his nose at me, eerie verdant orbs refusing to hide judgment.

"Sorry," I mutter, hating that this is his first impression of me after six years. "Please, come in." I wave him through the door, but he stays put. His hesitation puts the men behind him on high alert. They're clearly his security. One steps forward, glaring at me over Gambit's shoulder.

"Is everything alright, sir?"

"Everything is fine, Garrison. I am simply trying to discern if the Senator is well or not."

His eyes ghost over my brow, and I lift my hand, wiping the sweat away. "I'm not sick. The air condition is just out."

"Mmm." When he steps inside, Garrison and the other man try to move with him. He holds up a hand, and they pause. "The room is not big enough for all of us. Garrison, at the door. Woodard, in the hall."

He snaps his fingers, and they do exactly as he asks.

"Are you waiting for me to give you an order as well, Senator?"

"No."

"Good. Then please have a seat. I do not want to be inside this dreadful office any longer than I have to."

Since I feel the same way about the space, I can't bring myself to be offended. I take a seat behind my desk. "How can I help you, Mr. Gambit?"

"Straight to the point. I like that," he muses.

"Yes, well, I have a meeting in fifteen minutes."

"For the Environment and Public Works committee, correct? You all are voting on the leasing prospectuses for veteran outpatient clinics throughout Virginia."

The certainty with which he speaks gives me pause. I glance at the papers on my desk, wondering if he managed to read them while they were scattered on the floor or if he gleaned that information from where he's sitting.

"I already know I am correct, Senator. And I will spare you the stress of wondering if I had that information before I walked into your office." He pauses for dramatic effect then says, "I did."

"That isn't surprising. It's public information."

Most people don't go through the trouble of getting it though. But then again, Phineas Gambit isn't like most people. He's sitting in my sweltering office on a hot June day in a bespoke suit with three custom pieces to it, and he hasn't even broken a sweat. He glances at his watch, tsking when he sees the time.

"You will be late for your meeting if we do not speed this up. Quickly, Senator, ask me why I'm here."

"Why are you here, Mr. Gambit?"

His smile is a slow, sinister stretching of skin. "Because I need a favor from an old friend, and *you* need a man like *me* indebted to you."

* * *

JANUARY 11, 2018

"I just don't understand why you couldn't show up," Selene says for the millionth fucking time tonight. She's been home from her party for an hour, still in the floor length black gown she wore out because she's so busy nagging me about missing her special night to undress.

I turn my back to her, pulling covers up over my head. "I'm trying to sleep."

"You're behaving like a child, Aubrey. Don't you think I deserve to know why my husband wasn't there beside me, celebrating my accomplishments the way I always celebrate his? I mean, I could understand if you were working...."

She keeps droning on, but I tune her out, pulling my phone off the nightstand and smiling at a message from Susie or Sarah or Sasha. I can't remember her name, but I won't be forgetting the sight of her tits bouncing in my face anytime soon. The meet up wasn't supposed to last as long as it did, but I couldn't bring myself to cut it short. It felt good to be with a woman who appreciated me as a man. Who saw my power and revered it instead of resenting it.

That's all I get at home.

Complaints. Critiques. And the constant fucking nagging.

I just wasn't in the mood for it tonight. Couldn't stomach the thought of standing next to her while she smiled smugly and told anyone who would listen that winning a Global Tech Award wasn't supposed to happen for another ten years.

Throwing the covers off me, I sit up, glaring at her. "Why did you accept it?"

She's stripped down, the dress in a pool around her ankles. "What?"

"The award. Why did you accept it? According to your career plan, you're not supposed to receive one until 2028."

"I guess timelines change," she says as she scoops up her dress and disappears into the closet while I stare after her.

"Timelines change," I whisper, savoring the flavor of shifting expectations and free will on my way out of the bedroom. By the time I make it to my office, it's the only thing on my tongue, and I'm so distracted by it that I don't even notice when Phineas answers the phone.

"Senator Taylor."

Between the years we've known each other and the favors I've done for him, you would think he'd be inclined to use my first name, but he never does. I bypass greeting him altogether, skipping straight to the point the way he always does while I pour myself three fingers of whiskey.

"I want the Oval." The words burn on their way out. I knock them back in, washing them down with the amber liquid. Phineas is quiet, so I swallow and then repeat myself. "I want the Oval."

"What do you expect me to do with this information?"

Another heavy pour. This one four fingers or maybe even five. I'm too wired to care.

"The same thing I do with the tid-bits of information and instructions you give me: make it happen."

"You are not ready," he replies.

"Bullshit."

Years of doing his bidding and taking his advice has led to a major rise in my political profile. I've moved out of Cannon House and into an office with a view of the Potomac. I'm leading committees instead of just begging to sit on them. I am well known and respected among my colleagues, and most of all, I'm ready to make a play for the fucking Oval.

When I say all of this to him, he meets my explanation with an unimpressed hum. "And yet, none of the people who matter know who you are."

"None of the people who matter?!" I sputter, slamming the crystal tumbler in my hand down. "Who the fuck are you talking about? You and your rich friends? Because they most certainly know me. They've benefited from your connection to me, and now I'm ready for the proceeds to flow the other way."

"Please lower your voice, Senator. The people I am referring to are not my friends, or yours. They are the normal, every day Americans who need to know your name and your face. They need to feel connected to you, and they do not care what Senate committees you've served on."

"Tell me what to do," I plead, years-old desperation and desire caving in my chest. "Whatever it is, I'll do it."

"Come to my home tomorrow night, 9 p.m."

I'm still thinking about how abruptly he ended the call when I show up at the high rise where we met. To my shock, Phineas answers his own door, welcoming me into his space with a sweep of his arm. It's been close to two years since we've seen each other in person, and he's no less disconcerting to me now than he was the day all of this started. The man is an enigma and, to be frank, a bit of an asshole, which is why I'm not surprised to find that he failed to mention we wouldn't be dining alone tonight.

Phineas takes his seat at the head of the table and gestures to the stout, blonde woman on his left who I recognize from the halls of the Capitol. "Senator Taylor, I am sure you know Senator Barnes."

She lifts a hand in greeting, and there's a deep Southern twang to her voice when she speaks. "Please, call me Cordelia."

"Cordelia, it's nice to see you in a more personal setting."

"And this is Travis Langham," Phineas tells me, tilting his head in the direction of the man to his right who salutes me.

"It's a pleasure, Travis."

"Pleasure's all mine, Senator."

Phineas claps his hands. "Now that we are all acquainted, let us eat."

The meal is delicious, but the conversation is stilted. No one seems to understand why I'm here, including me, and by the time we've reached the dessert portion of the night, I'm questioning whether I heard Phineas correctly when he told me to come over.

I'm in the process of bringing a scoop of vanilla ice cream to my mouth when Phineas looks to Cordelia. "Tell Senator Taylor the worst thing you've ever done."

My spoon falls out of my hand, clattering on the edge of my bowl loudly. Travis snickers, enjoying my shock, while Cordelia's expression remains smooth. She takes a sip of her water before shifting in her seat to face me head on.

"For the past two years, I've taken payments from a vendor who sells defective bulletproof vests to ensure they are awarded government contracts. Those vests are shipped to the Middle East and given to U.S.

troops who die from wounds they would have survived if their gear was effective."

I don't know what I thought she was going to say, what kind of dinner party icebreaker game I thought we were playing, but never in a million years could I have expected that. Travis chuckles, raising his hand gleefully.

"Can I go now, Phineas?"

"Of course. Thank you for waiting your turn this time."

His salacious grin sends shivers down my spine, but I keep my expression neutral. "I'm a cop." I don't quite get the joke, but he delivers it like a punch line, and both Phineas and Cordelia laugh. "It's my job to hunt down murderers," Travis explains. "But occasionally, I get paid to be one."

More than a little confused, I look to Phineas, waiting for his confession or an explanation, whichever comes first. He dabs at his mouth with a corner of his cloth napkin and then drops it on top of the dish, signaling the end of dessert. Members of his staff appear out of nowhere, sweeping away the dishes quietly.

"Are you wondering why we are telling you this, Senator?"

I nod jerkily, unable to speak. Phineas smiles, and it's another one of those predatory grins that spreads slow like molasses. "Because it's important to me that you understand no one here is going to judge you."

Finally, I find my voice. "Judge me?"

"Yes, for what you're about to do."

"And what exactly am I about to do?"

He snaps his fingers, and a woman appears at my side, sliding a folder in front of me. The outside is plain, no words or markings, but when I open it there's a timeline on the first page that lays out my life for the next eight years. It starts with the phone call to Phineas last night and ends with me winning the Presidential election in November 2024. Everything in between is details and logistics like hire a woman named Jordan St. James as my campaign manager and convince Selene to start straightening her hair, but all of that comes after the one thing that gives me pause.

I drop the folder, finally understanding why Phineas had Cordelia and Travis share the darkest parts of their souls with me.

"You want to kill my son?"

It's there in black and white: *October 19, 2019, Aubrey Taylor Jr. dies in a school shooting.*

I'm aware that some part of me should be disgusted, that some part of me should be outraged. Those parts are eerily quiet right now, though, if they even exist at all, and the only thing I am is curious.

I look up, meeting the expectant gazes of the only three people in the world I think truly understand me, and ask the only question that matters at the moment.

"Will it work?"

27

SELENE

Vomit splashes in the kitchen sink.

Hot, rancid chunks of a meal I can't remember consuming stare back at me from the bottom of a stainless steel sink that, seconds ago, was spotless. I cleaned it myself, and if I look past the mess, I can remember what it looked like before it was ruined.

Just like I can recall what I looked like, what I *felt* like, before I found out the truth behind my son's death. Before my grief was restructured, before the pain that runs like currents in the marrow of my bones was reshaped with Jordan's words, made over by the dark verity of Aubrey's soul.

A monster.

I married a monster. I made him a father. I bore him a child he turned into a sacrificial lamb, and I missed every sign that he was a butcher, that our home was a slaughter house.

My nails scrape against the underside of the marble encasing the sink. Strands of my hair cling to the faucet, caught in the fine grooves while I heave once again, spilling what little is left inside of my stomach.

It's the only sound in the room.

No one moves or speaks, and I don't know if I'm thankful for the silence or bothered by it. It doesn't matter. Nothing matters because my son is dead and his father, the man I loved, the man I married, the man *I* chose, killed him.

Killed him.

Our baby.

My baby.

My blood. My flesh. My bone.

A life that started with our love ended by his obsession with power. A body I built from scratch—hands, feet, fingers, toes, a precious face and my father's nose—rotting in a grave and for what? For money? For dominion? For influence and notoriety? How could any of it be worth our son's life?

The questions I mean to keep to myself flow out of my mouth. They are met with nothing but silence, which is fine because I don't want anyone interrupting me. I don't need a single voice or word of compassion getting in the way of the scream that builds inside of me, beating the bile up my throat and splitting the air.

It's not enough.

I spin, feeling strands of hair pull and snap as I go, and, still screaming, grab the closest thing to me and launch it at the wall. It's a glass vase filled with hydrangeas, and I watch the lovely purple petals explode into the air, raining down in a cloud of glass and water that lands at my feet.

Jordan flinches, and Sam steps between us, shielding her from me because I'm still screaming and looking for another thing to destroy. He's right to be concerned that the next thing might be her because she's the closest thing to Aubrey in this room. Glass crunches under my feet as I cross the space between the island and dining area, dragging water and crushed petals along with me. The scream is nothing more than a low whine in the back of my throat by the time I'm in Sam's face.

"*Move.*"

"I'm afraid I can't do that, ma'am."

"Get the fuck out of her way," Cal barks.

I can't look at him. I can't meet the eyes of any of the people I love in this room because I don't want to see. The judgment. The confusion. The questions about all the things I must have missed.

Sam looks at him though, and whatever he sees must be enough to scare him because he shifts out of my way, revealing Jordan's sunken eyes and hollow cheeks. She's so thin, fragile almost, but it doesn't stop me from drawing my hand back and bringing it down across her face. My palm stings, but there's no satisfaction in the pain. I have this horrible, sinking suspicion that nothing will ever satisfy me again.

To her credit, Jordan takes the blow like a champ. She covers the imprint of my splayed fingers with her hand and glares at me as she turns her head back in my direction.

"I understand that you're upset," she rasps.

I slap her again, gripping her hair before she can recover and forcing her up out of her seat because I need her standing. Tears bloom in her eyes, skating down her cheeks as she searches for compassion that doesn't exist inside of me right now.

"Is that all you have?" I growl. "White woman tears? My son is dead, Jordan. HE'S DEAD AND HIS FATHER KILLED HIM, AND YOU HAVE THE NERVE TO SIT HERE CRYING LIKE YOU'RE SOME KIND OF VICTIM?!"

"That's enough," Sam says, standing too close to me. "You're upset. That's understandable, but—"

"Step back, Granger."

Cal is closer now, and Beck is radiating rage from not too far behind. I don't know which one of them pulls Sam away, but he goes screaming. "She's pregnant! Please don't hurt her. She's pregnant."

"*Sam*!" Jordan gasps, cutting frantic eyes at him.

My fingers relax, and I stumble back, staring at the stomach Jordan now has a protective hand over. Suddenly, I'm lost in a sea of memories, drowning in flashes of a past that was never real, every image once colored in love now tarnished.

I swallow, tasting the remnants of my regurgitated meal. "How far along?"

"Who cares?" Monique mumbles. She's slouched down in her seat, tears streaming down her face that she doesn't bother to wipe away. It's such a clear demonstration of grief, a tangible representation of the promise she made months ago to carry the weight of my son's loss with me. Neither of us knew then that we'd be starting the process all over again.

"Eleven weeks," Jordan whispers. "We were keeping it quiet until I made it past the first trimester."

"Makes sense why you've looked so awful lately. Between the pregnancy and guilty conscience, it must feel like you're being eaten alive."

An embarrassed blush rides high on her cheeks. "I didn't know what he was, Selene. When I started working with him, I thought he was like every other candidate. Entitled. Egotistical. A little sadistic, maybe. But I had no clue he was…"

"Capable of killing his own child."

She nods, lips trembling. "He didn't tell me the truth about AJ until the night of the debate. Do you remember?"

"I remember saying Sanders would keep digging and you telling me that there was nothing left for him to find."

The look Cordelia and Aubrey shared that night passes through my mind, reminding me that I knew Jordan was wrong. I just had no idea how wrong.

"I believed it when I said it," Jordan insists.

"I know you did. How long did they wait to tell you the truth?"

"Not long. After you went back to bed, Cordelia forced Aubrey to fill me in. He was almost…excited to tell me what he'd done. How Gambit laid it all out for him, explaining that killing Aubrey Jr. would raise his profile immediately, that suddenly voters would know him, like him, *feel* for him in a way they hadn't previously. The school shooting angle was an added bonus, allowing them to take it from a regular tragedy to a political issue he could build a career off of."

"*I was in the next room.*"

A wave of nausea sweeps through me, but I push it down, knowing it doesn't matter now. That it wouldn't have mattered then. My knees are weak, and they shake as I return to my seat. Monique grabs my hand immediately, but I still can't look at her. Jordan lets out a weary sigh. She looks tired, but she remains standing, leaning against the back of the chair I pulled her out of.

"It didn't matter to them, Selene. Cordelia said it was the only way I would understand the gravity of what we had to do next."

"Get rid of Sanders."

"Yes, they knew you were right about him digging deeper. I was adamant that if Sanders had caught even a whiff of what they'd done he would have put all of his focus on that instead of the affair."

"Absolutely. He probably wouldn't have gone public, though."

"No," Jordan agrees. "He would have used it to take Aubrey off the board completely. Maybe even parlayed it into a lifelong blackmail situation."

"And I would have never known the truth."

"Probably not."

"How did they do it?"

The question comes from Cal, and now that I finally have the courage to look at him, I'm able to see that neither he nor Beck are holding on to Sam anymore. They're all standing back, giving Jordan and I space to talk. Sam is still fuming about me abusing Jordan, shooting daggers at me from afar.

"Langham injected him with something while he was drinking his morning coffee on his patio," she says. "I didn't ask for specifics, and they didn't offer any. After they sent me to pay off the coroner to leave the puncture wound behind his ear off of the report, no one ever mentioned it again."

"How do they know each other?" Monique asks.

"I think he went to college with Phineas or something? I don't know. They're thick as thieves, though, and Phineas trusts him implicitly."

Beck snorts derisively. "He would have to in order to send him to assassinate a President."

"It's not just trust," Jordan says, some unnamed emotion swirling through emerald eyes. "It's a shared sickness. Phineas takes great pleasure in pulling people's strings, but Langham is the one he sends to sever them, and he *loves* it. The violence. The fear...."

I can't reconcile the man she's describing against the one who I met that day outside of Beaumont High. The one who appeared genuinely sad at my son's funeral. How had I missed it? The darkness lurking inside of him? Inside of Aubrey?

Monique gestures at Jordan's throat. "Langham is the one who did that to you."

"Yes."

"Then you're really on the outs with them," Mo replies. "And now you're here hoping Selene can save you from the monsters you gladly climbed in bed with."

Her succinct summary makes Jordan's hackles rise. "I'm here to help, Monique."

"But all you've done so far is hurt, Jordan. You've broke my best friend's heart with these stories—"

"They're not stories!" She yanks her collar down, baring her neck once again. "Langham almost killed me. That's the truth. Aubrey conspired with Cordelia and Phineas to have his son killed. That's the truth. They assassinated a fucking President to keep him and everyone else from finding out. THAT'S THE TRUTH!"

"You're here to cover your ass," Monique shoots back. "That's the truth too."

Frustrated, Jordan shifts her attention back to me. "Marsh is dead."

The revelation lands like a bomb, sending shock waves through the entire room. Everyone besides Sam and me begin shouting questions. Jordan deals with this inquisition much better than she did the one during the press conference, probably because she's not lying. She explains, mostly to Cal and Beck because the majority of the inquiries are coming from them, that Phineas wasn't on board with Aubrey's idea to break Marsh out to take care of me. He wanted Langham to do it, but Aubrey was insistent, saying that they needed someone with a clear motive, not another mysterious death. Of course, things didn't go to plan, and Phineas ordered Woodard and Garrison to kill Marsh because he kept demanding more money for a job he wasn't motivated to complete.

"They posed his body on White House grounds. The story will run tomorrow, and they'll say that he was killed while attempting to breach the perimeter to get to you."

I rest my elbows on the table, holding my head in my hands. "What happens now? Do I wake up with Travis Langham on top of me with his hands around my throat?"

"That's not going to happen," Beck assures me.

"No," Jordan says. "What happens next is you do the one thing I can't."

"Expose them."

A heavy sigh from Monique follows my words. I know she's suppressing the urge to launch into a speech about white women depending on Black women to be brave enough to dismantle the systems they've benefited from their entire lives. I understand her frustration. Jordan could easily expose the world she's been a part of for so long. She could take the recordings she's dangling over my head and go straight to the press.

They'd believe her before they'd ever believe me.

"Listen, Selene. I wouldn't be bringing this to you if I felt like there was anyone else who could take them on and not be bought, bribed or killed in the process."

I drop my hands, staring into her earnest expression. "Like they bought you."

She rears back. "Selene, I—"

"You don't get points for being here, Jordan. You don't get an award for running to a trusted adult when the wolf you brought home and hid under your bed decides it wants to eat you for dinner. You are complicit in all of this, and maybe you didn't know everything at first, but when you found out, you did nothing."

"I'm doing something now."

"WHEN IT'S TOO LATE!" I shout, slamming my fists on the table. "Too late for Sutton and President Sanders and whoever else they've hurt along the way." My chair flies out from under me as I stand, voice shaking, heart pounding with the injustice of it all. "It is too late for my baby, Jordan, but congratulations on being able to save yours. Maybe the prison guards will let you hold them before they carry it away and send you back to your cell."

Her eyes go wide, and Sam steps forward now, wrapping an arm around her shoulders as the image I've just painted sends her into hysterics. I want to laugh, to ask her if she really thought there was any amount of information she could give, any plea she could make that would spare her from the hell I'm about to rain down on all of them. Maybe she thought the news of her pregnancy would save her, but somehow knowing she's carrying new life while the one I nurtured and grew in my womb was stolen from me by a man she's protected for months makes it all worse.

My palms twitch with the desire to slap her again. Sam must see the desire because he urges her back.

"Let's go," he whispers. No one tries to stop them as he guides her out of the room, but just before they disappear from view, Jordan pauses.

"I'll send the files," she says, wiping away tears that don't move me at all. "They'll be in your inbox before the end of the night."

"Great."

"And Selene?" I arch a brow, urging her to continue. "For whatever it's worth, I'm sorry."

A bitter laugh breaks the tension in the room. "Oh, Jordan. Your apology isn't worth a God damn thing to me."

28

CAL

Jordan sends the files an hour after she and Sam leave.

They were just as extensive as she said they were, but no one had the energy to go through them after everything we'd learned. Beck and I cleaned up the aftermath of Selene's emotional destruction, Monique took her into the living room, holding her on the couch while her wails filled every crevice of the vast space.

She cried for hours. Monique cried with her, sobbing the way someone only can when they've lost what you've lost, when they hurt how you hurt, when their heart knows how to read the map of your pain. I've shed tears for Beck that way, wrapped him in my arms the way Monique did for Selene, cradled him like a baby and rocked him like one too.

I wanted to be able to do that for her as well, and the same desire rolled off Beck as the minutes ticked by. I was proud of the way we held it together. The way we sat and watched and waited, witnessing pain we couldn't be a part of soothing until we carried her to bed and crushed her sadness with our love. Slashed her doubts with our reassurances. Ripped the blame she was trying to carry out of her hands and replaced it with acceptance.

Hopefully, it was enough.

"When do you think they'll be up?" Beck asks, sitting a cup of freshly brewed coffee beside me. We've been up since six, going through the files Jordan sent and taking notes because neither one of us could sleep. Selene left the bed when we did, but she headed straight to Monique's room. It's almost two in the afternoon, and I haven't heard so much as a peep from either of them.

No footsteps overhead.

No soft murmurs.

No sobs either, which is a good thing.

I take a long sip of the steaming liquid. "I don't know."

"Should we wake them? I mean, they've got to eat."

"They'll eat when they get up, Beck."

His leg bounces, the scent of his anxiety curling in the air. "Selene threw up her dinner. She's probably starving."

"Beckham."

It's a gentle warning accompanied by the presence of my hand on his thigh. Onyx eyes fly to mine, glazed with regretful tears. "I hate that we were right," he whispers.

Months have passed since we first floated the idea of Aubrey's involvement with Selene's kidnapping and AJ's death. She refused to consider it, even going so far as storming out of the room to avoid having the conversation. We didn't bring it up again, but every time we uncovered a new piece of information, I braced myself for it to lead back to that theory. When so much time went by without it happening, I started to hope we were wrong, even though I knew we weren't.

"Me too."

Beck covers my hand with his, fingertips kissing the inside of my palm when he turns it into something of an embrace. "I can't believe she thinks this is somehow her fault."

"That's just the guilt talking. You, better than anyone, should understand that."

"I do, it's just hard to…" he trails off, searching for words to convey a thought that's echoed in my mind at least once a day for years.

For as long as I've known him, I've watched Beck carry the same weight Selene started to shoulder last night, loving him through that pain makes me feel more equipped to care for her as she navigates it. It's still scary, though. Knowing that there's hurt inside of someone your love might not be able to touch. I have to keep reminding myself that it touched Beck's. That it broke down walls and watered gardens left for dead long ago. And if it did it before, it can certainly do it again.

This time the process will move faster because I'm not the only one working toward the goal. Beck is right beside me, pushing love and understanding, dismantling harmful beliefs, meeting every what if with the gentle reminders of what was and what will be.

"See someone you love blame themselves for something that was completely out of their control?" I ask, finishing the sentence he abandoned with an arch of my brow that says 'welcome to my world'.

He balks, pushing my hand off his leg. "Shut up, Drake."

"You only resort to telling me to shut up when you know I'm right."

"I only resort to telling you to shut up when you're being an obnoxious ass," he retorts, slamming a finger down on the space bar to resume the recording he was listening to. There are hundreds, maybe even thousands, of them, and we've split them up. Beck is responsible for the later years, taking notes on everything pertinent to our investigation while the recordings play on the air-gapped laptop Selene insisted we keep copies of everything on. I've got the early years, and so far, I've learned a lot. Like the fact that Phineas Gambit recommended Jordan to Aubrey, instructing him to hire her after he was elected for his third term as a U.S. Senator because he liked her ruthlessness. I also learned that capitalizing off the sympathy and national attention he'd gained from AJ's death was always a part of the plan to get him to the Oval.

Jordan loved the idea.

Even over audio, it's easy to tell how thrilled she was by the prospect. As soon as Aubrey said he had no qualms about discussing his son's murder or his wife's devastation, she started spouting off ideas, never stopping to consider why a father who'd just lost his child would be okay with any of that.

The other thing that's become abundantly clear as we've listened is how much and for how long Aubrey has harbored a deep hatred for Selene. Not once is he heard speaking of or about her in anything other than a disparaging manner. And what's worse, is when she's in the room, when her soft voice is heard over the recordings and her genuine questions and concerns are caught on audio, and that version of him is nowhere to be found. It's like he transforms into a loving husband. I mean, he's still an entitled son of a bitch who talks out of the side of his neck sometimes, but it's nothing like when she's not around.

Hearing the switch up, witnessing her being subjected to such manipulation, fills me with the kind of rage that's useless to me right now because it craves action and violence and at the moment all I can do is be still and listen to a woman who only ever says what she means —and believes the same to be true of others—be lied to by the man she trusted with every piece of herself.

Last night she asked us how she didn't see it, how she missed the signs, and now I know I was right when I told her there probably weren't any. Aubrey played the role of the dutiful husband and grieving father so well when Selene was around, it wouldn't have made any logical sense for her to do anything other than believe him. The illusion fell apart when the affair with Sutton became public. His mask slipped, and he never bothered to put it back on, completing his transformation into bitch ass motherfucker on the TV screen right now.

As Jordan promised, the news of Marsh's death broke this morning. All day, we've listened to segments about the assassination attempt that landed him in prison, his son's death and the grudge against Selene that led to his escape and eventual death on White House grounds. Psychologists have been interviewed to speak to his state of mind, the warden from his prison has made a statement addressing the death and refusing to speak on the escape, old clips from his days leading the Brothers have been aired to give context to his hateful existence, political pundits have speculated about whether his death means Selene will return to the public eye and discussed whether the President feels safe in the White House after the breach.

Lots of conversation, speculation and endless mentions of his name, but not once today, have I seen Aubrey live and in color.

It's an odd sensation, seeing his face, watching him smile and wave like he's innocent when I know what he's done, and I catch myself glaring at the TV as if he can feel my hate through the screen.

"Where is he?" Beck asks, forcing me to look away from the man and at his surroundings. He's fielding questions from a small press corps in front of a motorcade that's blocking black, wrought iron gates that feel far too familiar. I pause the recording on the laptop, disbelief curling into a ball in my chest.

"Is that—"

Beck holds up a hand to stop me, grabbing the remote to turn the volume up.

"President Taylor, you're supposed to be hosting a Cabinet meeting at the White House today. What are we doing here in Bethesda?"

My heart sinks. "*No.*"

"How the fuck did he find us?"

On the television, Aubrey is spouting off some bullshit about being eager to reunite with his wife now that the danger has passed. His voice is annoying, grating on my nerves, but it doesn't even compare to the sensation of hearing it pass through the speakers of the intercom near the front door.

"You've got two seconds to open this gate," he growls into the box, which makes no sense because on the TV he's still taking questions while Woodard and Garrison stand behind him.

Beck looks between the front door and the TV, processing the same information as me and coming to a conclusion quickly. "There must be a delay."

He's right because TV Aubrey is only now approaching the box while the real life one presses the button again. "Tick tock, mother-fuckers."

"What do we do?"

There's only one option. I know it just as well as Beck does even though his question suggests he's hoping for some alternative outcome.

"Get Selene and Monique. I'll open the door."

"Fuck that, Drake. I'm not leaving you down here alone."

"What are they going to do, Beckham? Execute me on national television?"

I feel the weight and heat of his anger on my back as I head to the door, slamming my hand on the button that opens the gate. The one small action turns my body into a live wire. Suddenly, I'm on high alert, adrenaline pumping through my veins as I remove my gun from the holster and pull back the slide to check the chamber even though I know it's loaded.

"On your six," Beck says from behind me. I don't know if he went up the stairs to warn Selene and Monique, and there's no time to ask as the gravel of the driveway crunches underneath the tires of the vehicles of Aubrey's motorcade.

"He didn't bring the press up."

"We should have left his ass outside of the gate with them."

"That wasn't an option, Beckham."

Aubrey had brought the cameras and reporters specifically to force his way in. He knew we wouldn't be able to deny him entry without it turning into a national incident, one that would likely end with Beck and I being branded as kidnappers who infiltrated the safe house he provided for his wife and her best friend and turned one dangerous situation into another.

Resignation lives in the puff of air that leaves his nose when I grip the handle to open the door. I glance at him over my shoulder. "You ready?"

He nods, training his weapon on the space where Aubrey's head will be in a matter of seconds. I'm distantly impressed by the accuracy of his prediction when the door swings open and Aubrey's head is in perfect alignment with the barrel of Beck's gun. Of course, I don't get to appreciate that fact because now I'm looking into the eyes of the smuggest bastard on Earth.

My hand twitches, begging me to raise my weapon and end all of this. I could do it, aim and fire twice before Garrison and Woodard even bothered to react. Beck would take care of them, a bullet through each of their skulls that would sail clean through and pierce the tires of the vehicles behind them, depositing their blood and brain matter into the rubber while their fellow agents look on helplessly.

Aubrey lets out a low whistle as he passes over the threshold. "Nice digs. A major upgrade from that shack you were in the last time I made a house call."

Every step he takes forward, results in me taking one back. I'm not running from him, though I can tell by his expression he thinks I am, just keeping enough distance between us to avoid my weapon being taken by the fuckers behind him.

"You can lower your guns," Aubrey says, holding out turned palms up. "I come in peace."

"Walk out the door now, and you can avoid leaving here in pieces," Beck offers.

Garrison laughs. "More threats, Beckham? Do you plan on following through at some point or are you just talking?"

"I was more than willing to follow through the day I promised you that ass whooping, Garrison. Your boy Woodard is the one who decided to delay the inevitable."

"Today's not the day for a fight either," Woodard says, tugging at the sleeves of what is clearly a new suit. Gambit must have given them some generous bonuses for disposing of Marsh.

"That's exactly what you're about to get if you think you're walking out of here with Selene," I warn him.

Beck and I are side by side now. Garrison and Woodard have stepped around Aubrey. He lingers behind them, grinning at the promise of looming violence, and he actually claps when Beck and I holster our weapons. I don't see his reaction when Beck swings on Garrison, though, don't care to know what he thinks about his men not pulling the first punch. As soon as that first blow lands with a thud and crack that indicates the fracturing of Garrison's jawbone, I only care about one thing: driving all my anger through Mason Woodard's face.

His eyes go wide when he sees my fist coming, and I laugh at his confusion as blood flies from his nose, spilling all over that pretty new suit. "Did you think this was a fucking game?"

He stumbles back but manages to keep his hands up, firing off several shots when he advances on me. Only one connects, and my head snaps to the side, the taste of copper blooming on my tongue. I run it over my teeth, painting white with red so my smile bleeds wrath and rage when I turn back to face him, returning the cheap shot with multiple jabs to the center of his face.

Aubrey curses as drops of Woodard's blood land at his feet. I can't even relish his fear, can't tell him that he's next, because I'm too focused on the way Woodard's head keeps snapping back when I hit him, like if the next punch is hard enough it might fall off altogether. It doesn't take me long to overwhelm him, and when he starts to sway on his feet, arms flailing through the air as his knees buckle, I grab him by the collar with both hands kneeing him in the stomach before tossing him into the wall, shattering a mirror in the process.

Pained groans fill the air when he hits the ground, and it takes me a second to realize they're not just his. I shake my head, clearing red from my vision to get a full view of the hall, and find Beck standing over Garrison who, like his partner, is bloody and defeated.

A slow, applause fills the hall, drawing our attention to Aubrey and the men in the doorway behind him.

"What a display," he says, placing a heart over his hand to feign sincerity. "I'm truly impressed. Unfortunately, your efforts and their injuries are worth nothing because Selene is still leaving here with me."

"You'll have to kill me first," I growl, stepping forward.

All at once, the agents, who are probably more of Gambit's henchmen, draw their weapons, their motions fluid and synchronized. Aubrey looks around, a wide, triumphant smile stretching out his thin lips.

"*That* can be arranged."

"But it won't be necessary."

The voice comes from behind us, but I'd know it anywhere. I'd know *her* anywhere. Sugared wild berries and the nectar of peaches. Sable skin and gentle eyes that snag on mine for just a second, holding an apology she doesn't lend her voice to as she moves to her husband's side.

"No one needs to get hurt, Aubrey. I'll come with you."

29

SELENE

I t rained the morning AJ died.

Fat, angry drops of water falling from dark clouds, covered my windshield, landing with heavy splats that competed with the sounds of a YouTube video coming from his phone. Before he got out of the car, I told him to take the umbrella I kept in the backseat. He had refused, saying he didn't want to lug it around all day. I insisted, even went so far as to try to reach it when I pulled into the pick-up line, but he rushed out of the car before I could force it on him. I watched him dodge raindrops as he ran the short distance between the car and the door being held open by Mr. Manetti—his chemistry teacher— annoyed by his stubbornness and proud of his ability to advocate for himself.

I don't know which emotion was more prominent when he looked back and waved at me, initiating a goodbye neither of us knew was going to be forever, but I like to think it was the pride.

God, I hope it was the pride.

"Do you remember the last time you saw him?"

My voice is a haunted, rasping whisper from all the screaming and crying last night, but the car is quiet so Aubrey hears me. His brows jump in surprise that I'm the one who broke first. We've been in the

car for a little over fifteen minutes. I haven't said a word since I agreed
to come with him, and he had his men drag me out of the house. I don't
know why this is the opener I've decided to go with, but it feels right
because the only thing I want to discuss with Aubrey is AJ.

"Who?"

After everything I've learned about this man over the last twenty-
four hours, nothing he says or does should surprise me. And I'm not
surprised by his question; I'm *enraged* by it. I fly across the seat
screaming curses as I scratch and claw and punch whatever part of him
I can get my hands on. Beating the fuck out of him is much more satis-
fying than slapping the shit out of Jordan, but it doesn't last nearly as
long as I'd like because a cocked gun appears at my temple after I send
his head flying into the window a second time.

The cool metal awakens the quiet fear I've carried in my body
since November, and I shrink away from it as fast as I can. I crawl
back to my seat, noting how my knuckles ache and the skin on my
forearms burns from Aubrey digging his nails into me like the little
bitch that he is.

"WHAT THE FUCK IS WRONG WITH YOU?" he roars, unrav-
eling the knot of his silk tie with one hand while he pinches his nostrils
closed with the other. He's squeezing hard, but drops of blood still
escape, splattering on the crisp white of his shirt the way the raindrops
did to my windshield that day.

I smile at the correlation, finding an odd kind of peace in it even
though there's still a gun pointed in my direction and a man who's
proven he's capable of murder glaring at me from across the seat. He
balls up his navy silk tie, wincing as he presses it to his nose.

"You're a fucking lunatic, you know that?"

"Me?"

"Yes, Selene, you." The blood is flowing faster than the silk can
soak it up, turning the luxurious fabric a deep purple. Aubrey throws it
down and punches the headrest of the driver's seat. "Fuck! Why can't
you just be normal for once?"

"What exactly would that entail, Aubrey? Orchestrating the murder
of my only son in order to advance my career? Conspiring to assassi-

nate a sitting President to protect that secret? Being dumb enough to say no to the man who bankrolled all of those endeavors and getting my girlfriend killed?"

The slap happens so quickly I don't even see it coming. One second, I'm pushing the last syllable of my question out of my mouth and the next his knuckles are colliding with my teeth. *That's* when it becomes real to me. The decision I've made. The danger I've put myself in. The distance between the man I married and the one who just back handed me.

Black spots float in my vision as I bring trembling hands to my stinging lips and wobbling chin. Tears. There are tears skating down my cheeks, squeezing under my fingers, salt searing split flesh.

"You *hit* me."

All these years. All these secrets. All the pain he's caused and goodness he's stolen from me, and still, I'm shocked. Hurt. Broken. My lashes flutter rapidly as I process this new reality that shouldn't feel new at all. He's proven himself a monster, so why am I surprised that he has claws?

"You've never hit me," I whisper, voice breaking stupidly. He's been flirting with idea of it for so long. His hands too tight around my arms in the hotel room after the debate. His eyes wild and angry as he shoved me against the wall. His fingers splayed wide and reaching for my neck in the East Sitting Hall.

The desire is not new.

Not at all.

But there's a difference between seeing it on his face and feeling the force of his fury when he's finally found the courage to act on it.

"You fucking attacked me, and you're surprised that I hit you?"

A crazed laugh spills out of me, using the spaces between my fingers to find their place in the tense air. I drop my hands, sending blood and saliva flying in his direction when the laugh morphs into a cough because my throat is raw.

Aubrey's disgust is palpable. "What's so funny?"

I clutch my ribs, ignoring the way the cut on my top lip burns a little more with every passing moment. "You, Aubrey. You're funny.

Yesterday I found out that you had my son killed, and *you're* surprised that *I* hit you? I should have done a lot worse. I'm *going* to do a lot worse," I promise him.

His nose is no longer actively bleeding, but the evidence of my anger is still there. In the welts on his face and neck. In the red crust around his nostrils and dried blood on his shirt.

"AJ was my son too, Selene. Don't forget that."

Anger swells in my chest, pushing against my ribcage, and threatening to crush what's left of my heart if I don't let it out. It leaves me in a guttural scream that's wrapped in maternal outrage.

"DON'T YOUR DARE SAY HIS NAME!"

"You need to lower your voice, ma'am," the man with his gun still trained on me says.

"It's fine," Aubrey tells him. "Let her get it all out of her system. It's best for her to be calm when she meets Phineas."

"Phineas?"

"Yes, he wants to meet you."

Threads of fear stitch together my organs as a wave of cool dread caresses my spine. Phineas Gambit is not a man I want to meet. Aubrey reads the panic in my eyes and smiles, settling back into his seat now that I've been neutralized. The pad of my thumb finds the side of my index finger and before I can even get through the first flick, he sighs.

"Don't start that shit, Selene."

"Fuck you, Aubrey," I spit, completing the motion he interrupted and doing it over and over again. Not because it's soothing, because nothing could be soothing right now except the sight of Cal and Beck appearing to save me, but just to annoy the fuck out of my husband while he delivers me to the man who made it necessary for me to bury my child.

"Why did it have to be him?" I keep my focus on the city streets we're now navigating, counting the buildings blurred by my tears to keep my composure. "It could have been anyone in your family. One of your nieces or nephews, your awful parents or your idiot brothers. *Me.*" My throat aches, throbbing around a sob I refuse to set free. "You could have chosen *anyone.* Why did it have to be him? Didn't you see his sweet little face in your mind? Remember what it was like the first time you held him? Did you think about who he would have grown up to be? What he would have accomplished? What he and all those other people might have done with all the years you stole from them?"

The sob builds and finally breaks, caving my chest in, and I have to look at him. I have to see his face when I say this next thing.

"Didn't you think about how much you loved him, Aubrey? Did you ever love him?"

He drums his fingers on his thigh then flicks guiltless blue eyes in my direction.

"Of course I loved him, Selene. I just love me more."

There are no words after that. Just acceptance for what has happened and what is to come. I married a monster and birthed him a victim, and I'll have to live with that for the rest of my life.

However long, or short, that may be.

A chill runs through me at the realization that how much time I have left on this Earth isn't up to me. My life, my future with Cal and Beck and Isis and Imani, it's all in the hands of the men who destroyed the last family I built, and just like last time, I'm powerless to stop them. What's different, though, is seeing it coming. It's standing face to face with the designer of your demise and forcing yourself not to flinch when he examines you with empty, green eyes from the other end of his dining table.

"Your husband sat in that same chair some years ago," Phineas says, swirling around a goblet full of blood red liquid with lazy rotations of his wrist. "When was that, Mr. President? January 2018?"

Aubrey, who chose a seat to the left of Phineas, nods. "The 12th to be exact."

Everything about their tone suggests significance, and they wait patiently for me to figure it out. It doesn't take long, of course, because there's only one reason that date would mean anything to them and me.

My stomach rolls. "That's the day you decided."

"And we had the loveliest meal."

A fond smile pulls at the corners of Cordelia's mouth, and Travis Langham hums his agreement with her statement. I look around the table, no less disgusted by the people surrounding it than I was when I sat down minutes ago. They're all immaculately dressed, eating and sipping wine. Aubrey has changed into a clean suit and gotten his wounds cleaned and covered with makeup. Meanwhile, I haven't touched my plate and am still wearing Beck's boxers and one of Cal's t-shirts. I don't even have on a bra or shoes.

And if I could feel anything besides the blue flames of anger licking at my ribs, I'd be humiliated, which is probably what they wanted me to be.

Phineas sits his glass on the table and steeples his fingers. "There was not much to decide. The Senator wanted to ascend quickly. I presented the most effective path."

"Which involved taking the life of my child and twenty-seven other people."

"There weren't supposed to be that many casualties," Langham explains, chewing loudly and with his mouth open. "The kid got a little trigger happy, if you know what I mean."

"No, Officer Langham, I don't know what you mean."

He pulls a face, cutting his eye at Aubrey. "She really isn't any fun, huh?"

"None."

My hand clenches into a fist that Phineas studies with vivid interest. "I can only imagine the frustration you are feeling right now, Mrs. Taylor. All your enemies here in one place, and yet, you can do nothing to punish us for the crimes you worked so hard to prove we committed."

"It is frustrating."

The admission comes easily because I can't see the point in lying. Being dishonest now would only be in service to my ego, and my focus is on getting out of here alive.

His eyes light up. "Honesty. *How* refreshing. If your friend Ms. St. James had been as forthcoming as you have been in this moment, she and the father of her child might still be alive."

Horror fills me even as hope tries to take root, convincing me that if I continue to be honest I can make it out of this alive. "Jordan's dead?"

"Do not grieve for her, Mrs. Taylor. She revealed your location within seconds of Travis putting a bullet in her partner's head. She was willing to sacrifice you to save herself."

Cordelia lets out a tisk of disapproval, pointing at Aubrey. "I always told you that girl was a liability. She didn't have the stomach for this work."

A vein in the center of Aubrey's forehead begins to throb. "I know, Cordelia."

"So that's how you found me?" I ask, unwilling to be subjected to another one of Aubrey and Cordelia's spats. "Jordan told you."

"Yes." Phineas smiles then says, "You are not a fan of deviation are you, Mrs. Taylor?"

"No, I would prefer to stay on task. Things get done a lot quicker that way."

And I want this conversation, this experience, this entire day to be done. I want to go to the home I've made in Cal and Beck's arms and never leave again. I want to forget the sound of Cordelia's voice and Langham's chewing. I want to delete every memory I've ever shared with Aubrey from my brain and scrub every place on my body that has been touched by those green eyes.

"I wouldn't be in such a rush to get things done if I were you," Aubrey says, smirking when Langham pulls a syringe filled with a colorless liquid from a pocket inside his suit jack and sits it on the table.

Langham waggles his brows at me. "Potassium cyanide. Same stuff I used on Sanders."

The not-so-subtle threat snuffs out the flames of anger, leaving me cold and so fucking afraid I can't convince my features to convey anything else.

"Put that away," Phineas snaps, and the order hits Travis like the crack of a whip. He jumps into action, sweeping the syringe out of sight.

"She might as well know what's coming," Aubrey argues.

Cordelia nods. "It usually helps if they know they won't make it out alive."

"If I wanted either of your opinions, I would have asked for them," Phineas growls. "This is not your White House or the fucking Oval Office. This is my home, and I get to decide what happens with my guest."

"But I've already told you—"

"The last time I listened to you I wasted hundreds of thousands of dollars liberating a man from prison who could not be bothered to do the job I paid him to do and thousands more to get the men already on my payroll to clean up the mess you made, so you will forgive me if I do not give a *single fuck* about what you have told me."

Aubrey shrinks. Cordelia and Langham fall quiet. Phineas looks to me, huffing as he grabs his wine and takes a long sip. He swallows slowly, savoring it and the silence that only breaks when he wants it to.

"Mrs. Taylor, you have found me in a unique mood."

I will my voice not to shake, needing confidence and strength I don't possess to continue engaging with him. "Is that so?"

"Yes, I would like to open the table for a discussion."

"A discussion?"

He squints, tilting his head to one side as he regards me. "You are familiar with the concept, yes?"

"Of course." I roll my shoulders back. "Since this is your home, I think it would only be right that you start us off."

The offer is ridiculous. I wouldn't even know where to begin with brokering the terms of my freedom. I mean, if that's even what he's offering. I'm sure there's a world where this sick fuck thinks allowing me to choose the method of my murder would be a kindness.

"Showing such respect under these incredibly harrowing circumstances is admirable."

"Thank you."

"But playing to my ego will not save your life."

"I don't expect it to." The lie rolls of my tongue, smooth as silk. Phineas studies me, searching for signs of deception and coming up empty.

"Very well, let us begin." He takes another sip of wine, polishing off the glass and sitting it near the edge of the table. A woman appears out of nowhere to fill it, but he doesn't pick it up again. "Your husband seems to be under the impression that you are a threat to the freedom and livelihood of every person at this table."

"I am."

A slow, sinister smile spreads across his face. He claps his hands loudly, looking at Aubrey. "This woman is a delight, Mr. President. Why are you so determined to get rid of her?" His lips part, but Phineas shakes his head. "That is a rhetorical question. It does not require a response."

Aubrey bristles, but he does not speak.

"Ensuring you are no longer a threat," Phineas says. "That is my goal for this discussion. What is yours?"

"To leave here alive."

"These goals complement each other. I want to see you leave here alive as well."

The other three people at the table shift uncomfortably in their seats at the declaration, but relief is a soft tingle in the tips of my bare toes as I envision walking out of here. To freedom. To Cal and Beck. To Monique and the girls I adore. It's all within reach. Phineas—the most unlikely ally of all—is offering it to me. I just have to figure out how to get a firm grasp on it.

"You do?"

"Yes, we will already have our hands full with covering up Ms. St. James and Mr. Granger's deaths. Another death connected to the President would raise red flags and draw undue attention to him and, by extension, me. We are weeks away from closing the deal on the Qatari military base, and I need him focused on that not delaying work so he can pretend to grieve his wife."

"I wouldn't," Aubrey protests.

"*You would*, Mr. President. I would require it because it would be what the American people want to see, and if you speak out of turn again, I will have you removed from the room."

"I'm glad we're aligned, Mr. Gambit," I say, needing his attention back on me.

"As am I, Mrs. Taylor, and I only need one thing from you in order to make it a reality."

One.

A small number with huge implications.

A singular request that will give me my freedom but at what cost?

I wrack my brain for potential asks—grant him access to the computer Aubrey's men removed from the house in Bethesda when they ceased me so they can destroy Jordan's files and everything from my investigation, sign an ironclad NDA that prevents me from pursuing justice for my son and so much as uttering any of their names, agree to stay with Aubrey and birth another child.

Everything I come up with feels like too much and not enough all at once.

"What is it?"

My voice shakes, and I hate that. Hate the way those verdant pools Phineas calls eyes glow with delight at the tremors. Hate the way my heart keeps trying to sink and soar at the same time because hope and despair are battling for control of my body.

Phineas spreads his arms wide, encompassing the whole of the table within his impressive wingspan as he asks me to do the one thing I thought he never would.

"*Join us.*"

Aubrey scrubs a hand down his face. He is clearly outraged, but he is so afraid of Phineas making good on his promise to remove him from the room that he doesn't even breathe. He just sits there silent, seething along with Cordelia and Langham. They don't want me among their murderous ranks, which is fine because it is the last place I want to be.

"Why would I do that?"

"Because it is the only way to ensure your safety and that of your loved ones," Phineas explains, bringing his forgotten wine glass to his lips. "You know too much, Mrs. Taylor. Your only choices here are death or allegiance. As I explained before, death would be an inconvenience. I am also of the opinion that it would be a waste of a brilliant mind that would provide me with a foothold in an industry I have yet to make a name for myself in."

"You don't need my help to break into tech."

"Do you truly think it wise to try to talk me *out* of your usefulness?" The pointed edge of his tone conjures the image of Langham's syringe plunging into the side of my neck.

Death or allegiance.

Those are my choices.

"No," I breathe.

"I did not think so."

We stare at each other, neither of us blinking, and I feel it. His power. His influence. His cruelty. There is no way for me to win this. I drop his gaze, resenting the slow trickle of defeat that starts at the crown of my head and ends at the tips of my toes.

He celebrates my surrender with another round of solo applause, pushing to his feet to give me a standing ovation that doesn't end until he is in front of me, beaming triumphantly.

"Now that you have agreed to my terms, you are free to leave. My home. Your marriage. The White House and all the constraints that come along with it. It is obvious that you and the President make each other miserable, and I like to see my friends happy."

I blink up at him. "Friends?"

"Yes, very good friends." Phineas holds out his hand, and I take it allowing him to help me from my seat. His skin is cold and far too soft. I try to pull away, but he tightens his hold, baring his teeth in a smile that's all danger and no joy. "And you should know, Mrs. Taylor, that when I call on my friends, I *always* expect them to pick up."

30

BECK

Four Months Later

I've never spent Christmas with this many people.

The only memory I have that comes close is the one after I was adopted and parents invited everyone they knew to the house to celebrate. Since they were older, and all their friends were too, it was a subdued celebration and for most of it I was the only child in attendance. Eventually someone showed up with their grandchildren in tow, and I finally had someone to show my toys to that wanted to play with them as well.

After that year, holidays would be just the three of us. We'd take vacations or have dinner at home. The menu was always the same. The conversation never changed. There were never any new faces or laughter filled rooms or family flying in from out of town to spend multiple nights under your roof and constantly gathered in your kitchen.

When we bought this house, Selene and Cal fell in love with the kitchen first. I fell in love with the look in their eyes as they daydreamed about the exact moment I'm witnessing right now. Mama J at the stove, supervising Rae as she seasons the largest pot of greens

I've ever seen in my life. Al at the island carving the turkey him, Cal and Hunter insisted on using the smoker to cook even though it's as cold as fuck outside. Cal woke me up in the middle of the night, trying to talk me into trekking through the snow with him so he could turn the temperature down. I flipped him the bird and threw an arm over Selene while she laughed at our exchange.

She laughs so much these days.

On phone calls with her mom or FaceTime chats with her sisters and their kids. During visits with Isis and Imani who come over on the weekends whenever Joanna isn't in a mood. In the middle of the night when it's not nightmares that have woken us but desire. When Monique pops up randomly with a bottle of wine and enough food for all of us and we sit on the couch and watch the Hallmark movies we all got addicted to when we were hiding out in Bethesda.

Life is…good. It's warm, it's safe. It's happy and filled with acceptance I thought would be a lot harder to come by. After Selene walked out of the lion's den relatively unscathed, we decided not to leave another second of our lives to chance. We bought this big, beautiful house in the Great Falls area and sat among boxes in the living room, holding hands while we took turns calling the people we loved most to reveal the truth of us. Hunter and Rae were the least surprised, and Riley was just excited about having a new aunt. Erin asked why I didn't just tell her about Selene when I broke the news about me and Cal, and Mama J and Al said they didn't know a thing about a dynamic like ours but didn't care so long as we were good to each other.

At the time, I thought life was as good as it could get, but I was wrong. Because it's only gotten better. Every day it gets better, and today is no different.

A pair of arms wrap around my waist from behind, and I smile, leaning into Cal's embrace without a second's hesitation. "Where have you been?"

He kisses my cheek and then my lips when I turn around to face him. "Watching carolers on the front porch with Erin and Selene."

"People still carol?"

"Apparently."

"Sounded like that group should have stayed home," Monique quips from her spot on the couch in the living room. She's watching Riley play the video game Isis and Imani designed. It's still in the early stages with rough graphics and a few glitches once you get past the fourth level, but it has so much potential.

"They were just kids, Mo," Selene says, running a loving hand over the head of each child on the couch when she passes by.

"Kids who should have stayed home," Erin jokes, high-fiving Monique.

Selene shakes her head at them, an indulgent smile on her lips as she heads down the hall that leads to her office. There's nothing wrong with it. The smile, that is. It's bright and genuine, a true display of amusement and joy. But there's something underneath it. Something that makes the curve of her lips shake. Something that makes her legs move just a little bit faster when she gets close to the office, like she's impatient to get to the privacy of the room. Something that calls to Cal and to me and sends us down the hall after her.

When we enter the office, she's sitting on the edge of her desk, twirling the bracelet I gave her for Christmas around on her wrist while the diamond of one of the earrings Cal got her catches stray rays of light from the projector mounted on the wall behind her. We move to her side, bracketing her body with ours and casting large shadows that make it hard to see the schematics she's studying.

"You've been over this a million times, gorgeous."

She presses a button on the remote in her hand, and the projector clicks and shifts, displaying the same photo as before but this time zoomed in, focusing on an altitude limiter. "I just need to be sure I understand how it all works."

"But you won't step foot on the plane, pet. Everything will be done remotely."

The muscles in her face twitch restlessly, and she doesn't look at us. Cal and I exchange a look, knowing her brain won't allow her let this go. Not until she's studied the cabin pressurization system several more times. It's become something of a habit for her, going over the schematics of Gambit's plane, talking herself through the sabotage of this specific system. I know that when the time comes everything will go smoothly, but I also understand the anxiety driving her at the moment.

She left Gambit's home under the pretense of joining his little killer's club, promising to repay him for sparing her life by spending what's left of it waiting for a phone call from him that will result in her being asked to do something she won't. The stress of that promise, of that lie, has weighed on us since she made it, and now we all hear it. The ticking of the clock counting down to the day we can finally, truly, be free.

We just have to hope time runs out before the phone rings.

When Selene's anxious mind is satisfied, she shuts off the projector, plunging us into semi-darkness. "It's going to work, right?" She whispers the words, rambling on before either of us can say anything. "Not just the plane, but the rest of it. *All of it*. It'll work, right? It has to because otherwise…."

My mind fills in the blank.

Otherwise, we put our lives and the lives of everyone in our home at risk.

Otherwise, there's no justice for AJ.

Otherwise, they win.

And we can't let them win.

I find her hand in the dark, pulling it up to my mouth and laying a kiss in the center of her palm. "It will work."

31

SELENE

"I think I'm going to be sick."

Everything stops.

Well, Cal and Beck stop, pausing on the stairs that lead up to the bedroom I shared with Aubrey for so many years, but the nausea refuses. I pull in a breath through my nose and push it out in a quiet hiss through my teeth, willing my heart rate to slow. When the breathing doesn't help, I bend at the waist and study the disposable booties on my feet. They're an ugly gray color, connected to the white suit covering my body.

Spunbonded polypropylene.

That's what it's made of. I turn the words over in my head. The weight of the syllables drags me back into my body and keep me there. Relieved that the panic and nausea have subsided, I right myself and nod at the men in front of me, signaling that I'm good to continue. They both hesitate.

"We can—" Beck starts, his voice pitched low.

I shake my head. "No, it has to be now. It has to be today."

He glances at Cal. As they have one of their signature silent conversations, I thank my lucky stars that the group of hookers Gambit sent to Aubrey as a gift for finally closing the Qatari military base deal necessitated the dismissal of his security detail. Between that and Aubrey killing the cameras throughout the house to ensure his privacy, we couldn't have asked for better circumstances. All of which means, no matter what the two loves of my life decide, we're going up these stairs, and today, we're ending my husband's life.

It only takes them seconds to wrap things up, but it might as well be hours given how slow time is moving. Cal warned me that it would be this way. That the moments leading up to the mission would make me feel like I was swimming in a tank of molasses while my blood buzzed and my heart raced.

Nothing could have prepared me for how accurate that description was.

Last night, I couldn't sleep. I stayed up watching videos of AJ and staring at the clock that seemed to be moving at half speed. Every second, a minute. Every minute, an hour. Every hour, a lifetime. Beck had to force me to come to bed, carrying me over his shoulder while Cal followed us up the stairs asking how many orgasms it would take to get me to sleep.

"You're sure you're good?" he asks now, scanning my face.

"Yes."

I'm not good. Not by any stretch of the imagination, and I think he knows that. Just like he knows I won't be good until this is done. None of us will be.

Beck takes my chin in his hand. "It'll be over soon."

If peace can be found in a moment like this, it exists in the gentle way he cradles my chin. In the way Cal eases his way back down the steps and takes hold of Beck's free hand and one of mine. In the whispered 'I love you's we utter before he turns his gaze back on the landing ahead of us.

"Stay close and quiet."

We know Aubrey is here alone, but we move with caution. Clearing rooms and closets on this floor the same way we did on the first. It's strange, sneaking around in a house I used to call home, taking care not to leave a trace of myself in spaces I've existed in for most of my adult life. But the strangest thing of all is crossing the threshold into what used to be my bedroom and seeing Aubrey's sleeping form sprawled across the bed.

For a just a minute, my mind is caught between the past and the present. Between the blue-gray hue of this dawning day when I look at him with loathing and the bright warmth of a young sun on a Saturday morning when I watched him with a heart full of love.

I used to love him.

How fucking embarrassing.

Cal raises his gun, approaching the bed while Beck covers him from the door. I'm supposed to stand back, to stay out of the way and let them work, but I can't be bystander in this.

I rush across the floor boards on the tips of my toes, stopping him at the foot of the bed with my hand on his shoulder. When he looks at me, his features are tight with concentration. I've only seen this version of him once, when they came to save me from Jacob Marsh, and I don't know if I can reach past his tactical mind and get him to hear my needs.

He lifts a brow, asking for an explanation for the delay. My gaze drops to the gun in his hands, and he shakes his head immediately. I stretch my eyes, pleading silently only to be denied again.

"My dragon," I whisper, reminding him of what I said to Beck when he let his desire to protect me override my need to take care of some things myself. His worry is palpable when he relinquishes the gun, but I can't focus on that right now. I can only focus on me. When they insisted on teaching me to shoot—a skill I didn't want to acquire for obvious reasons—both of them said the only thing I should be thinking about when there's a gun in my hand is the power I'm wielding.

So that's where my mind goes, to the weight of the metal and the heat of Cal's palm still lingering on the grip. To my index finger curved around the trigger, resting there but not applying pressure. And then, when Aubrey rolls to his side, positioning himself perfectly for me to line the barrel up with his forehead, it goes completely quiet.

I allow the muzzle to ghost over his skin, pressing lightly but not hard enough to leave a mark. Aubrey flinches awake, and I take four measured steps back, knowing that it's important to stay out of his reach.

"What the fuck?" he mutters, throat clogged with anger and exhaustion. He scrubs at his eyes, blinking hard to make sure I'm real.

"Good morning, Mr. President."

"The fuck are you doing here?"

He starts to sit up, everything about his posture suggesting he's about to lunge at me, but Beck cocks his gun. "I wouldn't do that if I were you."

Aubrey freezes, neck rotating slowly as he takes in his surroundings. He tries to hide it, but I see the flickers of fear in those blue eyes when they finally land on me. "What is this, Selene?"

"You don't know a reckoning when you see it?"

He throws his head back, laughing loudly. "A reckoning? Please. At best, this is a case of breaking and entering. At worst, it's your signature on a death warrant for you, your boyfriends and everyone you love."

I glance at Cal, smirking. "I hope you're prepared to pay up, Drake."

"I'm always prepared, pet."

Aubrey grimaces at the exchange, and Beck laughs. "We made a bet. Selene and I knew you'd start with throwing around empty threats, but Cal thought you'd beg for your life first."

"Do you want to know what the winner gets, Aubrey?"

"No, Selene. I want to know what Phineas is going to think when he finds out your pledge of allegiance was a farce."

"You can ask him when he joins you in hell."

"Joins me in…" The cackle he lets out cuts his sentence in half. He slaps a hand to his chest when he recovers. "Joins me in hell. That's a good one." He cards his fingers through his hair. "You've gotten funnier, Sel."

"And you've gotten even more dense, Aubrey. I didn't think it was possible, and yet, here I am, explaining something to you that should be quite obvious."

"Which is?"

"That you're going to die today."

There it is again, that flicker. It stays longer this time, lingering in his irises as he eases himself into a sitting position and tosses the sheets back. The smell of sweat and bodily fluids waft up from the mattress, and I scrunch up my nose, disgusted.

"Still got an aversion to great sex, huh?"

"No, *we* have plenty of that," I retort, splitting a satisfied smile between my men. "I just have an aversion to you."

"Is that why you want me dead, *dear*?"

"Among other things." I use the gun to gesture for Aubrey to stand. "On your feet."

He groans, stretching languidly once he's up to draw attention to the fact that he's naked. "Is this the part where you take me out into the yard and shoot me like a sick dog?"

Every time Aubrey finds himself in a situation he is not in control of, he resorts to behavior like this. Fishing for information using questions that make it seem like he doesn't care while everything about his demeanor conveys that he does. Knowing that he won't stop talking until I give him something, I decide to gift him with the full truth.

"Oh, no, this is the part where you wash your face, brush your teeth, take a shower and get dressed for the day then go downstairs, put a gun in your mouth and pull the trigger."

As much as I want to be the one to take Aubrey's life, as badly as I want to beat him and bruise him and subject him to the same awful torture AJ faced, I know that I can't. There cannot be any signs of foul play. Cal, Beck and I discussed our options at length, playing around with various possibilities.

Ultimately, we landed on a staged suicide. It's the only way to be free of Aubrey and keep ourselves out of prison. It's also the only way to trigger the chain of events that will allow me to take everyone else in his orbit out.

"No one is going to believe I killed myself," Aubrey says.

He's in the bathroom now, freshly showered with his toothbrush hanging from his mouth and a towel wrapped around his waist. I'm just as surprised by how long it took him to formulate a response to my instructions as I am by how well he's following them. Cal and Beck haven't even had to step in. They've been hanging back, standing just inside the doorway watching and listening but saying nothing.

"People take their lives every day, Aubrey. You're not above suicide."

"Sure, but why would I off myself when my life is so fucking good?"

White foam gathers at the corners of his mouth as he brushes, I wait for him to spit and rinse before responding. "The guilt got to you."

"The guilt?"

"Yes, over what you did to AJ."

"If you tell anyone about that, Gambit will have your head."

I push my lips out into a faux pout, fluttering my lashes innocently. "*Me?* I'm not going to say anything to anyone. *You're* going to lay it all out in your suicide note. What's not covered there is explained in the email you sent to all the major media outlets this morning."

"I didn't send any fucking emails."

"Of course you did," I insist, knowing damn well it was me. "They came from your private computer and your personal account. You even made sure to attach the most incriminating of Jordan's files."

His jaw drops, and I watch in delight as the redness of agitation blooms on his chest and begins to crawl up his neck while he sputters, struggling to form a coherent thought. I'm sure it's overwhelming. I've thrown a lot of information at him all at once.

"Those files are gone," he spits. "We destroyed the originals, and the only copies were on the computer we took when I dragged you out of that shit hole in Bethesda."

"Oh, sweetie, you really believe that don't you?" He glowers at me, and I roll my eyes, sick of explaining the most obvious things. "You've never been thorough, Aubrey, and you've never paid attention. All the years you've known me, and you never noticed where I put the things I want to keep safe."

I've never been more thankful for that old laptop than I was the day I got back from Gambit's and realized Aubrey hadn't taken it. He hadn't even seen it because Beck had the foresight to hide it, leaving the newer one out as a decoy.

Cal clear his throat. "Time to get dressed."

Aubrey moves through the rest of his morning routine on leaden feet. I can't tell if he's given up completely or if he's plotting an escape, and truthfully, it doesn't matter because there's no getting out of this for him. Once he's dressed, I give Cal back his gun, so he can lead the march down to Aubrey's office.

"So this is where it happens," he muses, sinking into his desk chair with Beck's hand on his shoulder.

I open the third drawer on the right-hand side and pull out the old revolver he's had since his 18th birthday. Chip gave it to him, and he was supposed to pass it down to AJ. I never cared much for the tradition, but I think it's kind of poetic that the thing meant to link generations of Taylor men together will be the undoing of one.

"It seems like the kind of thing you would do," I say, carrying the small gun over to the couch he made me sit on when he took Cal and Beck away from me. They're standing in front of his desk like they were that day, exuding power none of us possessed then because Aubrey had it all.

"Why would I do it now?" he asks suddenly. "If the guilt about AJ was eating at me, wouldn't it make more sense for me to kill myself on the day he died?"

I stare at him for a full minute, wondering if he's serious. If he has his head shoved so far up his own ass he can't even be bothered to check a calendar. He looks back at me, growing annoyed the longer I go without speaking. When I finally find my voice, there's incredulity laced through it.

"Do you really not know what today is?"

"You woke me up with a gun to the face. I'm sorry I didn't have time to note the date."

"It's January 12th, Aubrey."

It doesn't take long for the significance of the date to sink in. With it comes startling clarity and the jarring realization that he really is going to die. All the bravado he's displayed leaves him. His shoulders drop, and the fear reappears. This time it sticks, refusing to leave even when he shakes his head to try to dislodge it. I relish every second, loving the way it makes him compliant enough to write the suicide note I dictate to him from across the room without argument, reveling in the way it leaks out of every part of him when the note is done and I slide the framed picture of AJ he's kept on his desk for years into his field of vision.

"*Selene.*"

He's shaking. Splotches of red interrupting the ghostly white of his complexion. I'm standing before him, the gun he'll use to kill himself in my gloved hand.

"Is this the part where you beg?"

He blinks back tears. "If you put that gun in my hand, I'll turn it on you."

My smile is so wide it hurts. "You won't do that."

"Why the fuck wouldn't I?"

Beck holds up Aubrey's phone, displaying the time and a slew of notifications. There are missed calls from Phineas, Cordelia and Langham as well as a breaking news banner from the Times that reads: CONFESSIONS OF A CORRUPT PRESIDENT.

"The article was published two minutes ago," I explain. "They haven't had time to go through all the files, so I'm sure it just says it's a developing story with more details to come soon. But your friends know what the details are, Aubrey, and they think you've sold them out."

His phone vibrates, and Beck laughs at the text. "Phineas says you're a dead man."

Aubrey's features are stricken. Every muscle frozen in terror as he considers what we've done to him.

"Do you think he'll do the job personally?" Cal asks, speaking to no one in particular.

Beck shrugs. "Maybe he'll send Langham."

"That's more likely," I say. "Aubrey, do you think he has any more of that potassium cyanide?"

He doesn't reply. I don't think he can. He's too busy crying, snot dripping down his nose, mixing with tears he couldn't muster for our son but of course, has in abundance for himself. Satisfied, I sit the revolver in front of him and place his phone that's still vibrating next to it.

"I thought I would have more to say when this moment finally came," I tell him. "But I've wasted so much time and energy on you in this lifetime that all there's left to say is goodbye, and you're not even worth that."

More tears fall, as he reaches for the gun, and suddenly, everything is moving fast. Cal grabs me around the waist, backing out of the room while Beck covers us, his gun trained on Aubrey as if he's a threat to anyone other than himself.

I know that he isn't.

I saw it in his eyes when his fingers wrapped around the handle of the revolver.

Defeat.

Acceptance.

Resolve.

That's why I'm not surprised to see the barrel of the gun in his mouth when Cal stops in the hallway and I can finally turn around. Why I don't flinch when he squeezes the trigger and there's a bright red flash of blood and brain matter across the back wall. Why I don't feel anything but triumph when his body goes limp.

I let out a sigh, tears gathering in my eyes as I realize I've finally had it.

A drink from the goblet of revenge.

A glorious mouthful of justice.

A taste of sin.

EPILOGUE 1: SELENE

"Thanks for agreeing to come in, Selene."

"I don't think I had much of a choice, Torrance," I pause, reconsidering the use of his first name in light of recent circumstances. "Or would you prefer that I refer to you as President Belford?"

He's been in the chair for three weeks, and I happen to think the role suits him. Despite being Aubrey's former VP, and something of a friend, he's never been anything like the man. If I thought differently, I wouldn't be sitting here with him today.

"Either is fine," he says, wiping a bit of the dressing from the salad he's having for lunch from the corner of his mouth. "Though, I think I might prefer Torrance."

"Haven't gotten used to the title?"

"Not yet. I know everyone thinks the VP is just chomping at the bit for the chance to drive the ship, but that's never been me. I honestly had no idea Aubrey was…"

"Suicidal," I supply, using my fork to push around the grains of my rice pilaf just to have something to do with my hand.

"Yes." He frowns, looking at me the way everyone does now that Aubrey is gone. It's a cross between curious and sympathetic, like they want to measure just how deep my sadness runs now that I'm a widow who was in the midst of divorcing her husband.

"I had no idea either, Torrance. Aubrey and I weren't on good terms before I left him, and we certainly weren't discussing his mental health struggles in the days leading up to his death."

None of those things are a lie, but I'm still self-conscious about my delivery. It was the same way when I talked to the FBI. They'd brought me, Cal and Beck in, subjecting us to a round of grueling questions that centered around our relationship overlapping with my marriage. Nothing came of any of it, but the investigation is still open, which makes me anxious.

"Yes, I was aware you two had ongoing struggles."

"He was a habitual liar and cheater."

Torrance shifts in his seat, uncomfortable with me disparaging the memory of his predecessor even though his legacy has already been well and truly tarnished. The media is dragging his name through the mud, and Cordelia, Phineas and Langham are right there in pig sty with him. Every day it's something different, but today the story surrounding them is both scandalous and somber.

Scandalous because Phineas had his personal pilot prepare his private plane so the three of them, plus Garrison and Woodard, could flee the country and avoid being convicted of their crimes.

Somber because pilot—a known alcoholic who regularly flew without a co-pilot or crew—failed to notice when I remotely accessed the system and switched the cabin pressurization system into manual mode, placing the control of the plane's airflow valve in his hands. His ineptitude led to everyone on board, including himself, suffering from hypoxia.

According to everything I read in the months leading up to the last leg of my revenge tour, it's not a particularly painful way to go. I'll always regret that, not making them suffer more, but I'll take solace in the fact that their bodies were burned to a crisp by the blazing flames that engulfed the plane when it crashed.

"I want you to know I never condoned his behavior," Torrance is saying now, covering his heart with his hand to indicate his sincerity.

"And if I had known what he'd done to your son, I would have never agreed to be his running mate or called him a friend."

"I know, Torrance."

We discussed this over the phone when the news first broke. He was shocked, and I had to pretend to be as well, sobbing like it was the first time I'd heard the truth. I've gotten good at it. The acting. The lying, the turning old pain and hurt into fresh outrage. I've done it for my parents and sisters and everyone else who can never find out what I knew, when I knew it and what I did with that knowledge.

"I'm sorry," he says, a self-deprecating smile pulling at the corners of his mouth. "I didn't ask you here to rehash things that have already been said."

Laying my fork on the napkin next to my plate, I arch a brow. "What did you call me here for then?"

Images of federal agents rushing in and arresting me flash in my mind, and I push them away, refusing to believe Torrance would be this cordial if that was the case.

"To let you know I've decided to have the investigation into Aubrey's death closed."

A swift, dizzying wave of relief hits me, causing me to stumble over my words. "Oh..okay. Is that what...you think that's for the best?"

Torrance nods. "Yes, after the discovery of Ms. St. James and Mr. Granger's bodies and what's happened to his co-conspirators, I think it's necessary. The longer it remains open, the longer our country is stuck looking at the ugly stain of his corruption. We need to start the process of cleansing our collective soul."

"That's a good line. Make sure they include it in your next speech."

He blushes and laughs. "Yes, ma'am."

The conversation is winding down, so I stand, extending my hand to him when he's on his feet. "You obviously don't need my approval or anything, but I agree that it's time to close this chapter of our lives."

"Your support on this matter means a lot to me," he says, and I know he genuinely means it. "Take care of yourself, Selene."

"You too, Torrance."

I leave the White House for a final time with a smile on my face that only grows larger when I arrive back home and find Cal and Beck in the kitchen with the scent of my daddy's chili recipe filling the air. Since I didn't eat a morsel of food during my lunch with Torrance, I'm starved. My stomach growling announces my arrival before I can issue either of them a greeting.

Beck spins around in the barstool at the island and opens his arms to me. I kick off my heels and walk into his embrace, taking his mouth in a filthy, licking kiss that's so good he growls when I cut it short. I dance out of his hold and over to Cal, who's tending to the pot on the stove.

I wrap my arms around his waist, kissing his shoulder. "You know you're supposed to just let it simmer at this point, right?"

"That's what I told him," Beck says.

"You're supposed to be slicing jalapenos for the cornbread, Beckham, not worrying about what's happening in my pot."

"I did that while you were busy doing all that unnecessary stirring, Drake."

Cal turns around to confirm his story, throwing me a distracted kiss in the process.

"Excuse me, sir."

He pulls his attention from the cutting board in front of Beck and gives it to me. "Yes, pet?"

"Do you want to give me a proper greeting or should I just pack my bags now?"

Beck snorts a laugh while Cal growls his displeasure at the suggestion. He scoops me up, plopping me on the island and positioning himself between my legs. His hands move to my face, cupping it gently as he treats me to a tender kiss. When it's done, I feel like Beck did when I ended ours, squirmy and dissatisfied.

"No fun being teased is it, gorgeous?"

"Shut up, Beckham," I gripe, squealing when his fingertips appear at my sides, poised for tickling. I immediately start laughing and trying to push him away. "I'm sorry. I'm sorry," I wheeze, and then when that doesn't work, "I have news! Don't tickle me. I have news!"

That does the trick.

He releases me and rounds the counter, coming to stand by Cal. "What is it?"

I split a wide grin between the two of their adoring, perfect faces. "They're closing the investigation!"

Four arms reach for me, pulling me into an embrace where I can't tell what hand belong to which man and it doesn't matter because every touch, every squeeze, every second they hold me is filled with the promise of a future where there will always be enough time, enough light, and enough love.

EPILOGUE 2: CAL

Two Years Later

"That's the last of it."

My announcement draws the attention of Selene and Isis. They're in the middle of the bedroom I've just officially finished moving Isis into, hands on their hips as they survey the set up and discuss what she wants changed.

I can't know for sure, but I'm certain Imani had Beck doing the same thing in her room earlier. We worked hard to make sure their individual bedrooms met the girls' standards and fit their personalities, but they're teenagers, so things are always subject to change.

"Thanks, Cal," Isis says, leaving Selene to step over the stack of boxes between us and give me a hug. The simple show of affection warms my heart. Selene beams at us, and I know we're both thinking about the many embraces we've shared with Isis and Imani that marked the end of our time together. For years, hugs meant goodbye, but now that Selene has officially adopted them, hugs are exactly what they're supposed to be.

Tender squeezes that end when you want them to.

This one is quick, ending when Beck shouts that the pizza has arrived.

"Thank God!" Isis shouts, stepping out of my hold and rushing out of the room.

"Don't run down those stairs," Selene yells when the hall is suddenly filled with the sounds of racing footsteps and the girls arguing about who is going to get the first slice of pepperoni.

They don't slow down at all. By the time Selene and I make it downstairs, the boxes are open and they're dancing around with triangles of melted cheese, meat and bread in hand.

"I tried to get them to wait for plates," Beck says, shaking his head.

"We were hungry!" Imani defends.

Isis pulls a pepperoni from the slice and pops it in her mouth. "Yeah, moving is hard work."

"Neither of you did anything," Selene points out as she takes a stack of plates from Beck and sits it by the pizza boxes. "I don't think I saw you lift a single box between the two of you."

While she's chastising them, I hand the girls plates and Beck sets about fixing drinks. I smile to myself, loving that we've already established a rhythm even though this is our first official night together as a family.

Imani's brows furrow. "What's the point of having two dads if we have to carry boxes?"

Questions like this activate this instinct in Beck, Selene and me. This impulse to pause and reiterate, to dissect and decode, to flat out ask Imani if she truly considers us her dads. Both she and Isis call us by our names, which has always been fine, but being referred to in that way, even indirectly, is significant and extremely meaningful.

We can't make a big deal of it, though, or else we risk making her feel weird or self-conscious about it. That's the last thing any of us want to do, so we share a brief look, just to acknowledge what the comment means to us and then move on.

"Damn, she's got a point," Beck says, sliding drinks across the island to each of us. The wedding band on his finger catches the light, and, on instinct, I rub the pad of my thumb across mine. It's been a little over a year since we took vows, legally binding ourselves to each other with Selene as our officiant and all the people we love, including our soon to be daughters, in the audience.

Conversation flows around me. Selene and Beck go back and forth with Imani and Isis about the amount of calories you burn supervising work you didn't perform, while I lose myself in the sweet chaos of the family I created and the beauty of a moment I will never have to leave.

EPILOGUE 3: BECK

"You know the whole point of running our own security firm is being able to end meetings when we want to," Cal chides, speeding through a yellow light that turns red as soon as we cross the line.

"Relax, Drake, we're not going to miss the reservations."

I try to sound certain about that, but I don't even know where we're going so my guarantees don't exactly hold weight. He cuts an eye at me, mild annoyance rolling off him as he breaks yet another traffic law to get us wherever we're going on time.

"We left the office thirty minutes late."

"I know. I'm sorry."

I've already explained that Shaw and Morgan delayed my departure with questions about overtime, so I don't bother mentioning it again. Instead, I resort to some basic guilt tripping to get him to forgive me.

"Are you really going to be mad at me on my birthday?" I ask, reaching over to grab his hand. He tries to hold out, gripping the wheel tighter at first, but eventually he caves, linking our fingers together.

"No, I guess I can't be."

Triumph curves my lips. "I knew it."

"Shut up, Beckham."

"Are you going to tell me where we're going?"

"We'd already be there if you weren't such a workaholic."

I roll my eyes, unable to admit that he's right. Me getting caught up at work is a common occurrence, but the same is true for him. The only thing that gets either of us out of the office on time is a commitment involving Selene, the girls or all three of the angels our world now revolves around. We should probably be just as rigid when it comes to making time for each other or ourselves, but I don't see that happening anytime soon.

Mainly because we love what we do so much.

I'd never pictured myself in the private security sector, but after working a job to repay the favor Cal called in with Hunter's friend, Russ, I got kind of obsessed with the idea of more money, lower stakes and the ability to fire a client whenever I felt like it. Cal, of course, was on the same wavelength, so we took the leap together, making Shaw and Morgan our first hires.

"Do we have much further to go?" I ask, scrolling through my texts to see if I've got any from Selene or the girls. They've been quiet for most of the day, which is odd. I would be worried except they all told me they'd be busy with work and school. Their demanding schedules are the reason Cal and I are celebrating my birthday alone for the first time in years.

"About five more minutes," he says.

"Can I really not know where we're going?"

"*Beckham.*"

The sharp warning has me sitting back and my seat and shutting the fuck up for the rest of the ride while Cal folds a satisfied smile between his lips. When we arrive at the restaurant—an authentic Italian spot that makes their pasta in house—that smile grows wider because he knows I've been wanting to come here since it opened.

We walk into the building hand in hand, drawing the attention of other diners, and I relish the absence of anxiety in my body as we follow the hostess to the back of the restaurant. I haven't felt it in years. The fear that used to cover our love, shrouding it in shame, making me want to hide something that should have only ever been celebrated.

As we stop in front of a pair of doors that lead to what I assume is a private dining area, Cal squeezes my hand and stops. His eyes are soft, his expression softer.

"Before we walk in here, I want you to know that you deserve this."

My lips part, and a request for him to elaborate begins to work its way up my throat. Before I can lend my voice to it, the doors open, revealing the faces of the people I adore most in the world. Selene, Isis and Imani are in the front. Behind them are Monique, Hunter, Rae, Riley, Mama J, Al and Erin.

"SURPRISE!"

They shout in unison as Cal leads me into the room. I follow him the way I followed him into deadly missions, career changes, and a love that forced me to stretch and grow in ways I never thought I could: with a certainty that as long as I stay by his side, everything will turn out beautifully.

THE END

ALSO BY J.L. SEEGARS

Passion and Politics:

The Illusion of Power (Book #1)

The New Haven Series:

Restore Me: The New Haven Series (Book #1)

Revive Me Part One: The New Haven Series (Book #2)

Revive Me Part Two: The New Haven Series (Book #2)

Revive Me Part Three: The New Haven Series (Book #2)

Release Me: The New Haven Series (Book #3)

Reclaim Me: The New Haven Series (Book #4)

The Fairview Novellas:

Again: A Marriage Redemption Novella

Speak: A Post Divorce Romance

ABOUT THE AUTHOR

J.L. Seegars is a dedicated smut peddler and lifelong nerd who's always had a love of words, storytelling and drama. When she isn't writing messy and emotionally complex characters like the ones she grew up around, she's watching reality TV, supporting her fellow authors by devouring their work or spending time with her husband and son.